BOOK ONE

BUCKED

USA TODAY BESTSELLING AUTHOR

HEATHER SLADE

bucked
/buhkt/

verb

to resist, oppose, defy

MORE FROM AUTHOR HEATHER SLADE

BUTLER RANCH
Kade's Worth
Brodie's Promise
Maddox's Truce
Naughton's Secret
Mercer's Vow
Kade's Return
Butler Ranch Christmas

WICKED WINEMAKERS
FIRST LABEL
Brix's Bid
Ridge's Release
Press' Passion
Zin's Sins
Tryst's Temptation

WICKED WINEMAKERS
SECOND LABEL
Beau's Beloved
Coming Soon:
Cru's Crush
Bones' Bliss
Snapper's Seduction
Kick's Kiss

ROARING FORK RANCH
Coming Soon:
Roaring Fork Wrangler
Roaring Fork Roughstock
Roaring Fork Rockstar
Roaring Fork Rooker
Roaring Fork Bridger

THE ROYAL AGENTS
OF MI6
Make Me Shiver
Drive Me Wilder
Feel My Pinch
Chase My Shadow
Find My Angel

K19 SECURITY
SOLUTIONS TEAM ONE
Razor's Edge
Gunner's Redemption
Mistletoe's Magic
Mantis' Desire
Dutch's Salvation

K19 SECURITY
SOLUTIONS TEAM TWO
Striker's Choice
Monk's Fire
Halo's Oath
Tackle's Honor
Onyx's Awakening

K19 SHADOW OPERATIONS
TEAM ONE
Code Name: Ranger
Code Name: Diesel
Code Name: Wasp
Code Name: Cowboy
Code Name: Mayhem

K19 ALLIED INTELLIGENCE
TEAM ONE
Code Name: Ares
Code Name: Cayman
Code Name: Poseidon
Code Name: Zeppelin
Code Name: Magnet

K19 ALLIED INTELLIGENCE
TEAM TWO
Coming Soon:
Code Name: Puck
Code Name: Michelangelo
Code Name: Typhon
Code Name: Hornet
Code Name: Reaper

PROTECTORS
UNDERCOVER
Undercover Agent
Undercover Emissary
Coming Soon:
Undercover Savior
Undercover Infidel
Undercover Assassin

THE INVINCIBLES
TEAM ONE
Decked
Edged
Grinded
Riled
Smoked

THE INVINCIBLES
TEAM TWO
Bucked
Irished
Sainted
Hammered
Ripped

THE UNSTOPPABLES
TEAM ONE
Furied
Merried

COWBOYS OF
CRESTED BUTTE
A Cowboy Falls
A Cowboy's Dance
A Cowboy's Kiss
A Cowboy Stays
A Cowboy Wins

Table of Contents

Chapter 1 1
Chapter 2 4
Chapter 3 13
Chapter 4 20
Chapter 5 34
Chapter 6 48
Chapter 7 60
Chapter 8 76
Chapter 9 88
Chapter 10 100
Chapter 11 111
Chapter 12 123
Chapter 13 135
Chapter 14 149
Chapter 15 157
Chapter 16 174
Chapter 17 196
Chapter 18 213
Chapter 19 227
Chapter 20 240
Chapter 21 250
Chapter 22 261

Chapter 23 272
Chapter 24 282
Chapter 25 291
Chapter 26 301
Chapter 27 309
Chapter 28 328
Chapter 29 337
Chapter 30 344
Chapter 31 348
Chapter 32 357
Chapter 33 371
Chapter 34 379
Chapter 35 385
Chapter 36 386
Chapter 37 393
Chapter 38 396
Chapter 39 404
Chapter 40 408
Epilogue 414
Irished 419
About the Author 423

1

Buck

"How are you holding up?" I whispered in the ear of the woman standing beside me.

"About as well as you are," she whispered back as we watched the woman I'd fallen hopelessly in love with walk down the aisle toward the man she was marrying instead of me.

My plus-one, Stella, and I had spent a couple of nights on the phone, drinking and drowning in our shared misery since she was equally in love with the groom. I was sure tonight would be no different.

We turned when Ali, the bride, reached Cope, the groom, who stood with the minister who would marry them. It wasn't the bride who captured my gaze, though. It was Stella. She looked so damn pretty today I almost swallowed my tongue when I picked her up at her apartment.

"Stop that," she'd said, punching my arm.

"Stop what?"

"Looking at me like I'm really your date."

I wanted to tell her she really was my date and that she was breathtaking. But I wouldn't put her on the spot like that. The woman, whose real first name I didn't know—I'd only heard her referred to as either TJ or Stella—had been in love with Sumner Copeland since the day I met her. It didn't matter that it was unrequited.

He had given her the nickname Stella. All the more reason for me not to use it. Maybe today would be the day I stopped. Maybe it would also be the day I told TJ how I really felt about her, and that instead of being her convenient plus-one, I wanted to be the real thing.

I shook my head at my foolishness. Not only would she carry a torch for Cope for-fucking-ever, she was a city girl. Born and raised. I was the exact opposite. I'd grown up on a ranch, shoveling shit and never able to get the dirt out from under my fingernails.

The thing we had in common, other than being in love with people who weren't in love with us, was that we'd both traveled the world for our jobs.

She was an award-winning journalist, and up until recently, I had been an agent with the CIA. I'd retired, but still worked in the business, just for a private intelligence firm instead.

That was how TJ and I met. She was covering a trial involving Cope, during which Ali's safety had been compromised. I'd been assigned to an op involving asset protection—for Ali.

I glanced at my date again when the minister began the ceremony. Instead of looking at Cope, TJ was looking at me, and she was breathtaking. From the day I first met her, I found it ironic that of all the women I'd known, she was among the most beautiful yet she was utterly unaware of it.

She wasn't just beautiful. She was smart, clever, and funny. There were times she made me laugh so hard I thought I'd split a gut. She was also a force of nature when she dug her heels into a story like the one she'd been reporting on when we met.

The woman was the total package, and I was lucky enough to get to spend time with her.

To think I'd met her through another woman I loved. But had I really? Or was it just lust? Somewhere along the line, even that had changed. Now when I looked at Ali, I was reminded of my younger sister, Flynn. Ali was no longer the woman whose pants I wanted to peel from her body. Now Stella—TJ—was the only woman whose naked body I wanted to hold next to mine.

2

Stella

"You clean up good," I'd said to Buck when he picked me up at my apartment. What I'd almost blurted out was he looked really fucking hot. So hot, I wanted to take his clothes off piece by piece and spend the afternoon exploring his naked body rather than attend the wedding of the guy I'd spent the last few years secretly in love with.

Was that even true? Had I been in love with Cope, or was it just lust? Before Ali was in his life, I'd had plenty of fantasies in which he was the star. *Porn star*, if I was honest. But it was more than that. There'd been a time I believed I had a shot at a relationship with him.

No point in going down that lane of memories on a day like today. Instead, I looked Buck up and down when I saw him doing the same thing to me.

The man was every cowboy fantasy I'd ever had, come to life. Add in his scruffy beard and long hair, and he was the exact opposite of Sumner Copeland. No less hot. Actually, more so. Way hotter.

Unfortunately, one of the things Buck and Cope had in common represented the reason my hot cowboy fantasies would never come to life. They were both hopelessly in love with Ali Graham Mancuso, who in about fifteen minutes, would add Copeland to her name.

Why had I agreed to even come to the wedding? Especially with Buck? If I'd said no, I wouldn't be forced to watch the man I wished I'd had sex with at least once get married while standing next to the man I wished I could have sex with right now. And by right now, I meant drag him back to that sexy-as-fuck pickup he drove us here in and ride him like the cowboy he was.

I clenched my thighs together when I felt Buck's hand brush against mine. That's all it took. One simple touch. Then he made it worse. He leaned over, put his mouth next to my ear, and whispered. It didn't matter what he said. I couldn't think straight enough to hear it anyway.

I turned my head before he pulled away. His lips were close enough that I could kiss them, if only I had the balls to do it.

Instead, I turned back in time to see Cope kiss the shit out of Ali when the minister pronounced them man and wife. *Damn.* I really didn't need to see that.

"What did you say?" I whispered to Buck.

He leaned into me like he had a minute ago. "I said, you look more beautiful than the bride, Stella."

"Thank you, Buck, but—"

"Way more beautiful." I could feel the heat of his breath on my neck.

What in the hell was Buck doing? I couldn't do this again. I couldn't go down the same road of a hotter-than-hell younger guy flirting with me to the point where I couldn't tell the difference between what was real and what was him just playing me.

"Excuse me." I brushed past him even before Cope and Ali had finished the recessional, and hurried off in the direction of the house, hoping no one had noticed me leave on the side aisle.

I raced into the restroom, wishing I could splash cold water on my face, but that would ruin the makeup it took me over an hour to put on, since I never wore it.

Instead, I took several deep breaths. "Buck the fuck up, buttercup," I said to the mirror, shaking my head at the use of the name of the man who had me so flustered that I'd made a jackass out of myself by rushing away from the wedding.

I squared my shoulders, took one last look in the mirror, and opened the bathroom door.

Just outside, there he stood. His arm was raised, and he leaned against the doorjamb. "Hey, Stella, you and me need to talk."

"What about?"

Buck looked down at his phone. "I, uh, gotta leave. I'm real sorry to do this to you, but there's an emergency at home."

"Oh! Of course. An emergency? Oh my God. Go. Don't worry about me. Is everything okay? Is there anything I can do? I mean, what kind of emergency?"

Buck gave me one of his lazy, panty-melting grins and put his hand on my shoulder. "Slow down, darlin'."

"I'm sorry," I muttered, shaking my head. I never got nervous and I never rambled. Not ever. I was a tough-as-nails journalist who'd never shied away from a story, no matter who or what it was about. I'd get in anyone's face—the most hardened criminals or the most corrupt politicians. Even Cope hadn't had the same effect on me that Buck did. Being this close to him turned my brain to mush. Not to mention making me feel like a damn cougar.

"Look, um, do you want me to arrange for a car service to give you a lift home later?"

"I can handle it."

"You sure? Cause—"

I raised a brow and folded my arms.

"Right. I better be on my way, then."

I took a step back and held up one hand in a half wave. "Goodbye, Buck."

"Bye, Stella."

As I watched him walk away, every fantasy I'd had about him and me and his sexy-as-fuck pickup, dissolved into an image of me alone at home with a jug of wine and a large pizza.

"Where's Buck?" asked Ali when she and Cope made the rounds, visiting guest tables after dinner.

"Emergency at home," I muttered, finishing off my third Manhattan.

"Damn," mumbled Cope, shaking his head. "That's too bad."

I looked at Ali, who seemed as confused as me. "What's too bad?"

"His dad must've died."

"And you know this, how?"

"He's been ill. I was afraid he might not make it to the wedding."

He'd told Cope he might not make it to the wedding but hadn't informed me, his date? "Men are such assholes," I muttered under my breath. "I'm out of here." I kissed Ali's cheek and saluted Cope.

"I'll walk you out," he offered.

"I'd really rather you didn't." I turned too quickly and grabbed the back of my chair when the effects of the alcohol I'd just pounded made me dizzy. Stumbling my way out of Cope's parents' yard would be the fucking cherry on the top of my ice cream sundae of a day.

"I've got this," I heard one of the other guys I'd met through Cope, say. The first time I met Ritter "Rock" Johnson, I was convinced he was Dwayne's twin although he swore there was no family connection.

"Let's get you home, Stella."

"Appreciate it, Rock." I put one arm through his and waved with the other. "Have fun, lovebirds."

"I'm sure Buck feels bad about having to leave like he did," said Rock as we walked out.

"According to Cope, his father died."

"I don't know for sure, but I do know he's been sick."

It made me sad that Buck hadn't talked to me about his dad. I mean, I get he wouldn't want to at the wedding, but he could've told me on our way here. Or even when we talked last night. I guess we weren't as good of friends as I thought we were.

"Hang on, and I'll walk you up," said Rock when he pulled up to my building.

I pointed to the three doormen, who looked like they were standing guard at the entrance. "I'm good."

"You sure?"

"Thanks, Rock." I waved behind me.

By the time I got to the elevator, my shoes were off and tucked under my arm. I couldn't wait to get the rest of this getup off and crawl into a nice, hot bath.

As if on cue, moments after I closed the apartment door behind me, my cell rang.

"Hey, Aunt Barb. I just walked in." There were times I thought the woman must have my apartment surveilled, or at least bugged, given how she always seemed to know when I was here.

"How was the wedding?"

"It was fine." My beloved aunt had always had an issue with my "inappropriate crush on a CIA handler," whom she refused to refer to by name.

Barbara Hunter was my mother's sister and the woman who'd raised me from the age of nine when my mom died from complications brought on by AIDS. Barb had been, and to a certain extent still was, one of the most revered female investigative reporters in the business.

The list of awards she'd earned over the years was lengthy, but the one she prized above all others was her Pulitzer for Public Service Reporting. She was given the gold medal for her early reporting on misconceptions about the causes of HIV and AIDS, as well as the predicted outcomes. Because of her exhaustive research, many of the stigmas associated with the virus were lessened.

My aunt had done that work while caring for my mother and me. After my mother's death, Barb took on raising me full-time. She'd still worked as a reporter, but on less hard-hitting news stories and ones that didn't require much travel.

"What progress have you made on what I've given you?"

I sighed. "Working on it."

"Hmm."

The three Manhattans I'd downed in rapid succession were now manifesting themselves in the form of a raging headache, not to mention a bit of nausea.

"We'll talk more tomorrow. Right now, there's a hot bath calling my name."

"TJ, I'm—"

"Barb, I'm tired. We'll talk tomorrow." I ended the call before she could say anything more and turned off my phone. She'd let me have it in the morning for hanging up on her, but I'd be better equipped to handle it then than I was now, when the last thing I wanted to do was talk about the litany of investigations she wanted me to follow up on. It was more than wanting me to take them on; she demanded I did.

I got it. I mean, I really did. Aunt Barb hadn't been ready to quit when her last big story ended her career in scandal. Ever since, she'd been living her life vicariously through mine.

3

Buck

"Can I get you another?" asked the bartender in the lounge at BWI, where I waited for my flight.

"One more. Thanks." I leaned against the back of the barstool and wondered if I should add a shot to the beer I'd ordered. By the time I landed in Denver, its effect would have worn off, and that's when I'd really need it.

My father was dead. It would take some time for me to wrap my head around him being gone, and not because I wasn't prepared for it to happen. I just figured the old man was cantankerous enough to whip cancer's ass for a few more months.

"What the fuck?" I mumbled under my breath before ordering the shot I wasn't sure I should have, but knew I needed.

I waited until the last possible minute to board the plane, wondering how pissed Stella was at me for leaving her at Cope and Ali's wedding by herself. I probably should've warned her of the possibility, but the doctors had given my pop six months to live four years ago.

Plus, Stella was a reporter, and a damn good one. The mere mention of my father would have led to questions I didn't want to answer. They'd start out innocently enough, but once she picked up on my discomfort, she wouldn't have been able to help herself; our conversation would have turned into an interrogation without her even realizing it was happening.

Stella. Wrapping my head around the idea that she and I were over before I'd had the balls to get anything started, was going to be hard too.

While I told her she looked pretty today, the words I'd almost said were "fucking hot." I laughed to myself. Why hadn't I? Stella, of all people, would've preferred the edgier comment. And maybe that was why I kept it softer—to see the blush on her cheeks at the word she didn't hear often enough.

I grabbed my bag and threw a twenty on the bar when I heard the final boarding call for my flight. What I'd give to not have to get on the plane that would take me to the home I'd never wanted to go back to.

Four agonizing hours later, I landed in Denver. Since it was already dark, there was no point in driving over to the ranch tonight; by the time I rented a vehicle and drove over, it would be past two in the morning. Instead, I'd try to get as far on the other side of Denver as I could. Maybe stop in Conifer or Bailey.

I stood to get my bag out of the overhead and banged into someone behind me. "Sorry about that," I said, turning around.

"It's okay," said the girl I'd bumped butts with. She was a cute little thing, all bright smiles and eager eyes. There might've been a time when I would've taken this kind of opportunity to flirt, maybe even get her number. Now, though, she just looked young. Too young. And vapid. When I saw she was trying to reach a bag in the opposite overhead, I grabbed it and handed it to her. "Go on ahead," I said, noticing the aisle was clear in front of us.

I waved a few more people by and then stepped out of my row, hoping the woman wasn't waiting for me at the end of the ramp that led from the plane to the terminal. This kind of thing happened to me often enough that I knew what to expect and how best to avoid it.

I put on my cowboy hat and walked off the plane. When I reached the terminal, I could see her waiting in the distance. I pulled out my phone, took a sharp left, and made a beeline for the men's room.

When I came out, I didn't see her, and even if I had, I'd made my lack of interest clear. I took the train to baggage claim and the airport exit. When I reached the top of the escalator that went from the platform to the main level, I saw a familiar face.

"Hey, man," I said to my brother Porter. "I didn't expect you." He and I moved out of the way and embraced.

"Couldn't just let you sit here at DIA," he muttered.

"I would've rented something and driven over."

"Is that all you've got?" he asked, pointing to my bag.

"That's it."

"Guess you aren't planning on staying long."

"I don't stay anywhere very long, Port." My attempt at a joke fell flat, not doing a thing to alleviate the tension that seeped from my brother's pores. "I also left behind a closet full of shit." The clothes I wore when I was at the ranch weren't a lot different than what I wore everywhere else, but the truth was, I traveled light.

"Gotcha."

"I appreciate this, Port."

"It isn't completely unselfish, Buck. There are things we need to talk about."

I'd expected there would be. "How's Flynn?" Of all my siblings, the youngest—my sister—would take our dad's death the hardest. I couldn't speak for my three brothers, but knowing they carried the same memories I did, I could understand if they didn't give a shit if the old man was burning in hell.

"Stoic," answered Port.

That didn't surprise me. Like our mom, Flynn held everything inside. I only hoped my sister could find a way to let the things that bothered her out. Otherwise, also like our mother, she might die of a heart attack before she hit thirty-five.

We didn't talk again until we were in Port's truck and on the highway.

"There's some stuff you need to know about the ranch, Buck. Finances in particular."

Roaring Fork Ranch, one of six hundred Centennial Farms in the state of Colorado—meaning owned by the same family for over one hundred years—hadn't always prospered. It was the second largest in Gunnison

County, and our family, like so many others, struggled with whether to divide the property and let a portion of it be used for development. It was something our pop had vehemently opposed, regardless of whether the ranch was profitable.

Stubborn didn't begin to describe Roscoe B. Wheaton, Sr. He did what he wanted, when he wanted, and how he wanted. He had no interest in hearing the opinions of his offspring or that of other ranch owners.

"How bad is it?" I asked.

"Bad enough that we might lose it."

Whether my siblings lost it or not would be dependent on how our father had divided the ownership. One thing I knew for certain was that none of it would be coming to me, and for that, I was thankful.

"You leave, and you won't be welcome back," the bastard had said the day I told him I was given a full-ride scholarship to a university on the East Coast. He took it a step further when I actually left. "You turn your back on it, you'll never own a square foot of Roaring Fork," he'd warned.

I didn't hesitate to tell him I didn't give a shit. I still didn't. But that was between my father and me. Nothing that had happened was Porter's fault.

"The brothers and I have some ideas."

"Look, Port, I'm happy to let you run stuff past me, or even give my opinion if you really want it, but what happens at the ranch isn't any of my business."

It was dark in the truck, but I could see the look of confusion on my brother's face.

"He cut me out, Port. You know that."

"I'm not so sure."

"What's that mean?"

"The lawyer is going to read us the will after the funeral, but we had to assure him you'd be here."

What the hell? What had the old man done? Left me a dollar to humiliate me? The fucker was dead, so I wouldn't be able to tell him that no matter what he did, he no longer had any kind of hold over me.

"What are your ideas?"

I laughed out loud when Porter turned his head and his face broke into a wide smile.

"I can't wait to hear this."

4

Stella

I knew better than to have so much to drink. Not only did I have a headache and feel sick to my stomach, it also gave me indigestion. Long gone were the days when I could consume whatever I wanted. Now, at the ripe old age of thirty-six, I had to stay away from things like pizza too late at night, alcohol any time of the day it seemed, plus a myriad of other things my digestive system used to be able to handle.

Even eating an apple, usually a fail-safe cure for heartburn, was no match for the combination of whiskey, bitters, and vermouth.

"Fucking Buck," I muttered. It didn't matter that it wasn't his fault I felt like shit. At least not physically. Scratch that. It wasn't his fault my stomach was bothering me. It *was* his fault I was so horny that even my vibrator, equally as fail-safe as the apple, did nothing to combat how much I wanted to feel his naked body against mine.

I'd hoped that after the wedding, he and I would end up back here, purging our desire for people who could never be ours by ravaging each other's bodies. I'd even managed to ignore the possibility that Buck might not be interested in having sex with a woman so much older. The last relationship I'd had was with a man sixteen years older than me. I hadn't had to worry about my age with him—I was practically a kid in comparison.

So here I sat with a huge itch that needed to be scratched. Buck was gone God knew where other than here, and it wasn't likely he'd be coming back. He'd only been in DC initially to protect Ali. When she went home to California, he went with her. It wasn't a job that had brought him here last week; it was the bachelor party and today's wedding.

I grabbed my laptop, got in bed, and searched for him on the internet. Nothing. Just like I expected.

"What the hell," I muttered out loud, pulling up the dating website I trolled from time to time. Given Buck was no longer an itch-scratching option, maybe I should consider doing what others did and find a stranger who could take care of it for me.

After a few minutes, I slammed my laptop closed, turned off the light, and opened up the reading app on my tablet.

When I opened my eyes again, the sun was streaming through my window. I reached for my phone, remembering then that I'd turned it off last night. I dreaded the idea of turning it back on enough that I let it sit on the nightstand when I went into the kitchen for a cup of coffee.

At the same rate the steamy brew filled my cup, guilt over Aunt Barb filled my chest. It wasn't just that I'd abruptly ended our call last night, today was Sunday—the day of the week I usually paid her a visit.

I'd so much rather stay in my pj's, read more of the book that had put me to sleep last night, and eat pizza early enough in the day to not have to think about its effects on my esophagus. But if I didn't visit Barb, the only other human contact she'd have all week would be Nancy, her housekeeper. I figured the two women looked forward to my visits just to escape each other's company for a short amount of time.

Why was I Barb's only other human contact? Because my aunt never left the confines of her apartment. She wasn't housebound for any physical reason. If she wanted to, she could do her own shopping, have lunch with friends, even visit me. It was her mental state that kept her from venturing out into the world.

It started a little over ten years ago, right after I'd graduated from NYU with my master's degree, that my aunt took a journalistic fall from grace. Her reclusion began almost immediately after she was accused of manufacturing evidence against then-Interpol president, Nicholas Kerr, a married man with whom it was alleged Barb had had a torrid affair.

In my aunt's career-ending story, which the AP had inexplicably passed on, she accused Kerr, along with the other members of Interpol's executive committee, of years of accepting bribes in exchange for a massive cover-up of what she'd reported as being called Operation Argead.

Days after the story ran, the AP ran their own piece, accusing Barb of being a spurned lover when Kerr ended the affair. The article alleged she'd falsely accused those named in it, out of spite. Within days of that, Kerr, along with the vice president and secretary-general of Interpol, sued her for libel. While that suit was later dropped, the damage had already been done.

Making matters much worse at the time, my aunt was unable to produce the evidence she'd said she had to back up her allegations. When pressed about it, Barb said her apartment had been burglarized and, suspiciously, all that was taken was every shred of evidence she had against Kerr and his co-conspirators.

The story took on a life of its own—not against Kerr, against my aunt. Her fellow reporters hounded her so relentlessly she remained locked inside her apartment, refusing to venture out for any reason. Even after the story died down, she'd refused to go out in public.

Her weekly therapist appointments continued, but over the phone, not that the woman had helped my aunt overcome or even battle her extreme agoraphobia.

The one thing the therapist had recommended, and that I agreed with wholeheartedly, was that Barb hire a companion, housekeeper, assistant—however my aunt wanted to define the position—in order to free me up to live my life.

I couldn't remember exactly where Barb had found her, but Nancy proved to be as invaluable to my sanity as she was to my aunt's. The arrangement worked out well for both women when she offered Nancy a salary to include room and board.

Online shopping became her favorite pastime, besides the endless research she conducted, which culminated in *assignments* for me.

I couldn't begrudge her, though. When my mother was first diagnosed HIV positive, my father had not only accused her of being unfaithful, he left the house one morning and never came back.

The following day, she was served with divorce papers. The day after that, Aunt Barb had shown up and never left. I was five. Four years later, my mother was gone, I had zero contact with my father, and my aunt had dedicated her life to caring for me.

My aunt was the one who'd first called me TJ when, right after my mom died, I told her I detested my first name—which I hadn't divulged to a single soul since. The J was for Jackson, my father's last name.

It wasn't long before my aunt adopted me and we legally changed my name to TJ Hunter. Hunter was Barb's last name, my mother's maiden name. The adoption was easy, given my father had relinquished his parental rights in my parents' divorce.

When it came time for me to go to college, she made sure I had every penny I needed to earn both my bachelor's and master's degrees. She sublet her apartment in DC and rented a place in Manhattan for the two of us while I attended NYU.

During that time, Barb, for the most part, quit working. When she did write, they were mainly fluff pieces.

The Kerr-Interpol-Operation Argead story was the first big investigative piece she took on after I graduated from college. I wondered now if the time off had made her rusty, diminished her previously honed skills, and resulted in her being sloppy. The idea that she blew the story for those reasons, only added to my already overwhelming sense of guilt.

With that burden firmly in place, I got my shit together, showered, and was on my way to her apartment an hour later. My laptop bag was slung over my shoulder, and I had Greek takeout in hand from the café in the lobby of Cope's building—the same place that had catered his and Ali's wedding yesterday.

"It's just me," I shouted, letting myself in.

"TJ?" she hollered back. Uh, who else would it be? She didn't recognize my voice after thirty years?

"I brought your favorite for lunch." I pulled plates from the cupboard and filled each with gyro, rice, tzatziki, and Greek salad. I looked up when she walked into the kitchen.

"I thought you meant Italian," she said with a sour face. For a moment, I considered dumping the food back into the takeout containers. Maybe it hadn't been such a great idea to come over. My hangover—along with my missed opportunity for post-wedding sex— already had my tolerance-for-shit level close to zero.

I stabbed my fork into the salad and took a bite. "More for me and Nancy, then," I said with food in my mouth. "Where is she, anyway?"

My aunt made a noise of disgust, picked up her plate, and sat at the dining room table. "In her room."

"You two have a spat?"

"I'm old as the hills, and that woman is ten years older than I am. It's time she retired and I said so."

Admittedly, my aunt was in her mid-sixties, which meant her housekeeper was seventy-five, at least. But if she retired, how would Barb get on without her?

"You were in a mood last night," she mumbled after we'd eaten in silence for several minutes.

"Still am." I finished what was on my plate and took it into the kitchen to clean up. "Do you want me to leave this or take it with me, since it's no longer your favorite?"

"You can leave it."

I peeked around the corner and saw her sitting with her chin resting in her hand. "What's up?" I asked.

She dropped her elbow from the table and leaned back in her chair. "I wish you were making more progress, TJ. By the time you report on some of the leads I've given you, the stories will either be old news or someone else will have gotten the scoop."

I sat back down at the table. "Why don't you write them?"

She rolled her eyes.

"I'm serious."

"No one would publish a word."

"Of course they would; you're a Pulitzer-winning journalist."

"Must we go down this road again, TJ?"

"The way I see it, you can do it yourself or stop giving me shit when I'm not quick enough for you."

The truth was, with few exceptions, Aunt Barb's "scoops" held little interest for me. I doubted any news outlets would find them compelling either. The subjects lacked the kind of sensationalism required for even AP to pick up the bylines. What might have been considered newsworthy ten years ago was hardly a radar blip now.

The worst part was that Aunt Barb held a personal vendetta not only against Interpol and even the CIA, but every journalist and media outlet that had disgraced her. She looked for and called out bias on a regular basis and expected me to report on it. The problem with it was, no one cared.

Everyone who watched the news, read a newspaper or magazine, knew exactly what the media outlet's slant was. Whether middle-of-the-road, conservative, or liberal, there was rarely an attempt to hide personal or collective opinions. I'd hardly be shining a light on anything not already widely accepted.

"You know I'm working on something else."

"For the love of God, please tell me you're not entertaining the idea of that book again."

Compared to the stories she wanted me to cover, the book was the one thing that would truly cause a stir, not just in the US intelligence world, but globally.

It all began when I got an anonymous tip about an arrest involving a CIA agent by the name of Paxon "Irish" Warrick, whose handler at the agency was none other than Sumner Copeland.

I covered the arrest and subsequent indictment, all the while believing Irish was a double agent who had been selling secrets to the Chinese government for almost a decade, which had resulted in the deaths of dozens of CIA agents, operatives, and assets around the world.

On the first day of his trial, I met Ali Graham—actually Ali Mancuso—who was undercover as a reporter also writing the story, but who I later learned was a CIA internal affairs agent brought in to see if Cope was in cahoots with Irish.

Much to my own heartbreak at the time, I stood on the sidelines and watched Ali and Cope fall in love.

When we both believed Cope had been killed in a car explosion, we not only became close friends, we also agreed to collaborate on the real story of what turned out to be a years-long mission undertaken by Irish, Cope, and a man named Decker Ashford to expose the true mole and his co-conspirators.

Like on the night I received the anonymous tip about Irish, my cell phone rang shortly after midnight. A computer-modified voice informed me that before dawn, multiple arrests would be made both in the States and around the world. I lay awake as reports of each hit the wires, the biggest of which was CIA Director Ed Fisk.

A few hours after that, I learned that Cope was alive. His death had been faked as part of the mission.

"TJ?"

I looked up and realized my aunt was studying me. "Yeah?"

"I would've thought after his wedding, you would stop following that man around like a puppy dog."

I sat back in my own chair. "You're on fire today, Barb."

"You need to walk away from it."

I leaned forward and rested my arms on the table. "From what? The book?"

"Yes, and lower your voice."

Now I was pissed. "Not on your life."

"Maybe on both of our lives."

"What does that mean?"

When Barb got up from the table and walked into the other room, I followed. She pushed aside the drape and looked out the window. "I have a bad feeling, TJ."

I turned my back so she couldn't see me roll my eyes. "Time for me to head out."

"Wait. We aren't finished talking about this."

With my fists clenched, I slowly turned back around. "Yes, Aunt Barb, we are. This book, this story, is important to me. Probably the most important of my career. There's nothing you can say that will make me change my mind about seeing it through."

"Even if it means the same thing will happen to you that happened to me?"

"*Jesus,* stop this. I don't know what kind of straws you're grasping at, but the situations have zero in common."

"You're wrong. They have a lot more in common than you think." After looking over her shoulder, presumably for Nancy, she walked over to the baby grand piano that had always been in her apartment but I'd never seen her play. I watched her lift the keyboard cover, count ten keys from the right, lift the one she had landed on, and pull out an entirely different type of key. She walked over and handed it to me.

"What's this?"

"It opens a safe-deposit box," she whispered.

"What's in it, Barb?"

"Keep your voice down." She looked over her shoulder again and motioned me closer. "The evidence."

I took the three steps between her and the piano, lifted the same key she had, dropped the one in my hand under it, and silently closed the cover. I approached my aunt and rested my hands on her shoulders.

"I love you, Aunt Barb. I appreciate everything you've done for me, and I can never repay you for it. That includes by me giving up my book. I won't do it. Don't ask me again."

My aunt's eyes bored into mine, but she didn't speak.

"Are we clear?"

When she didn't answer, I dropped my hands, walked into the kitchen, and grabbed my things.

"I'll call you tomorrow," I said before walking out and closing the door behind me.

5

Buck

"A dude ranch? Are you serious?"

I watched my brother's face fall. "You sound like the old man."

"Hang on a sec. I think it's a great idea."

"You do?"

"Hell, yeah!"

"We have another one."

"Go on."

"Stock contracting."

There was one other centennial ranch in the East River Valley, where Roaring Fork Ranch was located: the Flying R, owned by the Rice family. I'd heard they were raising roughstock—bucking broncs and bulls primarily—and that they were doing quite well. It didn't hurt that a past NFR bronc-riding champion had married into the family.

I had to admit, both of Porter's ideas surprised me, and not in a bad way. What didn't surprise me was that our dad shot 'em down without consideration.

"The problem is what it'll take to get them off the ground."

This was the part of the conversation I didn't want to get involved in. I didn't have the means—or the desire, if I was honest—to invest in the future of the ranch.

"Buck?"

"Yeah?"

"You're in favor of this, right?"

"Absolutely, Port. I wish you, Cord, Holt, and Flynn the best of luck. I just can't be—"

"I knew it."

"You knew what?"

"You're letting it go."

I rolled my neck, cringing when it cracked. "I have nothing to do with this, man. I'd love to see you make a go of it, be successful, but if you're looking for money, I'm not your guy."

"Right."

I tried to lighten the tension building between us. "You know somethin' I don't? Did I win the lottery and no one told me?"

"Close enough."

Porter drove past the gates of the ranch and pulled up to the main house. I jumped out, grabbed my bag from the back seat, and went inside through the front door that was never locked. I traipsed down the hallway to my old room. When I turned back to say goodnight to Porter, I saw his bedroom door close behind him.

I hadn't been in bed for a minute when my door flew open and my sister, Flynn, bounded over and planted herself next to me.

"What are you doin' up?" I asked, hugging her and messing her hair.

"Waitin' on you."

"How are you, Flynn?"

"Better now that you're here."

"Porter said you're bein' 'stoic.' I know Dad's death is hard on you, sis."

"Yeah. Well…"

"What?"

"I was never blind, Buck. I know how he was. I knew it then."

This wasn't a good topic of conversation ever, but especially not now.

Flynn put her arm around my waist and squeezed. "I'm just so glad you're here. It'll be great to spend time with you."

"It won't be great if you and I don't get some sleep." I moved her arm from around my waist. "We'll talk more in the morning, okay?"

"Sure." She stood to walk out but stopped at the door. "Thanks for being here, Buck. We need you more than you know."

After she left, I rolled over and punched the single pillow on my old twin bed. I got the feeling that both Port and Flynn expected me to stay a hell of a lot longer than I intended to.

When I woke up, the sun was high in the sky. I got out of bed, hit the bathroom, and walked into the kitchen. The house was quiet, which meant everyone was probably out doing morning chores.

After I made another pot of coffee, I went outside and sat on the porch. Crested Butte, Colorado, where the ranch was located, was close to nine thousand feet in elevation. That meant it rarely got above eighty even on the hottest summer days. It felt warmer than that today, though.

"Heard you landed last night," I heard another of my brothers, Cord, say from behind me. I stood and hugged him. Of everyone, he was the most like me.

Where Porter was the clean-cut cowboy, Cord and I let our hair grow past our shoulders, only shaved when there was a damn good reason for it, and always volunteered to handle the chores on Sunday so we could get out of going to church.

I put my hands on his shoulders and looked into the same blue eyes I saw every day in the mirror. "How are you?"

Cord shrugged. "Better now that you're here."

I'd seen three of my siblings, and each one had said the same thing—better now that I was here.

"I'm not sure how long I will be."

Cord cocked his head and took a breath as if he was about to say something when the last of my brothers walked out the front door.

"Buck," said Holt, pulling me into a tight hug. "You sure as hell are a sight for these sore eyes of mine."

He was the youngest boy but two years older than Flynn, who was the baby of the family and had just turned twenty-one.

Our mom had five kids inside ten years. No wonder she had a damn heart attack before her thirty-fifth birthday.

"You better get yourself cleaned up for the visitation later," said Cord, looking me up and down. "Looks like you just rolled out of bed."

I took a drink of coffee. "That's because I did. Port and I didn't get back from the airport until almost three in the morning."

"Where is Port anyway?" asked Holt.

"I'm right here." He walked out of the same door the other two had. "We'll need to leave in thirty minutes to go meet with the pastor."

I thought about begging off, but wasn't that what I'd been doing for the last few years? The least I could do was stand beside my siblings as we buried the old son of a bitch.

As I walked past Porter to go in and shower, I was struck by how much older he looked. I hadn't noticed it as much last night, but by the light of day, he looked ten years older than me with another twenty years' worth of worry piled on top of the age.

As it turned out, Porter and I were merely bookends for our younger sister, who had our father's funeral service planned out to the final note of the last hymn. I wondered how much the old man had done himself, but wouldn't ask her. Like Port had said, Flynn was stoic, and if that's what she had to do to hold it together, I wasn't about to shatter the walls she'd put around her heart.

The minister walked us out and said he'd see us later, at the visitation. I shook his hand and was about to get into my brother's truck when I heard someone calling my name. I turned and shielded my eyes from the sun.

"Hey, Buck. I was hoping I'd see you before tonight."

Bethany Strom—the girl who took my virginity—walked up and put her arms around me.

"Hey, Beth." When she held me tight and kissed my cheek, I had to admit I appreciated the comfort.

I watched as her eyes briefly met Porter's before he got in the truck, slammed the door, and she turned her focus back on me. "Whatever you need, Buck. I'm here."

I leaned forward and kissed her forehead. "Thanks, sweetheart. I'll see you later."

Arrangements had been made for the visitation to take place in the town's art center. I'd thought it was overkill until we drove up twenty minutes before it was scheduled to begin and there were already people lined up, waiting to get in.

If they only knew what the bastard had really been like, I doubted five people would've showed up. Then again, they weren't here for him. They were here for our family, who had been part of the Crested Butte community for almost one hundred and fifty years, and for my brothers, sister, and me.

An hour felt like ten as we stood side by side, thanking those who came, listening as they told stories about our father, our mother, or both.

Every so often, I'd catch someone from across the room staring at me, whispering to the person he or she was talking to. More often than not, they'd see me looking, turn their backs, and shake their heads. God knew what kind of judgment they were passing on me, and whatever it was, I didn't give a shit. They hadn't walked a single step in my shoes and had no idea what drove me to go off to college and never look back.

I excused myself to the restroom, went in, locked the door, and splashed cold water on my face. I unfastened the top button on my dress shirt, loosened my tie, and rested my hands on either side of the sink. I stared at the face in the mirror, the one that looked more and more like my father.

"Just a sec," I said when I heard a rap on the door. I dried my hands and walked back out to the room where my siblings were still greeting those who'd come to pay their respects. Like me, Porter must've needed a break, because he was no longer with them. I was just about to make my way over when I heard hushed voices coming from a side room. Though not loud, the tone was angry.

"Everything okay in here?" I asked, coming around the corner in time to see Porter reach out for Beth's hand and her yank it away. My brother swept past me without making eye contact.

"What was that about?" I asked.

"We were…uh…seeing each other for a while. It didn't work out."

That explained my brother's reaction this afternoon. "Listen, darlin', I appreciate you bein' here tonight, but I think it would be best if you head home now."

Her eyes filled with tears, but she nodded and turned to walk away.

"Beth, wait." I took two steps toward her. "You said things didn't work out. That had nothing to do with me coming back here, right?"

When she walked away without answering, a bad feeling settled in the pit of my stomach.

The second hour of visitation was more of the same. I thought for sure the crowds would dwindle down, but the stream of people remained constant. At the start of the third hour, I was ready to padlock the front door.

"Look who just walked in," said Porter. I turned my head in the direction he'd pointed and saw the Rice family coming toward us.

Bud and Ginny Rice had been good friends of my parents and grandparents. I was stunned by how much they'd aged since the last time I saw them.

"If there's anything at all we can do," Ginny said after she and her husband offered their condolences like so many others had before them.

"Same goes for Livvie and me," said their oldest son, Ben. Even though he had twenty years on me, I'd known him all my life. I'd watched from the sidelines as he and his band achieved moderate success, only for Ben to descend into a hellhole of drugs and alcohol.

Then I'd watched as he fought his way back, tooth and nail, until he achieved the kind of superstardom a man with his talent deserved.

The best part was that, along the way, he fell in love with Olivia Fairchild, world champion barrel racer, but more importantly, Ben's other half.

"It's good to see you," I said, returning his embrace.

"My turn," said Olivia when her husband stepped aside. Porter nudged me, and I shook my head.

"Let's just get through this," I said after they walked away. "There'll be plenty of time for us to talk to the Flying R after the funeral."

Thankfully, Porter acquiesced.

By the time we got home, I wanted no part of talking to anyone in my family and retreated straight to the bedroom. I pulled out my phone, hoping against hope there'd be a text from Stella. When there wasn't one, I scrolled through the old ones. They were from the night before Cope and Ali's wedding, and she'd been vacillating about going.

Oh, no, you don't, I'd written. *You promised to let me lean on you just like I promised you could lean on me.*

You'll be fine without me, she'd responded.

Rather than answer in another text, I'd picked up the phone. "I won't," I said when she answered.

We'd talked late into the night, until we both admitted we couldn't keep our eyes open.

God, I wanted to hear her voice. I'd gotten used to us either talking or texting just about every night. There was a two-hour time difference between Colorado and DC, but I knew she'd be up. Stella *wasn't* a morning person.

She answered before I heard the phone ring. "Buck?"

"Hey, Stella."

She was quiet, but I could hear her breathing.

"You mad at me?"

"I am."

"I'm sorry."

"Why didn't you tell me your dad was sick? I thought we were…Forget it. Anyway, I'm sorry for your loss."

"You thought we were what?"

"Friends," she mumbled. "Pretty stupid, huh?"

I realized then that Stella had had a few. "Not stupid at all, darlin'. I'm more than just your friend."

"Don't lie to me, Cope."

"Buck."

"What?"

"You called me Cope. I'm Buck and I don't lie, TJ."

"Don't call me that."

"You gonna tell me your real name?"

She laughed. "That is my real name, but I prefer Stella."

"You know what I mean, darlin'. The name you were given when you were born."

"Oh. That. Well, I swore I'd never tell a soul. You're a soul, so…"

"I miss you."

"You do?"

"Damn right, I do."

"I miss you too," she whispered as though, if she said it quietly enough, it wouldn't count. "I'm sorry about your father," she repeated.

"I'm sorry I didn't tell you about him."

"Why didn't you?"

I shrugged even though she couldn't see me. "He was sick for a long time."

"My mom was sick for a long time before she died too." She paused, and I heard what sounded like ice in a glass.

"Whatcha drinkin'?"

"Bourbon."

"Could use one of those myself."

"Go pour yourself one so I'm not drinking alone."

I walked into the kitchen, reached up to the cupboard over the fridge, and pulled down the bottle of Jack I knew I'd find there. I sloshed some of the brown liquid into a glass, tucked the bottle under my arm, and went back down the hallway.

"Cheers," I muttered.

"*Salut.*"

I finished what was in my glass and poured another.

Stella and I talked for another twenty minutes about absolutely nothing. By then I had enough liquor in my system that all I could picture when I closed my eyes was how her naked body would look under mine.

"I better call it a night. It was good to hear your voice, darlin'." I waited for her to respond but only heard the chimes of the call ending. It was the way she always ended our phone calls. I'd asked her why once.

"I don't say goodbye unless it's forever," she'd told me.

It hadn't occurred to me until now that when I left the wedding, those were the words she used.

6

Buck

My father's funeral was as much of a blur as the visitation had eventually become, with too many people I didn't know paying their respects to a man I hadn't respected since I was a child.

Now, I felt myself counting the minutes until the meeting with the attorney handling my father's estate would be over. As soon as it was, I planned to be on the first flight I could catch out of Colorado. Whether I could pick up another mission right away or not, my plan was to return to DC to see Stella.

While the town of Crested Butte was home to a few law firms, the Wheaton family attorney was in Gunnison—the county seat. The day after the funeral, that's where my siblings and I were headed.

"Hey, Buck," said a guy dressed in a suit and tie as he reached out to shake my hand when we pulled up and piled out of the two vehicles we'd driven over.

"Do I know you?" I asked.

Cord jabbed me with his elbow. "You don't recognize Six-pack Langley?"

I looked the guy up and down. Ol' Six-pack hadn't gotten his nickname from having washboard abs. It was from the six-pack he could down faster than one of us could finish a single beer. "You a lawyer now?"

"That's right. Took over the practice from my dad a few years ago." He looked over at Cord. "I go by Richard now."

I caught the glint in my brother's eye right before Porter jabbed him like Cord had me. "Let's get this over with," he said, motioning for us to go inside.

"As you know," began Six-pack after the rest of us were seated. "Your father's will is complicated. I'll get through it the best I can and ask that you hold your questions until I've finished reading it in its entirety."

That he'd used the word "complicated" seemed to come as no surprise to anyone but me. What the hell did that mean?

Six-pack cleared his throat and adjusted the microphone that sat on his desk.

"You recording this?" I asked.

"Yes, sir."

"Is that necessary?"

"It's our policy, yes."

I motioned for him to go ahead. Six-pack cleared his throat a second time, stated his name along with the names of my brothers, sister, and me.

"We're here today for the reading of the Last Will and Testament of Roscoe Buchtold Wheaton, Senior."

I looked at the document the man held in his hands. It was damn thick for the will of a man who didn't own much outside of a ranch that had been handed down through his family for several generations.

I zoned out most of what he said until I realized all eyes in the room were on me.

"Here's where it gets complicated," said Six-pack. He continued reading a bunch of legal jargon that didn't mean anything to me. He stopped, turned a page, and cleared his throat again.

"The distribution of proceeds of the estate will be reevaluated one year—defined as three hundred and sixty-five days—from the reading of this document. For the duration, the estate's assets will be held within the Roaring Fork Trust.

"That trust stipulates that my oldest son, Roscoe Buchtold Wheaton, Junior, must maintain full-time residency at Roaring Fork Ranch, defined as not being absent from the property for a period longer than for-ty-eight consecutive hours."

"What the hell?" I muttered under my breath.

"Let me finish," said Six-pack.

"If, at the end of the year, one of two things happen, either Roscoe Buchtold Wheaton, Jr., does not main-tain full-time residency as stipulated above, or, after an audit by the accounting firm named in Addendum C of this document, reports show that the ranch fails to earn a profit, then the proceeds of the estate will be distrib-uted at the discretion of the trustee, in their entirety, to include proceeds from the sale of the Roaring Fork Ranch, to local charities including, but not limited to, the Miracles of Hope Children's Charity of Crested Butte, Colorado."

The old saying of being able to hear a pin drop sure as hell fit the current situation.

Six-pack cleared his throat as though he had more to say. I held up my hand.

"Hang on. Is this legal?" I asked.

"It is."

"When was this will drafted? Was he even lucid?" The last time I saw my father, he'd been in and out of consciousness to the point where I wasn't sure he knew I was there.

Six-pack turned back to the first page. "Twelve years ago."

I shook my head. Right after I'd left for college. Or right before. Figures the old bastard was already planning how to get me back to the ranch and keep me there.

I looked around the room at my brothers and sister. Their comments about how happy they were that I was here made a lot more sense. Had they known about our dad's plan to hijack my life? As angry as the idea they did made me, I had no intention of asking in front of Six-pack.

"If you're finished, I'll go on," he said.

I pushed my chair back from the table and stood. "I've heard enough."

Six-pack stood too. "There's more I need to go over with you."

I walked out. When I said I'd heard enough, I meant it. Whatever the rest of the bullshit stipulations were, I didn't care.

"Are you okay?" Holt asked when he came outside with Cord a few minutes later.

"We'll talk when we get back to the ranch."

"That was fucked up," said Porter, storming past us. I'd ask which part, but more than not wanting to have a discussion in front of Six-pack, I didn't want to have one out on the street.

"Sorry," murmured Flynn.

I put my arm around my baby sister's shoulders. "We'll talk once we're home."

Her eyes met mine. "You said 'home.'"

"Don't make too much of that."

Everyone but Porter and I appeared to be walking on eggshells. I was pissed at our dad, but it seemed like my brother was mad at me.

"Where are you going?" Port asked when I walked through the front door and down the hallway.

"Taking a piss. Is that something the old man is monitoring? Does someone have to log every time I take a shit too?"

"Don't be an asshole."

"Yep, that's right. *I'm* the asshole."

Before returning to where I knew my siblings waited, I went into my childhood room and sat down on the bed. Never had I wanted to grab my bag, walk out the front door of this house, and not look back more than I did right now. The audacity of what my father had done was something I couldn't see a road to forgiving. Not that it mattered. He was dead, and yet, he still wanted to control my life from beyond the grave. Why? He had three other sons and a daughter who could run the Roaring Fork without my help.

"Buck?" I heard my sister's voice say from the other side of the door.

"I'll be out in a minute, Flynn."

"Can I come in?"

I stood and opened the door.

"I'm sure this is hard for you to accept."

I shook my head. "That is an understatement, sis."

"I know you and Pop never got along much, but I believe in my heart, he did what he thought was best for the ranch and best for our family."

"I'm not your savior. Not any of yours. If things are as bad as Porter says and the four of you want the ranch, you're going to have to work your asses off. I didn't bring any magic bullets with me."

"It won't matter how hard we work if you leave, Buck," Flynn murmured.

I looked up and saw my three brothers standing in the doorway.

"Are you leavin'?" asked Cord. I looked into his eyes then Holt's, Port's, and finally Flynn's.

I looked down at the floor. Did I really have any choice? My brothers and sister weren't to blame for what our father had done. In fact, they'd probably been trying to hold things together here for the last few years, with no help from me.

"Hell, no, I'm not leaving."

Flynn threw her arms around my neck. I looked beyond her to my brothers. Port was the only one of them not smiling.

"We need a minute," I said, brushing through the doorway and motioning for Porter to follow me back out to the porch.

I slammed the front door behind me and put my hands on my hips. "You wanna tell me what the fuck your problem is, Port?"

"Go to hell, Buck." He tried to get around me, but I shoved him up against the house.

"I didn't do this. The old man did. So whatever you're mad at me for, get over it."

My brother shook his head. "You can't see it from anyone's point of view but your own."

"Tell me how you see it."

"How do you think Cord, Holt, and I feel? We've been here, workin' our fingers to the bone while you've gone off and done whatever the hell you wanted to."

I backed up, and Porter walked around me.

"We should've inherited. Us and Flynn. You shouldn't even be here."

"You got that right." I stepped off the porch and walked toward the barn. When I was sure my brother wouldn't follow, I pulled out my cell.

"Hey, Buck. I was sorry to hear about your father," said Sterling "Hammer" Anderson, an attorney I knew the Invincibles kept on retainer.

"Thanks, Hammer."

"What can I do for you?"

"I need to talk to a lawyer."

"Then, you called the right place."

"I was hoping you could refer me to someone. It's about my dad's will."

"What about it?"

"I want to know whether it's legal or not."

"Who drew it up?"

I pulled out the business card Six-pack gave me and gave Hammer the firm's name.

"You know how to use those money-transfer things?"

I rattled off the names of a couple.

"Yeah, those. Send me $1. Do it now."

I pulled out my phone, opened an app, typed in Hammer's name, and shot him a buck. Seconds later, I received confirmation of his receipt.

"Now that I'm officially on retainer, I'll get a copy of the will sent over. I'll call you back once I've had a chance to review it."

I thanked him and ended the call. Before I could shove the cell back in my pocket, it rang.

"Hey, Rock, what's up?"

"Buck, I'm glad I reached you. There's a situation I thought you'd want to know about."

"What?"

"Stella's aunt along with her housekeeper were found dead."

"Fuck," I said under my breath. "How's Stella?"

"Not good, Buck. There's more. Both women were murdered. Whoever did it, was looking for something."

My phone slipped out of my hand and hit the ground. I bent at the waist, put my hands on my knees, and took several deep breaths.

"Buck? You there?"

I picked up my phone. "Yeah, I'm here. Where is she?"

"She's talking to DC Metro now."

"Who else knows about this?"

"I called you first. Should I try to get in touch with Cope?"

"No. Call Decker. Tell him I'll be there as soon as I can get a flight."

"Roger that."

"Where you off to, Buck?"

I spun around to see my brother Cord standing close enough that he had to have heard my side of the conversation.

"Listen, Cord, this is something I have to do. I'll be back as soon as I can be."

He scrunched his eyes. "Right."

"Back from where?" Porter walked over from where I'd left him on the porch.

"There's been a murder. A family member of someone I'm close to. I have to do this, Port."

He studied me. "Forty-eight hours, Buck. Either you're back by then, or there's no point in ever returning."

7

Stella

The police officer's questions sounded muffled, as though I had cotton stuffed in my ears. My response to just about every one was the same.

"Do you know why someone would want to harm your aunt?"

"I don't."

"It's obvious that whoever killed her and her companion was looking for something. Do you know what that might be?"

I looked around her ransacked apartment. "I don't."

I studied Rock, who was on his cell a few feet away. He'd shown up within moments after I walked into the apartment, found Barb and Nancy only a few feet apart, both lying in pools of blood, and screamed. Had he been following me? Why?

Someone had covered Barb's body with a sheet, but I could still feel her presence. It was as though her soul was calling out to me. "Do not tell them about the hidden key," she warned.

Rock walked over and sat beside me. "Decker is on his way."

I studied him. Decker? Why?

"You're your aunt's only surviving relative?" the police officer asked.

"That's right."

"Where were you—"

"That's enough," said Rock. "No more questions."

"If necessary, I can take her down to the station," the police officer threatened.

"Hold up," I heard another man say. I looked into the eyes of the person who was not only the DC Chief of Police, he was someone I'd once had a relationship with, Alder Jenkins. "There will be no taking Ms. Hunter to the precinct."

"Hey, Jinx," said Rock.

Jinx crouched down in front of me and took my hands in his. "I'm sorry about Barb, honey. Nancy too."

"Thanks." I looked around at the mess in the apartment.

"Let's get you out of here, TJ."

I nodded. "There are some things I'd like to take with me."

"What things specifically?"

Surely, I could tell Jinx about the key, couldn't I? I could trust him, right? Things between us had ended, but he'd always made it clear that if I ever needed him—or wanted him—he'd be there.

I closed my eyes when I swore I could hear Barb's voice tell me not to.

"Her laptop, along with some other personal items."

"For now, this is a crime scene, but I'll get you back in here as soon as I can." Jinx turned to Rock. "Got a minute?"

They stepped away, thinking I couldn't hear them, but I could. "I don't want her left alone."

"Roger that," Rock answered.

"Do you need support from Metro?"

Rock shook his head. "Ashford is on his way here. I'm sure he'll be putting a bigger team together. For now, I'll take her to her apartment."

"Good." Jinx walked back over to me, crouched down like he had before, and covered my hands with his. "We'll find who did this, honey. In the meantime, Rock will make sure you're safe. I'll come by later."

"Thanks," I mumbled a second time, not knowing what else to say.

"TJ, what about Nancy? Do you know if she has any family?"

I shook my head. I'd known Nancy for almost a decade, but had no idea whether she did. She'd never mentioned anyone.

Jinx stood. "I'll see what I can find out."

After returning to my apartment, I spent the next few hours making arrangements for my aunt to be cremated, per her wishes, once the medical examiner was done with her body. I had no way of knowing when that might be.

The other thing I did was try to recall every word Barb had said to me the last time I saw her. Given she seemed to think there was some correlation between my book and the story that had ended her career, I searched for everything about it I could find. When I came up with very little, I made a list of everything I could remember her telling me about it, hoping that once I was able to get a hold of her computer, I'd find more.

I was reviewing my notes, trying to piece things together, when I heard a knock at the door. Rock opened it, and Decker Ashford walked in. I closed my laptop and set it on the coffee table in front of me.

"Hey, Stella," he said, coming over to sit beside me. "I'm sorry about Barb."

I leaned against the back of the sofa. "Did you ever meet her?"

"I never had the pleasure, but I admired the hell out of her anyway."

I smiled. "She was formidable."

"If it's okay with you, boss, I'm going to head back over there and see what I can find out," Rock said to Deck.

"Copy that," he answered. Ashford waited until the door closed behind Rock before he spoke again.

"How are you holding up?"

"I could use a drink. Better yet, a bottle."

He stood. "Where do you keep your stash?"

"Under the breakfast bar." I put my hand on his arm. "Deck, is there any reason why Rock would've been following me?"

Before he could answer, there was another knock at the door. When Deck walked over and opened it, Buck walked in.

"What are you doing here?" I stood and asked as he strode toward me. He pulled me into his arms without answering. "Give us a minute," he said to Decker, who walked out and closed the door behind him.

Once he was gone, Buck pulled back and cupped my face with his palm. I moved out of his grasp and sat back down on the sofa. He sat beside me.

"I asked what you're doing here."

"Rock called. He told me about Barb."

"She's dead. So is Nancy."

"I'm sorry, Stella."

"Did he tell you they were murdered?"

Buck reached over and stroked my cheek with his thumb. "Yes. That's part of the reason I'm here."

I leaned back, out of his reach, and looked away in an attempt to get control over the emotions clogging my throat. I took a deep breath and looked back at him.

"Are you part of the bigger team Decker is putting together?"

He cocked his head. "Bigger team?"

"Jinx Jenkins asked Rock if he'd need Metro's help with my detail. Rock told him Deck was on his way here and that he'd put a 'bigger' team together."

Buck shook his head. "Rock called me first. I'm the one who told him to call Ashford. As far as your detail or a team, Deck and I haven't had a chance to speak yet."

"Were you the lead before?"

He leaned forward. "What are you talking about?"

"You left the wedding. Rock showed up. It was too convenient."

"I see. You think that's what the wedding was. I wasn't your date; I was your bodyguard."

I nodded and looked at the blue polish on my nails. It was already starting to chip.

"Stella?"

"What?"

"Look at me."

I looked up from my nails, but not at him. I couldn't. If I did, I might lose the tenuous hold I had on my emotions.

Buck put one arm behind me on the sofa. With his other hand, he turned my face so I was looking at him. "I did ask Rock to watch out for you when I had to leave on such short notice, but only because I care about you. He wasn't on your 'detail.' It was just a favor to me. He called to tell me that you found Barb and Nancy, and I caught the first flight I could to come here. Again only because I care about you."

"Please don't do this," I begged.

He lowered his arm to my shoulders and pulled me into him. When my eyes filled with tears, I buried my face in his chest. "Let it out," he murmured as I cried the tears I'd been trying so hard to hold in. Buck stroked my hair with one hand while he held me tight to him with his other arm.

"It's my fault," I whispered.

Buck brushed my hair from my face and looked into my eyes. "What makes you say that?"

I shook my head.

"It's okay," he soothed. "We don't have to talk about it now. We don't have to talk about anything right now."

I appreciated what Buck was trying to do, but I had to get this out. "She warned me." I reached for my laptop and handed it to him. "That's everything I could remember."

I watched as he read over my notes and then looked at me. "Have you shown this to Decker?"

"He arrived a few minutes before you did."

Buck pulled out his phone. "Okay if I ask him to come back in?"

"Sure." I got up and walked over to the window and then thought better of it. I shuddered with the idea that whoever had killed my aunt and her housekeeper could be out there, watching me. I went into the kitchen, got out three glasses, and poured myself two fingers of bourbon. "Join me?" I asked Buck.

"Maybe later."

He walked over to the door but stepped out rather than let Decker in. Seconds later, they both came inside.

"What was that all about?" I asked, pouring myself one more shot before putting the cap on the bottle.

"I wanted to make sure we were free to talk." He made a circular motion with his finger. It reminded me of the other night when my phone rang as soon as I'd walked in the door. I'd wondered then if Barb had my place bugged. Evidently not.

I pulled out a stool and sat at the breakfast bar.

"You wanna give Deck the rundown?" asked Buck, pouring himself a shot. He held up the bottle, but Decker shook his head.

"You know I've been working on a book about you, Cope, and Irish taking down Fisk?"

"I do," said Deck.

"When I was last with her, Barb warned me to drop it. It wasn't the first time she did, but this time she said that if I didn't, the same thing that happened to her would happen to me."

"Meaning?"

"I'm not really sure, other than it might destroy my career. Then she took it a step further. She said that if I continued writing this book, it might be over both of our dead bodies." I shook my head. "I thought she was being melodramatic."

"Did she give you anything more to go on?" Deck asked.

I looked at Buck, who nodded for me to go on.

"There's a safe-deposit box. She said it contained 'evidence.'"

"Evidence of what?"

I gave Decker and Buck the short version of the scandal that had destroyed my aunt's career.

Of everything I told them, I only saw Decker write down two words—*Operation Argead.*

Buck's eyes flared. "So about this safe-deposit box. Do you know where it is?"

I shrugged. "She tried to give me a key, but I put it back where she'd gotten it from."

"Where was that?" asked Deck.

"Hidden in the piano. Under one of the keys."

Decker held up his phone. "Let's see what Rock can tell us about what's going on over there."

"Go ahead."

When Rock answered, Decker put him on speaker.

"Looks like they're wrapping up for tonight. They took bags of evidence out of here. FYI, Jinx is headed your way."

"Anyone within hearing distance?" Decker asked.

"Negative."

"Stella said Barb tried to give her a key to a safe-deposit box. She said it was hidden inside the piano." Decker looked at me. "Where?" he mouthed.

"Tenth key from the right. Lift it up. The safe key should be hidden under it."

"Roger that."

Deck ended the call. "Makes sense that whoever ransacked her place was looking for it." He looked over at Buck. "We need to relocate."

"Copy that."

"Stella, get a few things together. We're going to move you somewhere more secure."

"What about Jinx?" I asked. "Buck said he was on his way here."

Decker pulled out his cell. "I'll give him a call."

Buck stood, walked over to the window, and rolled his shoulders.

"What's up?" asked Decker, setting his phone back down.

"I can't stay."

"All right. Why not?"

"There's some shit goin' down back home." He took a deep breath. "It's complicated." He held up his phone, and it looked like a timer was counting down.

Deck cocked his head. "What's that?"

"When I have to be back in Colorado. If I'm not, my brothers and sister lose everything."

"What the fuck?" Decker looked down at something on his phone. "And another what the fuck?" he added under his breath.

"What else happened?" Buck asked.

"Nothing. Get back to you having to return to Colorado. What's that all about?"

"My father's will. I have Hammer taking a look at it, but unless he tells me it isn't legal, I can't risk it."

Decker walked toward him. "Enough with goin' in circles. What's your point, Buck?"

He looked over at me. "I want you to understand that, before now, I was not hired to protect you, Stella."

I nodded.

"I need you to tell me you believe me."

I looked at Decker, who appeared as confused by what Buck had said as I was. "I don't know why it's so important to you, Buck. But okay, I believe you."

"No offense to you or your team, Deck, but I don't trust anyone to head up Stella's detail but me."

"Even me?"

"That's right."

"Huh."

"It's just the way I feel, sir."

Decker turned to me. "What about you?"

When my eyes met Buck's, I could swear they were pleading with me. "I don't know what you're asking," I mumbled.

Buck walked over to me and held out his hand. "Come with me." I stood, and he led me toward the hallway. "Which one is the bedroom?"

I pointed to the door at the end of the hall. We went inside, and he closed it behind us.

"Do you trust me, Stella?"

I didn't even need to think about it. "Yes."

"Do you believe me when I say that my gut is telling me you need protection and I need to be the one to provide it?"

"Yes."

"You're sure?"

"Yes, Buck."

He smiled. "Your trust means a lot to me. Now, I need to ask you something else."

"Go ahead."

"Will you come to Colorado with me?"

"When?"

Buck pulled out his phone. "We have to be in the air by six tomorrow night. If I can get us a flight directly into Gunnison, it'll buy us another five hours or so."

"Twenty-four hours."

"That's right."

"There are things that need to be taken care of."

"Which of those things would require you staying here?"

I rubbed my temples. "I don't know." Was there any reason I couldn't leave? What the hell else was I going to do if I didn't go with Buck? Sit here, or wherever Decker stuck me, all the while feeling trapped? Hell, no. "What if I need to come back?"

"We'll work it out."

I knew Jinx would offer to stay with me, but in my gut, I trusted Buck more. I would also feel safer if I got the hell out of DC. Until Jinx or someone else figured out who'd killed my aunt and her housekeeper, I'd be afraid of my own shadow, and I wasn't the kind of person who lived my life in fear.

"Where would I stay?"

"On my family's ranch. With me."

I raised a brow, and he smiled.

"There's a cabin not far from the main house. You can stay there."

"How will you protect me, then?"

Buck smiled again. "I didn't say I wouldn't be staying there with you."

"All right. I'll go."

A huge smile split Buck's face. "Good."

He led me back out to the main room. Decker was sitting at the breakfast bar, working on his laptop.

"This your spread?" he asked Buck, who looked over his shoulder.

"Not mine. My family's."

"Is this right?" he asked, pointing to something on the screen.

"Yes, sir."

"Fifty thousand acres in a revocable trust."

Decker looked at me and then back at Buck.

"Not only do you have to fulfill the stipulation of full-time residency, the ranch also has to be in the black within a year of your father's death."

"How in the hell—"

"You'd do well to remember just exactly who you're dealin' with, young Buck."

Buck nodded.

"Tell me about these outbuildings."

Buck sat down and explained what each one was.

"That the bunkhouse?"

"One of them."

Decker slowly nodded and continued to study the screen. He sat back in his chair, removed his cowboy hat, and set it on the bar beside his computer. "I've got a proposal for you, Buck."

"What's that?"

Decker turned to me.

"I'll go pack."

"Thanks, Stella."

"Don't forget to call Jinx," I reminded him as I walked down the hallway.

8

Buck

I listened while Decker informed Jinx that we'd be temporarily moving Stella to the apartment the Invincibles kept in the building where Ali had lived when she was undercover. For now, that was the safest place for her. I didn't like him telling anyone outside of our team where we were headed, not even the DC Metro chief. It surprised me that Decker was comfortable with it.

"What's the deal with Jinx?" I asked when he ended the call.

"He and Stella had a…thing."

"Had?"

Decker glared at me and pointed to his laptop. "Your place doesn't have shit for security."

"Haven't ever needed it."

"Well, now you sure as hell do. And I doubt you have the capital to invest in it."

"I can keep her safe."

"It isn't just her, Buck."

"What's that mean?"

"Irish, for now. He, Cope, Ali, and Stella represent the front line in this thing."

"And you."

Decker shook his head. "I can take care of myself, and don't you ever forget it."

I pulled out the stool and sat down beside him. "It didn't end with Fisk's arrest, did it?"

"Doesn't look that way."

"And you think the murders are somehow related?"

"Don't you?"

"It's the only thing that makes sense."

He nodded. "That's right, young Buck."

I laughed. "You gonna keep calling me that?"

"As long as you keep acting like one."

"You said Cope and Ali; have you contacted them?"

"I have and they're secure. For now."

Given it had taken Decker less than ten minutes to find the particulars of my father's will, there was no way I was going to ask him if he was sure. I already felt like an idiot for actually saying out loud that I didn't trust him to protect Stella. It's a wonder he hadn't thrown me out on my ass.

"Here's what we're gonna do." Decker outlined his plan to contract the Roaring Fork to provide a secure location for asset protection. In exchange, the Invincibles would install a state-of-the-art security system, as well as provide a stipend to the ranch for as long as the assets remained on the property.

"This might not be enough to get your family's ranch into the black, but it'll help."

"We have some other ideas."

Decker sat back in his chair and folded his arms. "Well, what are they?"

"Just some stuff my brothers have been kickin' around."

"I'm beginning to think you aren't smart enough to handle this assignment, Wheaton. Have you forgotten I've been the ranch manager of one of the most successful operations in all of the United States for the last ten years?" With every word he spoke, Decker's voice got louder.

"Okay, okay. They've been talking about turning it into a dude ranch."

"Good thing you told me that. It'll impact the way we set up security." Decker zoomed in on the map on his screen. "This is the main house?" he asked, pointing.

"That's right."

"What's over here?"

"Can you zoom in more?"

When he did, I could see that three of the old cabins appeared as though they'd already been fixed up. "Looks like guest quarters."

"For now, that'll be where we set up our operation." I watched as he added perimeter outlines and notes to other sections of the map. "What else?"

"Roughstock contracting."

"There's someone else in Gunnison County I heard got heavy into that."

"That's right, the Flying R." My cell phone vibrated. "It's Hammer."

"Put it on speaker."

"Hey, Hammer, I got Decker here with me."

"Hey, boys. Buck, I gotta ask you, what the fuck did you do to your old man to make him do something like this?"

"I left."

Hammer laughed, and so did Decker. "That'll do it. Listen, I got bad news and worse news for ya."

"Great," I muttered. "Let's hear it."

"There isn't any way for you to get out of this. The terms are straightforward and the stipulations are legal. There are a few loopholes. For example, if you're dying and you can get a doctor to verify you only have a certain amount of time left, you can leave the ranch for medical care. However, it needs two additional doctors with no affiliation to the first to verify your impending mortality." Hammer cleared his throat. "That's the other thing that will render the stipulation moot."

"What's that?"

"If you're dead." There was a moment of uncomfortable silence between the three of us. Decker was the first to break it.

"Hey, Ham, I need you to draw up a lease agreement between the Invincibles and the Roaring Fork." He turned to me. "Who's got power of attorney for the ranch?"

"I would assume the same lawyer who handled the estate."

"You know this guy?" Decker asked.

"Went to high school with him."

"Tell me you didn't hang him in a locker during passing periods or some other shit like that."

"Nah, Six-pack and I always got along great."

"What kind of cash does the Roaring Fork have available?" asked Deck.

"Are you asking me or Hammer?"

"Whichever one of you knows the answer."

"That's the other bad news. Your father's trust has been divided into two parts. The first is the ranch; the second is the cash. It allows for a monthly distribution to keep things going, but not anything that would allow for capital improvement."

"Thanks, Ham." Decker reached over and hit the end-call button on my phone. He closed his laptop and stood. "Please ask Stella to come back out."

I rapped on the bedroom door, easing it open when I didn't hear her answer. Her eyes were open, and she was staring into space.

"Decker asked me to come and get you."

She got off the bed. "What a fucked up mess this is."

"If anybody can get to the bottom of it, you can, Stella."

Her head shot up. "What makes you say that?"

"You're not just Barb Hunter's niece. You're one of the best investigative journalists in the country. Hell, Stella, in the world. If you think I'm gonna let you sit on your ass and watch me cowboy all day once we're back in Colorado, you're wrong."

She smiled, and damn, if it wasn't a beautiful sight. "You gonna crack your whip on me, Buck?"

"If that's what it takes." I looked down at the carry-on bag sitting near the door. "This your stuff?"

"I wasn't sure what to bring."

"A couple pairs of jeans will do it."

"Jeans? You're kidding, right?"

I shook my head, afraid to say I wasn't, since I had no idea where she was going with this.

"I don't own jeans."

I almost laughed, but stopped myself by biting my tongue so hard I drew blood.

"Hey, you two," Decker called out from the hallway. "Rock says the coast is clear. He's headed in to see if he can find the safe-deposit key."

I motioned with my head for Stella, whose cheeks were flaming bright red, to follow me back out to where he waited.

"We'll head over to the Invincibles' apartment as soon as you're ready," Decker said to Stella.

She pointed to her bag. "I'm ready."

I walked over and closed the draperies I'd pulled open earlier. Decker checked the fridge that I wasn't surprised to see was completely empty.

I'd never seen the woman eat much of anything. My guess was she didn't weigh in at more than a buck and a quarter and that was on a frame that had to be five feet seven. Her dark hair wasn't quite shoulder length, and the way she kept it styled back, away from her face, highlighted her dark, almond-shaped eyes.

She was older than me by about six years, but my face looked more weathered. Hell, I had wrinkles from spending too much time in the sun by the time I hit my early twenties.

Stella had a tight little body with narrow shoulders and a waist I bet I could wrap my hands around, and boobs big enough that they could fill a C-cup bra.

And that ass? Damn, I couldn't wait to see how it filled out a pair of Cinch jeans.

When we arrived at the Invincibles' apartment, Rock wasn't there yet.

It was a nice place with a view of the Capitol building—especially beautiful at night. It had three bedrooms, but with Rock, Decker, Stella, and me all staying here, we were one short. I took my bag and set it near the end of the sofa. I put Stella's carry-on in the master bedroom after checking to see Rock wasn't staying in there.

Decker pulled out his laptop and sat at the kitchen counter.

"Why don't you see if you can get some sleep?" I asked Stella, who like earlier, appeared to be staring off into space.

"I'm not tired."

She looked dead on her feet, not that I'd tell her that. I'm sure I didn't look much better. I pulled her over to the sofa, sat beside her, and put my arm around her shoulders.

"What are you doing?"

"I need a hug."

"You're hugging me."

"It still counts."

"There's something I need to take care of." Stella wiggled free of me and went in the direction of the bedroom.

I couldn't help but watch her ass as she scuffled off. As much as I looked forward to seeing it wrapped in a pair of jeans, it looked damn good in the tight knit pants she was wearing. "Hey, Stella," I called after her.

She looked over her shoulder at me. "Yeah?"

"What do you call the pants you're wearing?"

"Leggings. Why?"

"I like 'em."

When I heard the bedroom door click behind her, I pulled out my cell, figuring it was past time for me to check in with Porter.

"Hey, Buck," he answered.

"Hey, Port. Listen, there's some stuff I need to talk to you about." I went down the same hallway Stella had and into one of the other bedrooms.

"I got a call from Six-pack. Something about a lease agreement."

"Yeah, about that." I told him everything I could about what had gone down since I arrived in DC. He knew enough about the work I did that he didn't ask too many questions.

"The money will help. That's for damn sure."

"I'm relieved to hear you think so."

"Why?"

"It all happened kind of fast. I wish I'd had time to run it by you."

"It's your decision, Buck."

"No, it isn't. We're in this thing together, Port."

"What can I do to help?"

"I'd like to make use of the three cabins that sit along the river."

"That's easy enough."

"It means that the dude ranch idea may have to stay on hold for the time being."

"I saw the numbers. What your company is paying us is more than we could make in a fully operational season."

"It'll buy us time anyway."

"How do you see this playing out, Buck?"

"What do you mean?"

"At the end of the year."

"The clock hasn't been runnin' two days yet. Let's hold off on figuring out the endgame."

"Whatever you say, boss."

"See ya soon, Port."

"When will you be back?"

"Before the clock strikes the forty-eighth hour. Don't you worry."

I breathed a sigh of relief that my brother sounded more lighthearted when we ended the call than he had when I left the ranch earlier today.

I still didn't know how bad off we were financially, but it was obvious that Ashford did. While Port seemed pleased by the amount the Invincibles would be paying us, Deck had warned that it might not be enough to get us in the black.

That wasn't all I had on my mind. The idea that my siblings knew what our father had done with his will made me uneasy. Why the hell hadn't a single one forewarned me?

9

Stella

There wasn't anything I needed to take care of; I just needed to get away from Buck. Since he arrived, he'd been so *affectionate,* hugging me or putting his arm around me. What was that all about? Did he think I needed to be coddled because of Barb's death? If anything, I'd prefer to be left alone.

I lay down on the bed and looked up at the ceiling. Who was I kidding? I loved having his hands on me. I'd been fantasizing about it long enough. Now that it was happening, why did I run from it?

That was an easy question to answer: Cope. Not because I still had a thing for him. I'd let go of that long before his and Ali's wedding. The humiliation I felt at his rejection, though, was something I'd never forget.

When I'd finally mustered up the nerve to ask him if he wanted to "hang out," he'd let me down easy. So easy that it made me like him more than I already did. But my pride had been sorely wounded, and that was something I'd never forget. Nor would I make that mistake again.

Guys like Cope—and Buck—were trained to make those around them feel comfortable. They were experts at winning people's trust, whether it was to get information out of them or to get them to do their bidding.

The day I realized Cope's flirting was nothing more than that, my heart broke a little, but more importantly, I learned my lesson. I could still talk big, tell myself Buck was different, even fantasize that he and I might've shared sheets a time or two, but in my heart—and my head—I knew better than to take the cowboy's flirtation seriously.

"Yeah?" I said when I heard a knock at the door. Buck eased it open. "Heard from Rock."

"And?"

"He found the key."

"Thank God." However, this meant I couldn't go to Colorado with him. Didn't it? On the other hand, all I had was the key. I had to figure out which bank the safe box was located in, and I needed the death certificate along with a copy of her will before any bank would let me access it.

Buck came inside the bedroom and closed the door behind him. He leaned up against the wall. "Wish you were thinking out loud."

I looked up at him. "Did he find a laptop?"

"Not that he said, although if one was found, it was probably taken into evidence."

That made sense. "I need to contact Barb's attorney. He's in Manhattan. I can take care of that in the morning."

He nodded but made no move to leave.

I propped myself up on my elbows. "Was there anything else?"

"Yeah." He looked down at the floor. "Jinx is here."

I sat up and ran my hand over my hair. "Oh."

"You wanna see him?"

"I should."

Buck raised his head. "I could tell him you're already in bed."

"That's okay. I need to talk to him."

He put his hand on the doorknob but looked like he was waiting for something.

"What?" I asked.

"You comin'?"

"Please just send him back here to the bedroom."

Buck's nostrils flared, and his eyes scrunched. He opened his mouth as though he was about to say something. Instead, he opened the door and walked out.

So much time passed, I decided Jinx must have left. I was about to turn off the light and close my eyes when the door opened.

"Hey, TJ." Jinx walked over to the side of the bed I was stretched out on. "How are you doing?"

Let's see…my aunt was murdered, I was the one who found her, she was probably killed because of a story I was pursuing—what did he expect me to say? That I was fine? God, how had I forgotten how much Jinx annoyed me? "Not great, Jinx. Was that all you wanted to talk to me about?"

"Who's the guy with the ponytail?"

Now I wished I would've followed Buck out to the main room instead of asking him to send Jinx to the bedroom. At least then I could've walked away. "You know who he is."

"I don't."

"Buck Wheaton. He works with Ashford and the Invincibles. He was on Ali's detail."

"Doesn't look familiar."

How was this guy the chief of a police force the size of DC Metro's? "He's on my detail now. That's probably all you need to know."

"Decker said you're leaving tomorrow. I don't think that's a good idea."

I shrugged. "Safer than staying here."

Jinx held out his hand. When I took it, he pulled me to my feet. "I'm going to miss you, TJ," he said, embracing me.

I heard the door open. "Everything okay in here?" Buck asked.

"It's fine," I said, backing away. "Jinx was just leaving." I looked from Buck back to Jinx. "Before you go, I'm assuming you took Barb's laptop into evidence. How soon can I get it back?"

"We didn't find a computer, laptop or otherwise."

My eyes met Buck's.

"I'll walk you out," he said to Jinx.

"You won't reconsider?" he asked.

"Reconsider what?"

"Sticking around here."

"I didn't realize you were really asking."

"If I was?"

I shook my head. Jinx leaned down and brushed my lips with his. The kiss was chaste but made me uncomfortable nonetheless.

When Buck cleared his throat, Jinx studied me.

"You should go," I mumbled.

"I'll be in touch," he said before leaning down to kiss me again. When he left, I walked over and closed the door behind him. For a moment, I thought about locking it but turned off the light and got back in bed without doing so.

As I expected, within a couple of minutes, the door eased open.

"You okay, Stella?" asked Buck.

"I'm fine."

"Goodnight, then."

"Goodnight, Buck." Was it my imagination, or was there an edge to his voice?

I wasn't sure how long I'd been lying awake, staring into nothing, unable to sleep, when my phone vibrated. I picked it up from the bedside table and swiped the screen with my finger.

You still awake? said the text from Buck.

I smiled. *Yeah. Guess you are too.*

Can't sleep.

Why not?

I have this friend. She and I talk every night. I have a hard time sleeping if I don't hear her voice.

Maybe you should call her.

I smiled when his call came through a few seconds later. "Hi," I answered.

"Hi."

"So, Buck, are you saying the sound of my voice puts you to sleep?"

He laughed. "That isn't what I'm saying at all."

"What are you saying?"

"You soothe me, Stella."

"You soothe me too." I took a deep breath. "Can I ask you something?"

"Always."

"Why was it so important to you that I say I believed you weren't on my detail before?"

"I needed to make sure you know I wouldn't lie to you."

"I do. So. Colorado?"

"Yeah. Ever been?"

"Never. What's it like?"

"Depends on where you go. Denver is like any other big city, just more spread out. Out east is just like bein' in Kansas."

I laughed. "What does that mean?"

"Flat as far as the eye can see."

"And to the west?"

"The Rocky Mountains, darlin'."

"Which part are we going to?"

"Heart of the Rockies, to a place called Crested Butte."

"Tell me about it."

"It was a great place to grow up—most of the time. Gets damn cold there in the winter, though, and if you live or work on a ranch like I did, it doesn't matter if it's thirty below zero; you still gotta get the chores done."

"What was good about it?"

"Everything else. Best skiing in the world as far as I'm concerned. A main thoroughfare that's straight out of the Old West with bars that have been there longer than there have been roads. Wide-open spaces with endless trails you can hike. Streams and rivers for fishing. Some of the best hunting in the state. The largest Aspen grove in the world sits on top of Kebler Pass. It's also where the Roaring Fork River begins. The headwaters are on our family's ranch and are what it's named for."

"The only thing you said I could identify with are the bars."

"You'll like the rest just as much, I promise."

"Hiking? Hunting? You really don't know me at all, do you?"

"You may surprise yourself. Somewhere inside, I bet there's a mountain girl just dying to get out and explore a place like Crested Butte."

"I doubt it, but we'll see," I murmured.

"You gettin' sleepy?"

"I didn't think it was possible, but yeah, I am."

"Me too. Sweet dreams, Stella."

"Sweet dreams, Buck."

I closed my eyes and tried to picture myself in a place like Crested Butte.

"Hey, sleepyhead," I heard someone say. "Time to wake up."

I opened my eyes, and Buck was sitting on the bed, beside me.

"What time is it?"

"A little after ten. Decker, Rock, and I have been up goin' on three hours."

I pulled the blanket over my head. "Heathens, all of you."

"That may be true, but there are some things we need to take care of today."

I pulled the blanket away from my face and then thought better of it. Even I avoided looking at myself in the mirror right after I woke up. It definitely wasn't something I wanted to subject anyone else to—especially Buck. "Go away."

He laughed. "Okay, but if you aren't up and about in thirty, Decker may be the next person lookin' for you."

"Is there coffee?"

"There will be."

After I showered, I called my aunt's attorney's office, expecting to leave a message. Instead, Mr. Owens came right on the line.

"TJ, I was so sorry to hear about Barb."

"I'm surprised you heard already."

"Yes, well, I've been your aunt's attorney for quite some time."

"Who contacted you?"

"You and I have some things to discuss. I'll have my secretary set up a meeting. When can you come to the office?"

"I…uh…can't. I'll be out of town for a while."

"It's important, TJ."

"I'll have my lawyer get in touch with you." I ended the call. On my way out to the kitchen, I took it a step further and turned off my phone. There was something about the exchange that didn't sit right with me, especially when he blew right past my question about who had contacted him.

"Everything okay?" Buck asked, handing me a cup of black coffee.

"I just got off the phone with Barb's attorney."

Decker looked up from his computer. "And?"

"Someone contacted him about her death."

"I thought we were keeping this quiet," said Buck.

Decker looked from him to me. "Did he say who?"

I shook my head.

"Rock, you wanna see what you can find out?"

"On it." Rock pulled out his phone and left the room.

"Who's he calling?" I asked.

"Jinx." Decker turned back to Buck. "To answer your question, we're keeping the lid tight on this one."

"What else did he say?" Buck asked me.

"He wanted to set up a time for us to meet."

"Your response?" asked Decker.

"I told him I'd be out of town, and I'd have my lawyer contact him."

Decker nodded. "Good. We'll engage Hammer."

Buck took a step closer to me. "Did you mention the safe-deposit key?"

"I didn't."

"Also good," said Decker.

Rock came back to the kitchen. "Jinx said it wasn't anyone from Metro."

"Stella, can I see your phone?"

I pulled it out, handed it to Decker, and watched as he took it apart. "Rock will replace it before we take off."

Decker put his laptop in his bag. "Time to head out. Rock?"

"Irish and I will meet you at the airfield at thirteen hundred."

"Airfield?" I asked.

"All this damn travel," mumbled Decker. "If K19 can have their own plane, so can we."

"K19?" I whispered to Buck.

"Another private intelligence firm. I'll explain more later."

10

Buck

We'd been in the air almost two hours when Decker tapped me on the shoulder and motioned toward the back of the plane.

I shifted Stella so she rested her head against a pillow rather than my shoulder, relieved when she didn't wake up. I went into the aft stateroom where Deck waited with Irish and Rock, and closed the door behind me.

"I've been looking into the mission Stella's aunt stuck her nose into," Deck began.

"Operation Argead?"

"That's the one."

"What have you found?"

"Absolutely nothing." Decker looked up at me with a glint in his eye.

"Sounds like Burns may have had a hand in making it disappear."

"You're reading my mind."

"What's your plan?"

"Here's how it's gonna go. I've got a crew headed to your ranch now. They should already be there by the time we land. I'll get them started on setup, and then Rock can take over until I get back."

"Rock? Shouldn't that be something I work on?" Given my education in tech and the kind of work I did for the agency, it only made sense I should do it over Rock.

All three men looked up at me. Each one had a smirk on his face.

"What?"

"You're gonna have plenty to keep you busy."

Decker turned to Irish. "Your job is to find out everything you can about Kerr and his tenure at Interpol."

When I returned to my seat, Stella was awake.

"What's going on?" she asked.

"Decker has a plan for when we land."

"Anything I need to know?"

Deck sat down in the row of seats facing ours before I had the chance to answer. "I was hoping you and I could chat," he said, looking straight at her.

"What about?"

"Kerr and the Operation Argead story."

"I don't know much."

"You said Barb had an affair with Kerr?"

"She was accused of it. She never admitted it to me."

"It was almost like she was burned. She lost everything but her identity," I muttered.

Decker studied me and then turned back to Stella. "Whoever went after her, made sure she lost all credibility. Who was she working for at the time?"

"She was always independent. Up until that one, every story she wrote got picked up, usually by AP."

"They didn't back her?"

"They didn't even run it. Worse, they published a follow-up, accusing her of manufacturing evidence. She became *persona non grata* overnight."

"Does the name Burns Butler mean anything to you?" Deck asked her.

"Of course it does."

"In what context?"

"If you're asking if Barb ever spoke of him, the answer is no. Cope did, though."

There wasn't an agent alive, especially among those like me who worked in technology, who didn't revere Laird "Burns" Butler. Other than Burns' oldest son,

Kade, also known as Doc, there were few people in the business as close to the man as Deck was.

Years ago, when Decker was a teenager, he was adopted by MI6 Chief Z Alexander, who at the time, was living in Texas and running the King-Alexander Ranch, which he'd inherited from his late wife. Seeing something promising in Ashford, Z had contacted Burns, who'd agreed to mentor the teen in intelligence technology.

Many would argue that Deck had surpassed Burns in capability long ago, but the man himself never would. He humbly relinquished the "best in the world" title to Butler and always gave credit where he believed it was due. I didn't have an opinion either way. Given my degree was in information technology, both men intimidated the hell out of me.

The scholarship I'd received to attend the University of Maryland was a combined academic and sports scholarship—for football. I'd played for the Terps all four years, as a tight end. I was big enough to be a monster blocker and quick enough to catch passes. I'd gotten a couple of offers to play in the NFL, but I wasn't interested. By that time, I was far enough along in my degree that the agency had sent out a couple of feelers.

The way I saw it, I had a far better chance of never returning to ranch life if I got a job with the Central Intelligence Agency. When assignments started popping up first with just Ashford and then with the Invincibles, I was always first in line to get them, even if the jobs were only for asset protection.

In this case, it wasn't spy-tech Decker needed Burns' help with, though. The man was also considered the best in the business when it came to making an op, or an entire mission, look like it had never happened.

"Buck, you still with us?" said Deck.

"Yeah, sorry. What did you say?"

"After we arrive in Colorado, I'll be heading to California to meet with Burns."

Working with Burns, or just having an opportunity to meet him, was something I'd never dreamed possible. Still didn't. For all intents and purposes, the man was retired. I sure as hell wished I could go to California with Decker, but that was out of the question with the shit my father had pulled. Not to mention, there was no justifiable reason for me to go.

"Whatever Stella can recall about the story will be helpful to know in advance."

"I've never known much outside of the fact that it ruined my aunt's life."

Decker nodded and stood.

"I don't suppose there's a chance in hell I could go with you?" said Stella, echoing my earlier thoughts.

"None whatsoever, unless you can convince this guy I'd be an okay number two on your detail." Decker motioned at me.

"Oh no, you don't. You can forget making me the bad guy."

He laughed. "Tell you what, if Burns knows anything about Operation Argead, I'll try to talk him into coming to Colorado. Fair enough?"

Stella's face fell, but it appeared more in acceptance of the situation than disappointment.

"How long do you anticipate being there?" I asked.

"That depends on what Burns knows. Not more than a few hours would be my guess, but then I have to return to Texas."

Stella put her hand on my arm. "It's okay. Maybe another time."

It wasn't like her to give up so easily, not on anything, but I wouldn't ask her about it now, with Decker standing right beside us.

The rest of the flight was bumpy enough that the pilot suggested everyone stay put with our seat belts fastened. When I felt Stella tense beside me, I slid my hand into hers.

She looked down when I wove our fingers together. "What are you doing?"

"I'm holdin' your hand, Stella."

"Why?"

I angled my head so I could look into her eyes. "I've waited a damn long time to be able to."

She looked away, but she left her hand where it was.

"It's so beautiful," she commented on the drive from the Gunnison airfield into Crested Butte. It was a typical "Bluebird" day in the state that boasted more than three hundred days of sunshine a year.

"It's the next right," I told Rock after we'd driven past the entrance to the Flying R on the left. The road that led to the Roaring Fork went through a gated golf course community, something my father had tried to stop from being developed by bidding on the land himself. That he had been outbid at the last minute by a developer out of Texas was something that ate away at him for the rest of his life.

The road narrowed and went between two large red-rock formations surrounded by aspens. Just beyond that, was the ranch's main gate. As the road curved around, the first structures we came to were the original barn and farmhouse. The house hadn't been lived in during my lifetime, and the barn was only used for overflow hay storage, but both had always been my two favorite buildings on the property. There was a time I'd thought about restoring them and living in the farmhouse.

My father shot that idea down in the same way he had most ideas my brothers and I had. My mother was still alive at the time and ran interference when the old man threatened to tear them down. She'd issued her own threat, telling him that if he tried, she'd see to it that they were declared historic landmarks.

I shook my head and laughed at how she'd always been the only one not intimidated by him.

"What are you thinking about?" Stella asked.

"Ancient history," I mumbled.

The road came to a three-prong fork. "That way will be where we set up the dude ranch," I said, pointing to the far left. "The middle goes to the main ranch house and to the three refurbished cabins. Stock contracting will be to the far right."

"Nice of the geography to play along," said Rock, looking over at Decker.

"It does make our job easier."

Ten minutes later, we came to a crest and the wide expanse of our ranch opened up before us. Stella gasped. Even I had to admit, on a day like today, it was breathtaking.

Rock looked over his shoulder at me. "How did you ever leave this place?"

"It wasn't the place; it was the people. One person in particular."

Stella's eyes met mine, and in them, I could see the questions I'd tried to avoid when I didn't tell her about my father being ill.

Two SUVs, identical to the one we were riding in, were parked in front of the house. "Is that your crew?" I asked Decker when we exited our vehicle and walked toward the house.

"Affirmative," he muttered, looking at something on his phone. "How many cabins did you say were on the river? Three?"

"That's right."

I led him, Rock, Irish, and Stella into the house, shocked at how quiet it was. "Hello?" I called out.

"Hey, Buck," said my sister, coming around the corner.

I stepped forward and hugged her. "Where is everybody?"

"Out surveying." Flynn turned and looked directly at Irish. "Who are you?"

He stepped forward and extended his hand. "Paxon Warrick."

"Flynn Wheaton."

"Great name," said Irish.

"Yours too."

I suddenly felt like the rest of us in the room were invisible. I tapped Flynn on the shoulder. "Hey, sis, I'd like you to meet my friend, Stella. Stella, this is Flynn."

The two women shook hands.

"And this is Decker Ashford and Rock Johnson."

"It's nice to meet you both." Flynn was polite, shaking the hands of both men. However, I caught her looking over her shoulder at Irish more than once. And Irish? He hadn't taken his eyes off of her.

"Stella and Irish…err…Paxon are going to be spending some time here on the ranch."

"You may have one other joining you," I heard Decker say to Stella.

"Who?" she asked with scrunched eyes.

He leaned forward and whispered in her ear. Whatever he said made her eyes open wide. "No!"

"I'm going to head out and see if I can meet up with my crew," said Deck. He tipped his hat to my sister. "It was nice to meet you, Flynn."

"What was that all about?" I asked Stella once he was gone.

"Ali."

"What about her?"

"She may be staying here too."

11

Stella

"I see," said Buck.

I studied his face, trying to read something—anything—into the two words he spoke. Was he happy Ali would be staying here? Particularly since there was no mention of Cope joining her? "Too bad about their honeymoon."

"Deck hasn't said anything to me about this."

I shrugged. "I guess we'll have to figure out who will stay where."

He shrugged like I had. "Nothing changes as far as I'm concerned."

"What does that mean?"

He took a step closer to me. "It means you are my first priority, and that's what you'll remain. It's up to Deck to assign someone to Ali and Irish."

I wouldn't say anything now, but I'd lay money down that once Ali arrived, she would fill the top spot for the handsome cowboy.

"Let's get settled. You too, Irish. Give me a minute." I watched him walk down the hallway and open a closed door.

"I should head out now too," said Flynn. "But I'm sure I'll see you later."

She wasn't talking to me, so I didn't respond. In fact, I doubted if Irish or Buck's sister even remembered I was in the room.

"I'd like that," he murmured, following her to the front door. Irish stood in the doorway and watched her walk away.

"Ready?" said Buck, coming back down the hallway with a travel bag in his hand.

"Where are you going?" Irish asked.

"I'll be staying in one of the cabins," answered Buck.

"Which one?"

"I'm not sure it matters, but if you're asking if I'm staying with you, the answer is no."

Irish nodded, and it was then I realized he was avoiding making eye contact with me. It was almost like I was invisible. It was one thing when Flynn was here, but now that she was gone, it was pissing me off.

"Hey, Irish, you do know I'm writing a book about the Fisk mission."

He nodded again, but still didn't look in my direction.

"I was hoping that since we're both here for the foreseeable future, you could tell me more about it," I said as we walked out the front door.

"You have other sources."

I looked at Buck. "What the fuck?" I mouthed.

The absolute last thing I expected when he took a step forward and brought his mouth close to my ear, was that he'd kiss my cheek. But that's exactly what he did.

"What was that for?"

He took my hand and led me out the front door and over to a truck that looked a lot like the one he'd picked me up in for the wedding. "I decided I need to do that more often."

"Why?"

He smiled. "Because eventually, I'll make my way from here," he touched my cheek, "to here." He ran his thumb over my lower lip and opened the passenger door.

"Is this the same pickup you had in DC?" I knew it wasn't, but I had to change the subject.

Buck blocked me from climbing in. "Is that all you've got to say, Stella?"

I looked away. "Don't play with me, Buck."

"Look at me."

I shook my head.

"Look at me, darlin'."

I folded my arms; Buck put his fingers on my chin and gently turned my face toward him.

"I'm not playin', Stella."

"Sure you aren't, Buck. This isn't exactly my first rodeo, cowboy."

He moved his arm out of the way. "Scoot to the middle, darlin'."

"You didn't answer my question about the truck."

"When I moved to Virginia, I bought one just like it. I don't think either one would make it from one state to another."

I wasn't thrilled when Irish climbed in beside me, given his rude comment from a couple of minutes ago. I shifted closer to Buck and looked up at him.

If anything, being on the ranch made him look even hotter. Here, dressed in his cowboy get-up, he looked like he belonged. When I first met him in DC, when he was on Ali's detail, I thought the whole flannel shirt, pressed jeans, and hat ensemble was pretty hokey. It didn't take long, though, before I found myself admiring how great his ass looked in those jeans.

Same with his beard. I'd never been a fan of them, but on him? *Lord have mercy.* And the long hair he kept tied back in a ponytail? He was everything I never dreamed I'd find attractive in a man. Now, I wanted to climb on his lap and straddle him as he drove to the cabin I hoped only had one bedroom. And here I'd just accused him of playing me. Maybe it was the other way around.

Before starting the truck, he looked into my eyes, winked, and smiled. "Whatever you're thinking about, pretty girl, I like it."

I could feel the heat flush my cheeks, and I looked away. Girl? I was old enough to be his…uh…older sister. He dropped one hand from the wheel and rested it on my thigh. When I looked down at it and then up at him, his fingers dug into my flesh.

He parked in front of one of the cabins and cut the engine.

"You're in that one down there," Buck said to Irish, pointing to the left. "And we're in this one," he said to me.

He got out and held his hand out to me. When I slid over, he put his hands on my waist and set me on my feet. Instead of letting go, he tightened his grip. "I knew it," he murmured.

"Knew what?"

His hold tightened more. "That I could wrap my hands all the way around your waist." When he let go, I immediately missed his touch. He grabbed both our bags. "This way," he said, motioning toward the door.

I stood, waiting for him to unlock it. Instead, he set one bag down and turned the handle.

"Ladies first."

I don't know what I expected, but it wasn't what I saw in front of me. The furniture looked like it came straight out of a Sundance catalog. Rustic, yet it appeared comfortable, with cushions, pillows, and throws in deep, rich colors that reminded me of time I'd spent in Taos. "This is beautiful," I murmured.

"I haven't seen it since my brothers and sister fixed it up." Buck walked into the hallway, opened a door, and set both of our bags inside. When he turned back toward me, I raised an eyebrow. "Is that the only bedroom?"

"The only one I'd hoped we'd need."

He took a step closer to me. The look on his face, in his eyes, was heated. He was so close I could feel his breath, like I'd been able to at the wedding. I'd run from him then. Did I have the balls to stand my ground now? Could I look him in the eye, challenge him to quit playing and kiss me?

I closed my eyes and leaned into him. We both went perfectly still when we heard a knock at the cabin door.

"Shit," mumbled Buck as he took a step back. He walked over and pulled the door open. Someone who looked like he could be his twin, walked inside.

"Stella, this is my brother Cord."

The man walked over to me and held out his hand. His blue eyes sparkled just like Buck's did. "Welcome to the Roaring Fork, ma'am."

Ma'am? Jesus. The reminder of how much older I was than the two men standing in front of me had the same effect as if I'd been drenched with a bucket of ice-cold water.

Buck put his arm around my shoulders. "What can I do for you, Cord?"

"Just wanted to welcome our guest to the ranch."

"Done." He dropped his arm and ushered his brother toward the door.

"You be sure to let me know if there's anything you need, Miss Stella. If Buck doesn't take good care of you, I guarantee that I will." When he winked, also like Buck had, I felt my knees go weak.

"Get the hell outta here," said Buck, closing the door behind him and throwing the lock. He rested against it. "You need somethin', Stella, you'll get it from me. Understand?"

"Buck?"

He took a step in my direction. "Yeah?" He took two more steps and wound his arm around me. "I'd really like to kiss you. You okay with that?"

I gripped the chair behind me. "Maybe you should show me around first."

"We'll get to that."

I twisted away from him when I heard my cell phone ring. Not many people had the number to the new phone Rock had secured for me. When I pulled it out and saw it was Jinx calling, I thought about letting it go to voicemail. I didn't, though. I needed a minute to break the spell Buck had cast on me.

"Hey, Jinx."

Buck scowled and stalked out of the cabin.

"Hey, TJ. I wanted to make sure everything was going okay in Colorado."

"It's fine." I walked over to the window to look for Buck. I didn't see him. "Was there another reason you called?"

"We lifted a partial print in Barb's apartment. My team is working now to see if it's enough for a match."

"That's encouraging and…surprising." It was incomprehensible to me that someone would be that sloppy. It wasn't as though it was a robbery gone wrong. Whoever had killed Barb and Nancy was looking for something, most likely her laptop, the key, or both.

"I agree."

Out of the corner of my eye, I saw Buck pacing out front. He was on his phone but turned toward the window in time to catch me watching.

"Jinx, I gotta go." I ended the call without looking away from Buck. He appeared to do the same thing and stalked toward the cabin's door.

"What's going on?" I asked.

"That was Cope. He said that something is off with Fisk."

"Meaning?"

"The federal prosecutor offered him a deal, which he refused to take."

I cocked my head.

"Cope thinks there's someone higher up, maybe more than one person, who Fisk is more afraid of than going to prison."

"Is he on his way here?"

Buck's eyes scrunched, and he shook his head.

"What about Ali?"

"I'm not sure when she'll arrive."

"I see." It occurred to me that I used the same words Buck had shortly after Decker told me she would be staying on the ranch at some point.

"Stella—"

"Excuse me." I walked in the direction of the bedroom, looking for a bathroom. Whatever he was about to say probably had something to do with her. While I didn't doubt she was head-over-heels in love with Cope, that didn't mean she wouldn't fall into old habits with Buck. The two had spent every day together for several weeks. The last thing I wanted to feel was jealousy, but even the thought of her being here brought it to the surface. How bad would it be once she was actually here?

I ducked into the bedroom and then into the en suite bathroom. When I came out, Buck was sitting on the end of the bed.

"I have something to say, Stella, and I'd appreciate it if you'd show me the courtesy of listening."

I folded my arms and leaned against the doorjamb.

"Would you please sit down?"

"I'll stand, thanks."

"Please?" he said again, this time patting the bed. "Come over here and sit beside me."

"Buck, I—"

"Jesus, Stella, could you please just sit the fuck down?" He took off his hat, threw it on the bed, and ran his hand over his hair. "Just sit. That's all I'm asking."

"Okay, settle down. God." I sat down.

"There's something I need to ask you."

"Go ahead."

"Why do you think I'm playin' you, Stella?"

I looked down at the floor, wishing so much that I could get up and walk away to avoid answering him. "You don't think I'm smart enough to figure out I'm not exactly your type, Buck?"

"Come again?"

"You heard me."

He opened his mouth, but before he could say something else, we heard a knock at the door. "Fuck," he muttered. "Who the hell is here now?"

He stood, walked out of the room, and I followed.

"Got a minute?" Irish asked when Buck opened the door.

"What for?"

"I need to talk to you."

Buck let out an audible sigh. "I'm getting sick of this shit. Whatever you have to say, you can do it in front of Stella."

"What's going on here?" asked Decker, who stood on the porch behind Irish.

12

Buck

I was beginning to think that if I wanted a minute alone with Stella, I was going to have to take her to one of the more remote cabins higher up on the ranch.

"Hey, everybody," I heard my sister say.

"What are you doing here, Flynn?" I asked.

She eased her way past Deck and Irish. "Holt asked if anyone would mind if Ben Rice and a couple guys from his band came over tonight."

"It would be better if Holt went there instead."

"But—"

The look I gave my sister shut her up. The last thing we needed before Decker's security system was set up was a bunch of extra people on the ranch.

Deck and Irish came inside. Both men pulled out laptops and sat down at the table.

"We're in the middle of something, Flynn."

She turned on her heel and stomped toward the door.

"I'll go with you," I heard Stella say from behind me.

"You need to stay here."

"I'm just going back to the house, Buck," said Flynn.

"I said Stella needs to stay here."

"Buck, I—"

I was getting pretty damn close to telling everyone else to leave us alone, tossing Stella over my shoulder, and tying her to the damn bed until I could finish the conversation we needed to have yet kept getting interrupted from. Instead, I took her hand in mine and pulled her into the bedroom with me. I closed the door behind us and locked it.

"What the hell, Buck?"

I got right in her face. "Dammit, Stella, you are my responsibility to protect. You won't be going as far as the cabin next door without me with you."

"You're overreacting," she mumbled.

"No. I'm not," I whispered, resting my forehead against hers. I couldn't resist, not for another minute. "Do you know how long I've wanted to do this?" I grasped the back of her neck and kissed her.

As if it was made of molten lava, her body melted against mine as my tongue wound around hers. I gripped her ass, pulled her against me, and lifted her up. "Put your legs around my waist, darlin'."

"Buck…"

"Shh. Just let me kiss you, Stella."

I thrust my tongue into her mouth, kissing her deeper than I had a few seconds ago. I couldn't hold back. I'd imagined how this would feel so damn many times. Now that I had a taste, I needed more. I needed it all. Everything from this woman. I ground my steel-hard cock against her heat.

"Damn, Stella, you taste so good."

"So do you," she murmured before I fused my mouth back with hers. I spun around and sat down on the bed with her on my lap. "Straighten your legs out, darlin'."

When she did, I lifted her perfect ass and put her pussy exactly where I wanted it.

"You feel me, how hard I am for you, Stella?" I whispered.

"I feel you, Buck," she whispered back.

"That's your first clue that I'm not playin' you."

She tried to tuck her head in my neck, but I wouldn't let her.

"Buck, they're waiting for us."

I'd give anything to make the two men sitting on the other side of the wall disappear. "I need one more taste of those sweet lips first, Stella."

She gave me a quick kiss, shifted her body off my lap, and rushed into the bathroom. I flopped back on the bed and looked up at the ceiling. What had I been thinking, starting something between us when Deck and Irish were sitting at the kitchen table?

I eased the door open, praying against hope they'd left. They hadn't.

"Where's Stella?" Deck asked.

"She'll be out in a minute."

"We're gonna need her."

"If I go back in there—"

Deck held up his hand. "That was the last thing I was suggesting. Believe me."

When Stella came out, I pulled out a chair for her then sat beside her.

"I spoke with Burns," said Decker. "He said he's heard rumors about Operation Argead but never had a reason to look into it. Which means he didn't burn it. He has theories about who did, though, and has promised to see what he can find out. For now, there's no reason for me to go to California."

"Copy that."

"There's more."

"What?" I asked.

"Settle down, young Buck. I'm getting to it."

"You do know that you're only a couple of years older than I am, right?"

"In age maybe, but infinitely older in wisdom."

I smiled and shook my head.

"He thinks it would be best if we kept this thing as far away from the Invincibles as possible. Mainly to keep the heat off Irish and Stella. Cope and Ali too."

"What did he suggest?" Irish asked.

"To pull K19 in."

I raised a brow.

"Yeah, I don't like it either, but hear me out."

It wasn't so much that I didn't like the idea; I was just shocked that Decker was going along with it so easily, especially given the mission that took down Fisk was as much his as it was Cope's or Irish's.

"And you," I mumbled.

"What's that?" Deck asked.

"Burns wants to keep it away from you too."

"Yeah, all right, you're a genius. Burns wants to keep the heat away from me too."

"What's the plan?"

Decker smiled. "This is the part I like." He rubbed his hands together. "Cope will contact Doc and get him to contract out a couple of undercover gigs."

"Where?"

"Inside Interpol for one."

"Who are you thinking?"

"Casper."

I smiled like Deck had. He had no intention of staying out of this op. Casper worked with the Invincibles far more often than she did K19.

"Who else?"

"I'll leave that to Doc."

"Why did you say you liked the part of the plan where Cope contacts Doc?" asked Stella.

"I'll answer that," I said. "Because Doc will think it means he's got a shot at recruiting Cope to join up with them."

"Does he?" she asked.

"Hell no," muttered Decker.

"Cope won't sign with the Invincibles either," said Irish, who I hadn't realized was paying any attention to the conversation.

"We'll see," muttered Deck.

"What'll Casper's assignment be?" I asked.

"To get inside the executive committee. If we can get her in place quickly enough, she can be set up in time for the end of quarter meetings."

Given Interpol was more of a clearinghouse for international crime intel, rather than an actual law enforcement agency, the organization only had as much power as its executive committee. Of the three positions—president, vice president, and secretary-general—only the latter was a full-time, paid position. The other two offices were advisory in nature and held by individuals who still worked for their respective countries' intelligence agencies. The committee only met officially at the end of each quarter. Everyone in intelligence believed they met far more often than that in an unofficial capacity.

"Any ties to Fisk?" I asked.

"Negative," Deck answered.

"What about Kerr?" asked Stella.

"Irish?" prompted Deck.

"Both Daniel Byrne, the current president, and Boris Antonov, his vice, served as delegates under Kerr. I haven't been able to find a connection to Kim Ha-joon, the secretary-general, yet. However, he's tight with Byrne and Antonov."

"What about a connection between Kerr and Fisk?"

Irish slowly raised his head and looked directly at Stella. "Need-to-know," he mumbled.

Decker cleared his throat. "Irish," he warned. "Answer Stella's question."

She didn't take her eyes off of him. The look on her face would've had me squirming, and not in a good way. But damn, it was hot, as long as I wasn't on the receiving end of it.

"They worked together at CFR."

"CFR?" I asked.

Stella pushed back her chair, stood, and walked over to the window. "The Council on Foreign Relations."

"Officially, it's a foreign policy think tank," answered Irish. "Unofficially, a place for its 'members' to meet without having to announce it as such."

"Which office?" Stella asked.

"Fisk was in DC. Kerr was in New York."

Stella turned toward us, and her eyes met mine.

"Barb too?" I asked.

She nodded. "New York office."

We'd drawn the line between Stella's aunt, Fisk, and Kerr at least.

"What happened to him?" I asked.

"Kerr?" asked Irish.

I nodded.

"He stayed on at MI5, but not as director general, the position he'd held for years."

"What did he do instead?"

"Became more of a consultant."

I looked at Decker. "I already have a call into Z about him."

I knew that after Z returned to England, once his son and Decker took over management of the King-Alexander Ranch, he took the DG position formerly held by Kerr. This was a few years before he took over as chief of MI6.

"Where did Kerr go after that?"

"Retired." Irish raised his head and looked directly at Stella.

"What?"

"He divorced his wife at the same time he left Interpol. He's been married to Sally Hennessey for nine years."

"Jesus fucking Christ," Stella muttered. I watched her stalk out of the cabin door.

"Who's that?" I asked as I stood to follow her.

"At the time, she was the executive editor at AP."

"Barb's editor?" Deck asked Irish. I didn't stick around to hear the answer. Stella's reaction already told me that's exactly who she was.

"You okay?"

"She fucking set her up."

"Makes sense."

"Barb never had an affair with Kerr. Hennessey did."

"Logical assumption."

"Buck, there's something you need to know before this goes any further."

"Before what goes any further?"

"Everything."

I took a step closer to her. "What besides the investigation, Stella?"

"What happened earlier."

"You mean, me kissing you?"

"Yes, Buck."

"What do you need to tell me?"

She had the same look on her face she did when she'd all but leveled Irish with her glare. "I'm going to destroy them."

I smiled and stepped close enough that I could wrap my arm around her waist. "Do you know how hot you are right now?"

"I'm not joking about this, Buck."

"I know you're not, and there's something I need you to know."

"What's that?"

"I'm going to be right there with you, darlin'."

"Why?"

"While I understand your desire to avenge Barb's death, which I'm as convinced as you are that they had a hand in, if Kerr is connected to Fisk, then the blood of several of my brothers in arms is on his hands."

"I'm going to devote all my energy to this, Buck. I can't afford to get distracted. I don't know what would've become of me if it weren't for Barb."

"I hear what you're sayin', Stella."

"So you understand that I can't…you know…start something with you."

My arm was still around her waist, and she hadn't pulled away. "You know what I think?"

She shook her head.

"We're going to have to spend all of our time together. We'll have to work on this night and day, and you know what that means."

Stella smiled. "I don't."

"It means we have to be together twenty-four seven. Awake. Asleep. Together."

"I don't know, Buck. I mean, I'll need my rest."

"Oh, I'll make sure you rest, darlin'."

She rolled her eyes.

"What?"

"If you're playin' me…"

"Now isn't the time, but I promise you, I'm going to get to the bottom of what I've done to make you think I would." I cupped her cheek. "Because I wouldn't, Stella." I knew she didn't believe me, but I was determined that, eventually, she would.

13

Stella

It wasn't anything Buck did or didn't do. It was Cope, and even then, it wasn't his fault. Sumner Copeland was a flirt. I'd seen it countless times, and certainly not just with me. That I'd been stupid enough to believe it meant he was attracted to me, wanted some kind of relationship with me, was what kept me from thinking anything serious would ever come of Buck and me. Off-the-chart sex was probably in our future, at least once, until he realized the implications of sleeping with someone so much older.

Buck was likely more accustomed to having sex with younger, more nubile women, whose asses were still high and tight, whose boobs hadn't yet sagged, and whose stomachs were flat and hard. I doubted he had any idea what happened to a woman's body when she aged. Well, he probably did, but that didn't mean he wanted to see one naked. Maybe if we left the lights off the first time, there'd be a second.

But like I'd just told him, I had every intention of going after Kerr and Hennessey. More, I planned to annihilate them the same way they had Barb's career. If they had anything at all to do with her death, I'd see to it they rotted in prison. To do that, I needed to focus solely on the investigation and nothing else.

There was one more thing I had to do, and that was get Irish to stop treating me like the enemy. I had no doubt he already knew things that would aid my investigation. Given his mandate from Decker had been to find out everything he could about Kerr's tenure at Interpol, I needed him to willingly share whatever he learned with me.

"Ready to go back in?" Buck asked.

"Before we do, I need to ask you about Irish. What's his deal with me?"

"I can't say for certain, but I don't think it's you specifically, Stella. You have to remember that for the last few years, there wasn't anyone the man could trust outside of Cope and Decker, and then, it wasn't just trusting them; he had to trust them with his life. Plenty of people hated Warrick enough to kill him because they believed he was a traitor to his country. On top of that, there were many others who wanted to kill him because he was getting too close to exposing them."

Admittedly, I was one of the people who had hated him. Early on, at the beginning of his trial, which I later learned had been staged as part of the overall mission, every time I looked at him, all I saw was a murderer. I had never gotten close enough to him to tell him about my feelings, but if he'd ever seen me look at him, he would've known exactly how I felt.

"I need to talk to him alone."

Buck nodded. "I'll wait out here."

"Hey, Deck, can I have a minute with Irish?" I asked when I went back inside.

"I was just getting ready to head out anyway." He put his laptop in his bag and slung it over his shoulder.

"Are you leaving the ranch?"

"As soon as I make sure Rock has the install of the security system under control, I'm headed to Texas."

I knew Decker's wife was pregnant, but not exactly when the baby was due. "Give Mila my best."

Deck walked over and kissed my cheek. "She'll appreciate that, Stella. I'll be in touch, but in the meantime, you let these fellas keep you safe."

"I will."

When I sat down at the table, Irish looked like there was nowhere he'd rather be less. "Look, Paxon, I owe you an apology, and it's long past due."

He nodded, but didn't say anything.

"I know you're a good man, and you deserve a lot better than has been doled out to you, including by me. But now, I'm part of the investigation. The same people you're after either killed my aunt or arranged for someone else to do it. I'm going to take them down, Irish, if it's the last thing I do."

"Copy that," he muttered.

"Can we figure out a way to work together on this?"

"I promised Decker I would," he said as he stood and walked toward the door.

"Where are you going?"

"I work better alone."

"But—"

He held up his hand. "Whatever I find, I'll share."

I watched Buck and Irish talk on the porch for a few minutes, wishing I could hear what they were saying.

I'd always been a nosy eavesdropper. Barb used to say that was what made a good reporter. She'd also say that as soon as my curiosity languished, I might as well hang up my press credentials.

She'd certainly never lost her penchant for sticking her nose into anything that caught her attention. She'd believed she lost the way to get her stories out to the world. She tried through me, and I'd shut her down.

God, what a selfish, unappreciative bitch I'd been to her. If only I could go back and do that last day over with her. There were so many things I'd change, starting with being a fuck of a lot nicer to the woman who had given up years of her life to take care of my mom and me. How had I thanked her? By telling her I could never repay her and that included by giving up my book. God, what was wrong with me?

I went into the bedroom to get my laptop. Instead, I sat down on the bed and put my head in my hands. I could say I was going to avenge Barb's death, but wasn't I the one who'd caused it? Hadn't I refused to give up writing the book even after she warned me of the consequences?

I fell back on the bed, rolled to my side, and sobbed. I was responsible for the death of the woman who had done everything for me. Me. No one else. Just me.

"Hey," I heard Buck say in a soft voice. I felt his weight when he got on the bed, behind me. He put his arm around my waist and pulled me against him and then rolled me toward him. I buried my face in his chest. "Shh," he murmured, stroking my hair. I cried and cried, and all the while, Buck held me.

When I opened my eyes, it was dark in the room and Buck was still beside me. "Better?" he asked.

"I must've fallen asleep."

"You wore yourself out, darlin'."

I put my hand on his shirt; it was wet. "I'm sorry."

He stroked my cheek with his thumb. "Nothing to be sorry for. I'm glad I can be the person who's there for you when you need to let out all that sorrow."

"There were so many things she wanted me to work on, and I disregarded all of them. In fact, I only read the first few she sent me. After that, I just ignored them." I looked into Buck's eyes. "Oh my God, I just *ignored* them. What if there were leads relating to Operation Argead? Or about Kerr or Hennessey?"

"When you say you ignored them, what do you mean exactly?"

"I filed them."

"Where?"

"In an email mailbox."

Buck breathed an audible sigh. "So you still have them?"

"I do." I started to get up, but Buck tightened his hold on me. "Hang on a minute, Stella. We don't have to dive in tonight. You've already had a long day."

I wriggled free. "This is what I was talking about, Buck. I can't get distracted by anything else. When I have to work, I have to work. Besides, I work better at night."

He sat up. "Let's get at it."

"You can sleep if you want to."

Buck stood, and so did I. He cupped my cheek with his palm. "I told you, I can't sleep if I don't hear your voice, Stella. I don't think it'll work if you just holler at me from the other room."

Four hours later, Buck and I had gone through every email Barb sent me, reading and re-reading them. If there were any clues in them, they were buried under more cloak and dagger than the Marvel comic books of the same name.

"This was a waste of time," I muttered.

"Maybe not." Buck pulled up an email that referenced a small town in France called La Chapelle-Saint-Maurice. I read it while he typed something on his phone.

It was one of the few I remembered reading when it was initially sent. In it, Barb said it was a place she'd always wanted to visit. Given she never set foot outside of her apartment, I'd chalked it up to nonsense.

Buck set his phone down.

"Oh my God, are you really going to make me ask who you contacted?"

He laughed. "I sent a message to Cope, but I haven't heard back yet."

"What about?"

"The name of the town is familiar."

"In what way?"

"That's why I need to talk to Cope. I can't remember the details."

"Do you even know where he and Ali are?"

"Need-to-know."

"You, or me?"

Buck smiled. "Both of us, Stella. I can assure you, there isn't anything relating to your aunt I won't tell you as soon as I learn of it."

"I appreciate that, Buck."

"Is there anything more you want to work on tonight?"

As much as I wished I could keep going, I was exhausted. Buck stood and held his hand out to me.

"Come on, Stella, let's get you to bed."

I put my hand in his, and he led me to the bedroom we'd been in earlier.

"You know where the bathroom is. There are towels in the cabinet under the sink. If there's anything else you need, let me know." He walked over and opened another door. "You can keep your clothes in the closet or in the dresser. They're both empty." Buck took a step closer, leaned in, and kissed my forehead. "Goodnight, darlin'."

"Where are you sleeping?"

"I'll be in the room across the hall. If you need anything, just holler and I'll come running."

"I thought…"

"I know, but we're both dead on our feet, darlin'. When we're together for the first time, I want to be wide awake and I want you to be too."

This was unexpected. Earlier, when he held me while I cried, I didn't doubt for a minute that Buck and I would share a bed tonight.

This was better, though. I mean, we hardly knew each other. Having drunken sex after Cope and Ali's wedding would've been way different than him climbing into bed next to me in the cabin we'd be sharing for God knew how long. No, Buck was right to sleep in the other room.

"Goodnight, then."

He kissed my forehead again. "I'm right across the hall if you need me," he repeated.

I took a shower, brushed my teeth, and got in bed, wondering if I should've asked Buck to stay. Having his body wrapped around mine felt so good, so comforting, almost like it was made just for that purpose.

I fluffed the pillow under my head and rolled to my side. When I heard my cell phone vibrate, I rolled back over and grabbed it from the bedside table.

Still awake? Buck's text read.

Yes.

Wanna talk?

Always.

Seconds later, his call came through.

"Hi, Buck."

"Have I told you how much I love the sound of your voice, especially when it's low and sleepy?"

"I don't think you have."

"Well, I do."

"I like the sound of your voice too."

"Yeah, what do you like about it?"

I smiled. "How it gets gravelly late at night. It's really sexy."

Buck groaned.

"What?"

"It's really hard not to think about sex when you're right across the hall."

"It isn't any easier for me, Buck."

When he groaned again, I could hear it both through the phone and through my closed door.

"What do you wear when you sleep, Stella?"

I laughed. "Do you somehow think knowing is going to make it easier to not think about sex?"

"I was hoping you'd say flannel pajamas that cover every inch of your skin."

The idea that Buck slept naked planted itself firmly in my mind, making it hard to speak.

"You there?"

"Yeah, I'm here."

"Tell me, Stella. I have to know."

"I sleep in the nude, Buck."

"Damn. I knew it."

"What about you?"

"Boxer briefs."

"Take them off."

"Jesus, darlin', you trying to kill me?"

"Take them off, Buck."

"They're off."

"Your turn."

"For what?"

I put the phone on speaker and set it on the pillow. "Tell me what you want me to do."

"Let's see, where should I start? Hmm. I think I'll go straight to the best part. Put your hand between your legs, Stella."

"Just one?"

I heard his phone rustle and feared for a minute he was headed in here. I could handle doing this over the phone. I wasn't ready for in person yet.

"Okay, I'm back," he said.

"Where did you go?"

"I pulled the shades on the windows."

That made me smile.

"One hand for now, darlin'. Put it between your legs and tell me what you feel."

"I'm so wet."

"Describe your pussy to me."

"It's bare—"

"Okay, slow down. That almost made me lose it."

"Tell me about your cock, Buck."

"It's so hard I could pound nails."

"How big is it?"

"Length?"

"Mm-hmm."

"From the top of my middle finger to an inch past my wrist."

I shuddered. "And around?"

"Can't close my fingers. My turn."

"Okay."

"Reach down and put one finger in your pussy. With your other hand, spread your folds and put your middle finger on your clit. Press on it hard, Stella."

"Buck," I moaned, cursing myself for starting this. God, I needed to come.

"Add another finger. Go deep. At the same time, rub your clit for me."

"It's my turn," I whined.

"I'm all yours, baby."

"Stroke your cock, but slow."

"I'm way ahead of you."

"Imagine you're rubbing it against my clit. I'm so wet for you, Buck. I'm begging you to put it inside me, but you won't."

"I won't? Why not?"

"Because you're making me wait until I'm right on the brink, so the minute you thrust inside me, I'll come. Can you feel how wet I am for you, Buck?"

"Stella, I can't hold back anymore."

"I can't either."

When I heard him moan, I arched my back and rode the wave of the most powerful orgasm I could remember experiencing. It only made me wonder how much better it would be if it was Buck's cock inside me instead of my own fingers.

I could hear him breathing as I slowed my own.

"Stella? You there?"

"I'm here."

"That was so fucking hot."

14

Buck

I knew the minute she fell asleep. Stella snored. Not the loud, sawing-wood kind of snoring. This was soft and adorable, like a little bear cub.

It wasn't the first time she'd fallen to sleep while we were on the phone, but it sure as hell was the first time we'd had phone sex. Damn, it was so hot I was rock-hard again just thinking about it.

The idea that only two doorways and a hall separated us, somehow made it that much more of a turn on—like when she said I was making her wait, teasing her. And, Jesus, when she said her pussy was bare, I almost shot my load right then.

After ending our call, I got out of bed, eased the door open, and walked down the hallway to the bathroom. The bedroom Stella was in was the only one that had an en suite.

I turned the shower to hot, even though cold would've served me better, climbed in, and let the water pulsate against my shoulders. I kept my eyes closed, imagining Stella was in here with me.

I'd have her bend at the waist, put her hands on the tile, and pound into her from behind. Once we both came, I'd bring her to another orgasm with my tongue.

Admittedly, she'd surprised me when she initiated the sex-filled conversation. I was the furthest thing from a prude, but I could already feel my cheeks heating, imagining looking her in the eye tomorrow. Worse, how was I supposed to keep my hands off of her?

On my way back to the bedroom, I stopped outside her door. No way I'd go in uninvited, but if she could hear me and it suddenly opened, I'd be the happiest man alive. I stood there a few seconds before returning to the other room. I climbed between the cold sheets, wishing so much I could sink into Stella's warmth.

I'd been up for a couple of hours, sitting on the porch and re-reading some of Barb's emails I'd asked Stella to forward to me, when I heard the front door open. She came outside wearing a t-shirt I'd thrown into my bag yesterday before we left the main house. It fell almost to her knees.

"Good morning," she said, bringing a cup of coffee to the lips I'd spent most of the night dreaming about. "Sorry I fell asleep on you last night."

I set my laptop on the table in front of me and stood. If she expected me to be able to resist putting my hands on her, she was wrong.

"I would've been a whole lot happier if you had been sleeping on me." I snaked one arm around her waist and pulled her body against me. "Tell me, Stella, do you have anything on under my shirt?" I was just about to slide my hand down to find out when I heard someone clear their voice.

"Sorry to interrupt," said Porter, standing a few feet from the porch.

"Hey, Port. Meet Stella."

Instead of taking a step forward to shake his hand, she waved from where she stood. "Hi."

"You got a minute, Buck?"

"I was on my way back inside anyway," I heard her mutter and then the door close behind her.

"Damn," I heard Porter say.

"Whatever thoughts you're having about the woman who just went inside, bleach them from your brain."

He laughed.

"What brings you by this morning?" I asked, anxious to get this conversation over so I could go confirm Stella's bare butt—and pussy—were all that were under my shirt.

"I'd like to set up a meeting with the guys from Flying R Rough Stock. It seems like we'd have better luck getting started with bucking bulls and broncs than we would the dude ranch. At least until your boss gets the security system in place. Even then, you're occupying the only cabins we have ready to go."

"Have a seat," I said, pointing to one of the Adirondack chairs. As much as I didn't want to have this conversation now, it was long overdue. I sat beside him. "I have a few things I need to ask you before we start scheduling meetings."

"Fair enough."

"Port, did you know what was in Pop's will?"

He looked over at me with scrunched eyes. "No, Buck. None of us did. At least not the way he set it up. I can tell you, though, he did his damnedest to make each one of us aware that as the oldest son, the decisions about the ranch were yours to make."

I looked out over the land our father had used against each one of us in many different ways. "When I left for college, he told me that once I walked out the door, I wouldn't own any of it."

"He obviously didn't mean it."

"Well, I didn't know that. I walked away willingly, Port. I never wanted a piece of the Roaring Fork. I still don't."

"But you're here."

"I came to Crested Butte to pay my respects. I never intended to stay. Once Six-pack read the will, what choice did I have? Did you really think I'd turn my back on all of you?" I stroked my beard. "How bad is it?"

"With the money from the Invincibles, we aren't that far off, if we could shake some cash loose to invest, I think we could turn a decent profit by the end of the year."

"I don't have it, Port."

He looked away, out over the land, like I had.

"I'm sorry if you were under the impression I did."

"That isn't it."

"What is it, then?"

"Why'd he have to make it so damn hard?"

It wasn't just this. He'd made our entire lives hard. Roscoe Buchtold Wheaton, Sr., was the most manipulative, controlling son-of-a-bitch I'd ever known—and the most critical. There were agents, higher-ups, who had a reputation of being assholes to work for. Compared to my father, each one was a goddamn pussy.

"It was his way," I finally said when I realized Port was waiting for an answer.

"What about getting a loan?"

"We'd have to put up collateral to secure it. As of right now, I'm just an independent contractor. I don't have the steady income I had when I was at the agency."

"Can I ask you something, Buck?"

"You can ask."

Port laughed. "Why'd you leave?"

"The CIA?"

He nodded.

I had no business telling Port what I was about to, but he deserved to know. Particularly since it was the reason Stella and Irish were here. "There was some shit goin' down that I couldn't stomach. Worse, I could've easily been on the same firing line as other agents." I made sure my brother was looking me in the eye. "This goes no further."

"Understood."

"Agents—good ones—were being targeted. Irish, the guy staying in the next cabin over, was the one who started paying close enough attention to get suspicious. Decker, the guy you referred to as my boss, almost brought the whole mission down, but in the end, he joined up with Irish and his handler, a guy named Cope. When the CIA director was arrested, we thought it was over."

"It isn't?"

"Afraid not."

Porter shook his head. "Shit."

"That's why Stella and Irish are both here. Also why Decker and the Invincibles are investing in the security system. You should know we're expecting one or two other people. I mentioned Cope a minute ago. His wife is on her way here, but I have no idea her ETA. I'm also not sure if Cope will be staying here too."

"Thanks for telling me all this, Buck."

"I'd prefer not telling our sibs, but I'll leave that decision to you."

"I guess if there comes a time they need to know, I'll tell 'em. To be honest, I figured most of this out, just not the particulars. I'm sure they have too."

I laughed. "Deck can be over-the-top cloak and dagger, so I'm sure everyone has their theories."

"Back to the meeting with Flying R."

"Right. I guess it would be good to know what kind of investment we'll need if we want to make a real go of it."

"Billy Patterson, one of the partners, said there's also a possibility of going in on a few bulls. Broncs too."

"As in, get people to invest?"

"Exactly. If they're rank, we either buy them out at the end of the year when we can get our hands on more cash, or we sell and split the profit."

"I like the sound of this, Port."

"There's something else you should know."

I was getting damned tired of being blindsided. "What's that?"

"Bethany Strom and I were seeing each other for a while."

"She said."

"When you walked in on us at the visitation, she was ending it."

"If you're asking, I'm not interested in Bethany, Porter. Not the slightest bit."

He motioned with his head toward the cabin. "Yeah, I kinda got that impression."

15

Part of me felt guilty for cracking the window open so I could listen to Buck's conversation with his brother. Another part of me had accepted my incessant need to eavesdrop a long time ago.

I'd only gleaned bits and pieces from his earlier conversations with Decker about him not being able to leave his family's ranch. There was obviously a lot more to it, and I intended to find out exactly what it entailed.

When the two men stood, I went into the bedroom. For a second, I thought about getting dressed but changed my mind, remembering how Buck had reacted to seeing me in his t-shirt.

I heard the front door open and his footfalls in the hallway. I grabbed my laptop and met him halfway. Without saying a word, he took the computer out of my hands and set it on the dining table. He walked back over to me, wrapped his arm around my waist, and pulled me into him.

"I'm pretty sure this is where we were when my brother interrupted us."

"I think you're right."

"If I recall correctly, I asked a question you didn't answer."

"Maybe. I don't remember."

"I'll ask it again. What do you have on under my shirt, Stella?" He slowly slid his hand from my waist and was moving it to the hem of his shirt when we heard a knock at the door.

Buck looked up at the ceiling. "Are you fucking kidding me?"

If we were in the bedroom, I would've told him to ignore it, but from where we stood, we could see Irish and he could see us.

"I have a feeling he's here to talk to you, and as much as I wish you could stay dressed just the way you are, the idea of him—"

I reached up and touched Buck's lips with mine. "Answer the door. I'll be right back."

"Where did Stella go?" I heard Irish ask.

"To get dressed, asshole."

"What the hell?"

"You could see us. It didn't occur to you to take a hike and come back later?"

"Sorry to interrupt your little interlude, but while you're playing kissy-face with the reporter, there are agents out there in the world getting killed."

"Irish," I said, coming out of the bedroom. The only thing I put on were a pair of leggings, and the minute the man was gone, they'd be coming off. "Was there something you wanted to talk to me about?"

"I was able to obtain travel records for Kerr."

"And?"

"He flew from England to New York City two days before your aunt's death. According to the manifest, he was on the plane. Once Decker is at King-Alexander, he'll be able to delve into facial recognition in order to determine Kerr's whereabouts."

"Two questions."

"Go ahead."

"Can you please remind me what King-Alexander is again?"

"A large ranch in Texas that has been Decker's home since he was a teenager. It's owned by Z Alexander and his two adult children. Actually, I misspoke. Since Decker and Mila are married, they reside on her ranch, which is adjacent to King-Alexander. That reminds me, Decker heard back from Z about Kerr. He said there was nothing remarkable about him retiring from full-time duty with MI5 and becoming a consultant. It happens all the time."

I was pretty sure those were the most words Irish had ever said to me in one breath.

"What was your other question?"

"Any idea of Hennessey's whereabouts?"

"She's believed to still be in London. Again, once Decker is available, he'll track her."

"Was there anything else?"

"I thought you'd want to know about Kerr's arrival in the States right away."

"Thank you very much for that information."

"Thanks, Irish," I heard Buck say as he escorted him to the door. By the time he turned around, I had my computer open and was drafting an email to Jinx. Decker Ashford wasn't the only person able to access facial recognition systems.

That Kerr was in the States two days before Barb's death, made my blood boil. Had he gone to see her himself and, after being unable to find the proof I now believed she must have stashed away in a safe-deposit box, killed her? She and her housekeeper both died of a gunshot wound. Certainly the type of murder Kerr would be able to commit with ease.

Buck walked down the hallway and came back moments later with his own laptop.

"I have one or two sources I can check with while we're waiting on Decker."

"I already emailed Jinx." If I hadn't been looking right at Buck, I would've missed the quick scrunch of his eyes. "What?"

"Nothing."

"No. Not nothing. Say what's on your mind."

"You and Jinx."

"It was never anything serious."

"But it was a thing?"

"It was."

"Is it over?"

"Given I used the word 'was,' yes, Buck, it's over."

He looked back at his laptop and began typing, pounding the keys far harder than necessary.

"Is there anything else you want to ask me?"

"I got the impression he didn't think so."

"What are you talking about?"

"He kissed you. Not to mention, he was awfully possessive of you, given it's supposedly over."

I slammed my laptop closed and took it into the bedroom. I didn't slam the door, but I certainly locked it behind me. Jinx was possessive? Jesus, had Buck looked in the mirror lately?

We were friends, at least until last night when we crossed the line into something more. That was my fault. Hearing his sexier-than-shit voice, all I could think about was him naked in the bed across the hall. I knew better than to start anything remotely sexual with someone I was working with, and that's exactly what we were doing.

I sat on the bed and looked out the window. Damn Buck for using the word "supposedly." I wouldn't lie to him about being with Jinx, especially after last night, and I sure as hell wasn't a cheater.

I mean, not that I'd had many opportunities. It was rare for me to have one romantic relationship happening let alone more.

"Stella?"

"Go away, Buck."

"There's something I need to say."

"I'm listening."

"I need to say it to your face."

I wiggled off the bed, stalked over to the door, unlocked, and opened it. He took a step forward so he was standing on the threshold.

"Can you look at me?"

"I'm pissed at you, Buck."

"I know, and I owe you an apology."

"I'm listening," I repeated.

He cupped my cheek and looked deep into my eyes. "I'm sorry, Stella. I shouldn't have questioned you. I have no right."

I took a step back and moved his hand away from my face. "That's not why I'm mad at you."

Buck took another step forward. "I know it isn't. I'm sorry that I doubted you'd tell me anything but the truth. That's on me, not you. Will you accept my apology?"

"Yes." I drummed my fingers on my arm, a nervous habit I abhorred. "This is why I don't get involved with people, Buck. Not that we're involved or even…anything. But regardless, I don't have time for bullshit. More, I don't have the patience for it."

Before I realized what he was doing and could move away, Buck had his arm around my waist and my body pulled close to his. "I'd say we're something, Stella. Last night was something."

"Last night was phone sex, Buck. That doesn't count as anything."

Like earlier, his hand slid down from the small of my back to the hem of his t-shirt I still wore. The difference now was, I wasn't naked underneath it.

"Tell me what I would've found under my shirt earlier if we hadn't been interrupted."

"You'll never know."

"No?" He moved his fingers inside the top of my leggings.

"Knock, knock. Buck? Where are you? I know you're here. Irish said he just talked to you."

"I'll be right out, Flynn." He rested his forehead against mine. "I'm sorry we keep getting interrupted."

"Didn't you lock the door?"

"I did, but she knows the trick to open it."

"You need a better lock."

"One I plan to install later today."

"Go. Talk to her."

"Save my place," he said, brushing my lips with a chaste kiss.

I smiled. God, he was such a flirt. Hadn't I learned to be immune to men like him? Men like Cope? And why the hell were they the only type I was attracted to? Why couldn't Jinx do it for me the way Buck did?

Jinx was a man in a powerful position, close to twenty years older than me, handsome, smart, even charming sometimes. But I'd always had the upper hand in that relationship, and thus, more often than not, he bugged the crap out of me.

Was I only attracted to men I thought were out of my reach? It kind of seemed that way. I wondered what would happen if I ever caught one of them. Would I end up feeling the same way I did about Jinx? Didn't I only want what I was sure I couldn't have?

I stepped over to the bedroom door and opened it a crack.

"Come on, Buck, it'll be fun."

"I don't know, Flynn. I'm not sure I want to take the risk of leaving the ranch."

"Have you ever been on the Flying R? With as famous as Ben Rice is, I'd be willing to bet their security system is as elaborate as the one being installed here."

"I doubt it, but I hadn't thought about the fact that Ben would need something substantial."

"It'll mean so much to Holt."

"When did he become a member of their band?"

"A couple of years ago. Until he knew whether they'd invite him to go on tour, he kept it quiet."

I opened the door the rest of the way and walked into the front part of the cabin. "Did I hear something about going to see a band?"

"I'm trying to talk my overprotective brother into coming along and bringing you and Paxon with him."

I looked at Buck, who appeared as indecisive as he'd sounded a minute ago.

"What if we ask some of the guys working on the security system to go along?" I asked, knowing that Flynn didn't care if Buck and I went; it was Irish she wanted to go.

Buck stroked his beard. "That could work."

"Please," said Flynn, her hands clasped together.

"Let me talk to Rock first, and I'll let you know."

When Buck's sister left the cabin, I stood by the window and watched her walk toward the one Irish was staying in.

"What do you think about Flynn and Irish?"

"She's a kid," Buck answered absentmindedly.

"She's a woman."

Buck looked up at me. "Irish is old enough to be her father."

"That's an exaggeration, and you know it."

"Not by much."

"Some women find older men attractive."

"Women like you?"

I shrugged. "Not exclusively."

"I'll call Rock," Buck snapped, walking out the front door.

I opened the refrigerator, surprised to find it well-stocked with food. None of it, though, looked like my usual "heat and serve" fare. I checked the cupboard, found a loaf of bread, plugged in the toaster that sat near the coffeemaker, and while it did its magic, went back to the fridge to look for butter and jam.

As I waited for my breakfast to pop up, I watched Buck outside, pacing like he had before when he went out to make a call.

He was usually so good-natured that when he wasn't, it was jarring.

I sat down with my laptop to take another look at Barb's emails and rubbed my temples. It wasn't going to be easy to do the kind of research I needed to online, and I doubted very much Buck or Decker would see fit to provide security for me as I gallivanted around as I normally would with any other investigation.

No, my best bet would be if I could figure out where Barb kept her safe-deposit box. As her sole heir, the bank would be required to give me access, right? At least after I was able to show them a death certificate and a copy of her will.

I looked up from my computer when Buck came back inside. His sunny disposition hadn't returned.

"Just say no."

"What?"

"If you don't want to go to this other ranch tonight, just say no. I'm sure it's far more complicated than Flynn or even I know."

"It's fine." He walked over and opened the refrigerator. "You hungry?"

"I had a piece of toast."

I watched as he pulled out a carton of eggs and different kinds of produce.

"How's an omelet sound?"

"Um, good. Although I'm not that hungry."

"You had a *piece* of toast, and you're not hungry?" Unlike before, Buck wasn't teasing me. He sounded irritated.

"That's right."

"That's ridiculous."

I realized that, like Irish had done, he was hardly looking at me. "Buck?"

"What?"

I got up and joined him in the kitchen. Before he started chopping vegetables, I put my hand on his arm. "What's going on?"

"Nothing."

"Then, why won't you look at me?"

Buck shoved the food back into bags and put them and the eggs in the refrigerator. "I've lost my appetite."

When he stalked out of the cabin, I didn't follow or even go to the window to see where he went. I sat down in front of my laptop and continued my research. Like I'd told him—and myself—I didn't have time for bullshit distractions. I not only had a job to do, I had to figure out who killed my aunt and why.

I wasn't sure how long Buck had been gone when I heard a knock at the door. I thought about hollering for whoever it was to come in, but I was here under the auspice of needing protection.

"Hey, Rock," I said when I saw it was him standing on the porch. "What can I do for you?"

"Buck had a few things to take care of, so he asked me to cover for him."

"I see. Do you want to come in?"

"Thanks." He walked past me and over to the refrigerator. "Buck told me to make sure you eat something."

For God's sake. Seriously? "As I told him, I'm not hungry."

Rock walked over to the table and pulled out a chair. "You don't eat enough."

"And this is your business, how?"

I caught his grimace and felt a tinge of guilt for snapping at him. However, I was a grown-up and hadn't starved to death yet. On the other hand, I did exist on a diet of almost exclusively takeout food.

"Just let me make you something to eat."

"Thanks, Rock."

He brought me a sandwich and salad and sat down beside me. "How's the research going?"

"I'm coming to a lot of dead ends, but that's what I expected."

"I can dive in if you'd like."

"I'd appreciate it."

"What time is it?" I asked, looking up from my laptop.

"Almost five," answered Rock.

I wasn't asking about the time as much as I was about Buck's whereabouts. He'd been gone most of the day.

"Have you heard from him?" I asked.

Rock looked at his phone. "Yeah."

What was it with these guys that they insisted I ask a question when the information I was looking for was obvious? I mean, Rock knew who I was asking about without my saying Buck's name.

When he didn't say more, I played along. "And?"

"Me and one of the other guys are supposed to accompany you and Irish to the Flying R Ranch at six."

"Will Buck be going as well?"

"I can't answer that, Stella."

"Which means you know, but you can't tell me?" Jesus. And Buck told me he wasn't going to play games. Actually, that wasn't exactly right. He said he wasn't going to play me. Those were two different things, weren't they?

I wasn't sure what I should wear to visit this other ranch, except that I shouldn't wear Buck's t-shirt. I closed my laptop, went into the bedroom, and took a shower. When I came back out, Rock was looking at his phone.

"Ready?" he asked when he noticed I'd walked in.

"To be honest, I'd rather just stay here."

"You wanna get me in trouble?" he asked with a smile.

"Never."

"Let's get out of here, then."

When we walked out the front door, Irish was waiting on the porch. Rock opened the front passenger door for me. "I can sit in the back."

"No, I will," muttered Irish, reaching for the door handle.

"We have one more to pick up," said Rock, as if that made a difference.

When we pulled up to the main house, Irish's desire to sit in the back made more sense. He got out, walked around to the other side of the vehicle, and opened the door. Flynn came out the front door and got in.

We pulled out behind another SUV identical to the one we were in. I looked in the side mirror and saw another followed. Was Buck in either of them?

If he wasn't, or if he didn't show up at the other ranch at all, I would regret agreeing to come along. I had no desire to listen to some band I didn't know, or hang out with any of these people. I would've much preferred continuing my research.

16

Buck

Earlier, I'd stormed out of the cabin in a ridiculous fit of jealousy over the idea that Jinx Jenkins had spent any time at all with Stella. Making it worse, I'd just apologized for doubting her when she said it was over. But the idea that he'd had his hands on her naked body when I hadn't, pissed me the fuck off. The only way I could stop from making a complete jackass of myself was to leave.

I went in search of my brothers and found them helping Decker's crew with the security system installation.

"Hey, Buck, how are ya?" asked Zane "Rip" Kailor, one of the guys who had been with the agency like me, but now worked as a contractor for the Invincibles.

"Not too bad. Good to see you, Rip." I looked beyond him and saw three more former agents I'd worked with on several ops: Mick "Jagger" Reynolds, Breckin "Ink" Ryan, and Hayes "Press" Preston.

"How's it looking, boys?"

"We should be able to finish in a day or two."

"In that case, you should take a break and come along with us tonight. From what I've heard, CB Rice is giving an impromptu concert."

The three guys looked at Rip. "Okay with me."

When he motioned for me to follow, the men went back to work.

"Deck asked us to stay on and see what else we can do to help."

"By help, do you mean asset protection?"

"That too."

"What else?"

"The four of us formed a side business a couple of years ago, flipping houses. We've gotten pretty good at it. We could get some of the other cabins fixed up, move the dude ranch along quicker."

"I appreciate the offer, but money's pretty tight around here, Rip."

He shrugged. "We're gonna be here anyway, and we're gettin' paid, so we might as well keep ourselves busy."

"I'll give Decker a call this afternoon and find out what he's thinking."

"You want me to give you a rundown of what we've got goin' on out here?"

I spent the next few hours working with Rip's team. Most of what we did was place and/or bury sensors that were all part of an elaborate network of communication devices. What the sensors picked up determined the main system's response, ranging from camera-monitoring all the way to the deployment of weapon-equipped drones.

What blew my mind was the size of the sensors. No way in hell could they be detected by anyone, including those of us who installed them, unless they had the app Decker wrote to monitor the entire system. If, say, an animal unknowingly dug it up or it was disturbed in some other way, a camera on the sensor itself would immediately be activated.

Before I knew it, it was seventeen hundred hours. I waved at Rip. "Time for me to head out. You guys coming along?"

When the caravan of SUVs pulled through the gates of the Flying R Ranch, I wondered why I'd agreed to come out tonight. I would've preferred staying at the cabin alone with Stella. At least I would've known that all the assholes who kept showing up and interrupting me every time I was about to get my hands on her would've been here while we were there.

Hell, she probably wasn't speaking to me anyway after the jackass move I pulled by walking out on her.

We pulled up to the barn where Flynn said we were supposed to meet up with the band. Before I could get to the SUV Stella was riding in, I saw Press get out of the first vehicle, open her door, and escort her through the alley doors. As I walked closer, I could hear the band had already started playing.

"Hey," said Port, walking up with two bottles of beer. "Want one?"

I looked around for Stella but didn't see her. Where the hell had she gone?

"She's dancing." Port pointed at her and Press.

Instead of taking the bottle from my brother, I stalked over to where several other couples were dancing in front of the stage where CB Rice was playing. I was within a foot of them when I saw Cord do the very thing I was about to and cut in. I thought about doing it anyway, but I'd only make myself look like a dick. I returned to where Port waited, holding out the same bottle to me, this time with a smirk.

"Not a lot of dance partners here tonight," he muttered.

I looked around the room; guys outnumbered women at least five to one. When I turned back, Porter had walked away.

"Hey, Buck," I heard a familiar voice say from behind me. "Would you like to dance?"

There were two reasons I shouldn't dance with Bethany—Stella and Porter. But the look on her face outweighed both. While my brother might be pissed at first, later he might not be if I told him the only reason I'd agreed was to talk to Beth about him.

"It's nice to have you back home," she said, wrapping her arms around my neck. I took one and set it on my shoulder and the other on my waist. "Why'd you do that?" she asked as I danced her around the floor.

"You know why, Beth. My brother."

"It wasn't anything, Buck. We went out on a couple of dates, is all."

"It was something to Porter," I murmured, remembering I'd said the same thing about myself to Stella. I cleared my throat. "You should know I'm with someone else now."

I felt her stiffen in my arms. "Oh. Who?"

"That woman right over there, dancing with Cord."

"Doesn't look like she's that into you, Buck."

She was right. Stella only had eyes for Cord, and whatever he'd just said, made her blush. It was all I could do to not leave Beth standing alone while I went and ripped my brother's arms off.

"We had a disagreement," I muttered, wondering why I felt the need to explain this to my former high school sweetheart. "Look, Porter cares about you. If the only reason you broke things off with him was because of me, I'm off the market."

"Do you love her?"

"We aren't to that point yet, but I plan to get there."

Bethany looked over at Stella and Cord at the same time I did. This time, Stella was also looking at us. "She's a lucky girl," Beth mumbled.

That was the thing, Stella wasn't a girl; she was a woman. She told me not to play her, which to me, meant she was interested in exploring this attraction between us. "Thanks for the dance, Beth," I said when the song ended. I left her standing where she was and walked over to my brother, who still had his arm around Stella's waist. "Excuse me," I said, squeezing Cord's shoulder hard enough that he wouldn't dare ignore me. "I need to talk to Stella." The band started playing another song. It was one of my favorites, and I'd be damned if I wasn't going to hold Stella in my arms for it. I held my hand out to her. "May I?"

When she nodded, my brother walked away. I gathered her in my arms and softly sang along to the song that had catapulted Ben and his band, CB Rice, into superstardom.

> *Sweet beauty on the steps, waiting, like me*
> *Sun masked by clouds, so free*
> *Beautiful, if only you were able to move,*
> *To go, to ride, to smile, to fly, to kiss, to fall*
> *I know how deep your smile, if only you could fall*

"It's beautiful," Stella murmured, resting her cheek against my shoulder.

"Ben wrote it for the woman who is now his wife."

"She wasn't then?"

"No. In fact, she was in a coma at the time."

She pulled back to look at me.

"Olivia is a barrel racer, and she took a fall that could've killed her." I kept singing along.

> *I know how wild your passion, if only you*
> *would fall*

I know how deep your longing, if only you
 could fall
I know your fear, I know your tears
But that smile, so sweet, that longing so deep
Your eyes burn into my heart, my love, my joy,
 my fall
You know my longing deep, you know my
love, so hard
You know my longing deep, you know my
passion, so wild
You know my fall
To see you here then, in the midst of your fall
To know your joy, so deep, to know your
 passion, complete
To know your longing, my all, and then, my
 sweet, you fall

"The melody is haunting," she murmured.

I spun her around and pointed over to where Olivia stood, swaying to the music and singing along with her husband. "That's her."

"You'd never know she came close to dying."

The song ended and another began. Since it was also a slow one, I kept my arm tight around Stella's waist.

"You disappeared today."

"I had some work to take care of." She tried to pull away, but I tightened my grip. "Where do you think you're going?"

"I asked you not to play me, Buck. I guess I wasn't specific enough, because it appears you don't realize that also means no games and no *lies.*"

I rested my head against hers. "I'm sorry."

"What set you off?" she murmured.

"Seems I've got a jealous streak I didn't realize I had."

She snickered. "Right. I remember you weren't at all jealous of Cope and Ali."

"It wasn't the same."

She shook her head but didn't say anything.

"Thinking about you with Jinx…"

"I told you that was over."

"I know you did, but I got to thinkin' that he knew how it felt to hold your naked body against his and I don't." I put my finger on her chin and lifted it so I could see her eyes. "I really want to know how that feels, Stella."

"What happens if you don't like it as much as you think you will?"

"Not a chance in the world."

"I'm older than you, Buck."

"What's that got to do with anything?"

"Seeing me naked might not do it for you the same way it would with her." Stella motioned to where Bethany stood off to the side, watching us.

"That was over a long time ago."

"It looks like she might want a second chance."

"As I told her a few minutes ago, I'm with someone else now."

"Is that someone supposed to be me?"

I shook my head. "That someone is you, Stella."

"We're hardly together, Buck. Unless you're just using me to get her to back off."

I looked up and saw Rip headed our way. If he thought for one second that I was going to let him dance with Stella, he was dead wrong.

"Come with me." I took her hand, led her off the dance floor, and out of the barn. Once outside, I maneuvered her over to the corral fence, backed her up against it, and leaned my body into hers. "You want to know what I don't understand?"

She looked down at my arms that had her pinned where she was. "I don't think I have any choice but to listen."

"When we're on the phone, we don't have any trouble talking to each other. After our last conversation, I'd say we don't have any trouble with intimacy either."

"What's your point?"

I was done trying to make a point by talking. I grabbed the back of Stella's neck, leaned down, and kissed her. I pushed my tongue between her lips and angled my head to go deeper.

"Hey, Buck? Oh, sorry to interrupt," I heard Rip say from behind me. I ignored him and kept kissing Stella. I would've continued doing so if I didn't hear more voices headed our way but from the other direction. I broke off the kiss, turned around, and called out to Rip.

"Yeah?" he answered.

"I need the keys to one of the SUVs."

He walked over and handed them to me. "Where you headed?"

"Back to the Roaring Fork."

"Hang on, and I'll get a couple of the guys to go with you."

I had no intention of waiting. "Let's go," I said to Stella, taking her hand in mine.

"Buck, I—"

I spun her back to the fence like I had earlier, angled my head, and kissed her again. With both hands, I cupped the cheeks of her ass and pressed my hard cock against her heat. "Yeah, Stella? What were you going to say?"

"I don't remember." Her voice was thick and low, like she sounded on the phone.

"Come on." I pulled her over to the parked vehicle and opened the door. I closed it behind her after she climbed inside.

"I like your other truck better," she said when I got in the driver's side bucket seat.

"I do too." I reached over to put one hand on her thigh after I started the engine and put the SUV in gear. When she moved my hand between her legs, I thought about pulling over and moving us both to the rear bench seat. I wanted her that bad.

"Are you going to answer that?" she asked when my cell phone rang.

"Hell, no."

"What if it's important?"

"There isn't anything more important than what is happening right here, between you and me."

"Come on, Buck, I'm serious."

"They'll leave a message." I waited for the ranch gates to open, pulled through, and waited for them to close behind us. Stella was quiet the rest of the drive, but I could feel the heat of her arousal through the thin, knit pants she wore.

She waited for me to come around to the passenger side when I pulled up to the cabin, parked, and climbed out. I reached for her and slid her sweet body down the front of mine. Stella groaned.

"Let's go inside," I said, taking her hand in mine. I unlocked the front door and, after we were inside, double-checked the damn thing to make sure the deadbolt was thrown.

I walked over to where Stella stood by the fireplace. "I want to share your bed tonight, darlin'. Would you like that?"

"Very much," she answered, barely above a whisper.

"I'd also like to take a shower."

Stella made a face.

"I guess that means you don't want to join me."

"I'd rather take a bath."

While I wasn't much of a bath guy, taking one with her sounded damn good. "Can I join you?"

"Um…sure. I'll go get it started."

When she tried to walk away, I grabbed her hand and pulled her back. "We need to get something straight before we share anything—a bath or a bed."

"Okay," she murmured.

"I want you so much it hurts, Stella. I've felt that way a lot longer than I bet you even realize."

"You have?"

"Back before we knew Cope was still alive, when I was still on Ali's detail and you and I used to talk, I think I knew then."

"No, you didn't." She tried to wriggle out of my arms, but I held her tight.

"I did. Don't you realize that's when I started texting you before we both fell asleep?"

Her eyes scrunched like she was trying to figure out if that was true. It was. I was sure of it. I was also sure that my attraction to her began before then It started the first day I met her.

Sure, I'd been as wrapped up in Ali as Stella was in Cope, but there was a big part of me that wished things were different. Mainly, that Stella wasn't in love with him. The more she and I talked, the more I wanted to be the man she thought about *first*. I wanted to be the man she *wanted*. My reaction to her having a relationship with Jinx made a lot more sense to me now that I'd thought about it from that perspective. He became another man who I believed she thought about—wanted—more than me. Now, I was done being second in line.

"Every single night that we talked until we couldn't keep our eyes open any longer, I'd pull the damn pillow into my arms and pretend it was you."

"I did the same thing." She tried to bury her head in the nook of my shoulder, but I pulled back.

"I'm not going to let you hide from me, Stella. If we're going to talk about sex, it's going to be face to face. Tell me you understand."

"Buck, I…"

"Whatever it is, just say it."

"I'm thirty-six years old."

"Do you think that means I won't find you attractive?"

She put her hands on my chest and pushed, but I wouldn't let her go.

"Unless you tell me no, I'm about to learn everything there is to know about that thirty-six-year-old body."

"Oh."

"And you're about to learn quite a lot about mine." I took her hand and rested it where my cock strained against the buttons on my jeans. "First lesson. That's how much I want you." I took a step back when I got an idea. "There's this fantasy that I haven't been able to get out of my head all damn day."

"What is that?"

"You. My t-shirt. Me finally finding out exactly what you had under it."

When she smiled, I knew she liked that idea.

"Wanna make my fantasy a reality?"

"Be right back."

While I waited, I lit the fireplace along with a couple of candles I noticed earlier on the mantle. When Stella returned, I hit the switch to turn off the hallway lights. I grabbed her hand, pulled her body into mine, and slid my hands down to the small of her back—where they'd been each time we were interrupted.

With the fingers of one hand, I grasped the hem of the t-shirt and held my breath as I put the palms of both hands on her bare ass. Damn, she felt good. I lowered my mouth to hers and kissed her. In a split second, it became frenzied. Both for her and me. I pulled the shirt over her head and took a step back, running my eyes up and down her naked body. "So fucking beautiful," I murmured, reaching out to cup her breast.

"Buck, I want to see you," she said, sliding one hand under the waistband of my jeans.

"All in due time, darlin'. I want you there, on the floor." I pointed to the throw I'd laid out on top of a thick rug. "On your back, legs spread."

Her breath hitched as she knelt down with the grace of a dancer. Before she was stretched out the way I wanted her, I placed a pillow under her head and leaned in, close to her ear. "Legs spread, Stella."

I knelt between them, spreading them wider. "Bend your knees." I grabbed one of her hands and put it under her leg. "Hold yourself this way," I said, moving her other hand behind the opposite knee.

Leaning forward, I used my tongue to separate her perfect, wet, hot folds. I put both hands under her, digging my fingers into the ass I'd waited all day to make mine. I wanted to slide my cock into her heat, but I couldn't. This was my first time making love to Stella, and I wanted her to feel it, see it, know that this was more than a quick fuck between two people who'd teased each other mercilessly.

"Hold on tight," I said when I saw her hand slipping from her knee.

Her glazed eyes looked into mine. "Please, Buck," she whispered.

"Did you say please? What are you asking me to do, darlin'?"

"Fuck me." It came out as a needy whine. Would it be best if I warned her she had a long time to wait before I'd give her what she begged for? No. I'd let her go along for the ride instead.

I moved her hands, took her legs one at a time, and stretched them out on the floor but open for me. I licked her clit with my tongue. As much as I wanted to linger there, I didn't. I ran my tongue up the center of her body to her belly button.

She jerked and giggled as if it tickled, but she wasn't smiling. Her body was strung tight with tension I would eventually relieve, but not yet. I kept going, taking as much of her breast into my mouth as I could while I plucked and pulled at her other nipple.

I released both her breasts and did the thing she least wanted me to do. I studied her body. I lifted her breasts and let them fall. I ran my tongue and lips down her side. I raised her arm over her head and kissed the smooth skin above her elbow. I kissed her neck, the soft lines on either side of her mouth, the harder lines on the edges of her eyes.

I came back to her mouth and kissed her with all of the fervor I'd felt for her every minute I listened to her voice before I fell asleep. I kissed her hard and deep and, at the same time, trailed my hand back down her body to settle between her legs.

I stopped and looked into her eyes—her pleading, insecure, frightened eyes. "Trust me," I whispered.

Stella nodded, just slightly, but enough for me to know that despite her fear, she was still with me. Still willing. I kissed my way down her body, moved between her legs, and settled there. I watched her as I used my mouth and hands to give her enough pleasure that her back arched, her eyes rolled in her head, and she pulled my hair with the fingers she'd woven into it.

When her breathing evened out, and she dropped her hands from my head, I kissed my way down her leg. I took my time, trailing my tongue down the soft flesh on the inside of her thigh to her knee, then down her calf to her ankle. As I made my way up her other leg, I put my hands on her waist. My thumbs met in her center and I stretched my hands until my middle fingers met behind her. I flipped her then, so I could get to know the back of her body the same way I was learning the front.

She groaned when I trailed my tongue down her spine and when I kissed the tender cheeks of her ass. I was torturing her, mentally more than physically, but after tonight, I wouldn't allow Stella to ever again question my attraction to her. She would understand that every inch of her excited me. Every breath she took, every thought I could see rolling around in her beautiful brain, turned me on.

When I stood, Stella looked over her shoulder at me. "You better be taking your clothes off."

I didn't answer. I sat on the couch and took off my boots and socks. I kept my eyes fixed on hers as I unbuttoned my shirt, pulled it from my body, and tossed it on the floor. I stood again and unfastened my belt.

"Roll onto your back," I said and waited with my hands on the waist of my jeans until she rested her head on the pillow. My cock strained against the denim as I popped the grommets and pulled the fly open. When I lowered my jeans, my hardness sprung forth. Stella's eyes trailed down my body and settled between my legs.

"I want to touch you."

"I'm all yours."

She got on her knees and reached out for me. As much as I wanted to feel her mouth on my cock, I couldn't. Not now. I wouldn't last, and the first time I came with Stella, I wanted to be balls-deep inside her. "Changed my mind. Stand up, darlin'," I said, holding out my hand.

She grasped it and stood, her eyes fixated on mine like they were earlier. I pulled her into my arms and twisted my tongue with hers. When I pulled back, I put my hands on either side of her face. "I need to make love to you, Stella. I need you to understand that's what this is between us. This means too much to me for you to think any less of it."

Her eyes darted back and forth between mine. "Buck…I'm…"

"What? Tell me. Talk to me. What we're about to do is too important for me not to know how you're feeling."

"You're scaring me," she whispered. "I'm scared."

I knew what she meant, but I had to be sure. "Of me? Physically?"

"No."

"What, then?"

"Why are you making this matter so much?"

"Because you matter that much to me."

She looked away. "Why?"

I put my hand on her chin and turned her face toward me. "If you think I'm going to let you keep me at arm's length by allowing you to call this casual, meaningless sex, you're wrong. You're important to me."

She brought her hand to her hair and ran her fingers through it. "This is too much. Too fast."

I dropped my hands from her face. "Then, we'll wait."

"What?" she all but shrieked.

"You heard me. If intimacy is off the table, so is fucking." I eased by her and walked toward the hallway.

"Where are you going?"

"To bed."

"But…but…"

"If you're willing to give yourself to me the way I'm giving myself to you, say so." I waited, watching the conflict she was feeling play out on her face, in her eyes. When she didn't say anything, I kept going, into the same bedroom I'd slept in the night before.

17

Stella

What in the name of God just happened? I was standing alone and naked in the main room of the cabin after, only minutes ago, Buck had made me feel like the sexiest woman alive. With every touch, every kiss, every stroke of his tongue, my insecurities fell away, one by one. I knew he wanted me. Me. Just as I was.

Now, he was gone. Behind a closed door. And I didn't know what to do. Should I follow? Knock? Ask if I could come in? Get in bed with him? Then what?

He was asking me for something I wasn't sure I could give. The bottom line was, I never had before. When Jinx pushed too hard for "more" from me, I ended the relationship. When Buck made it clear he thought the mutual attraction between us was "something" as opposed to nothing, I'd balked and told him I didn't have time for distractions. That wasn't it, though.

I was honest when I told him I was scared. It was more than that. I was terrified. My worst fear, the one that sat deep in my subconscious, the one I never allowed to come to the surface, was clawing its way out, and I couldn't let it. I left Buck's t-shirt on the floor, blew out the candles on the mantle, and went down the hallway to the room I'd slept in last night.

I crawled under the cold sheets, wondering how I'd ever sleep without hearing the comfort of Buck's voice. I hadn't been apart from him for ten minutes, yet the yearning I felt, hurt. I covered my eyes with my arm, but that didn't stop my tears.

The solution was simple. All I had to do was get out of this bed, walk across the hall, and tell Buck that he mattered to me too. I didn't have to tell him how terrified I was that once I allowed myself to care too much, he'd change his mind and leave. He didn't have to know any of that. All he'd asked me for, was to acknowledge that what we were about to do was making love, not having sex. That was all I had to admit, accept, allow myself to feel. He wasn't asking me to love him, only to make love with him.

I had no idea how much time passed while I lay there, trying to talk myself into getting up and going to him. Maybe it was two minutes, maybe thirty when I heard my phone vibrate.

I jumped up and grabbed it, almost afraid to look. If it wasn't Buck, my disappointment would be profound. I closed my eyes tight, turned my phone over, and slowly opened them. I gripped the phone as I read his simple words. *Please, Stella.*

I dropped my cell on the table and opened the bedroom door. There, leaning against the opposite wall, stood Buck, still naked. I held out my hand. "Please, Buck, make love to me." His eyes met mine.

"Let's make love to each other."

I was breathless when he pulled me into his arms and kissed me. He walked me backwards, our mouths fused together. "Get on the bed, Stella."

I did and scooted over so he could lie beside me. He reached over and turned on the bedside light.

"I want to see you."

I nodded and held my arms out to him. When he lay beside me, I looked over his shoulder and saw several condom packets on the table by the lamp I hadn't turned on.

I smiled and kissed him. "Thanks for not giving up on me."

"Tell me this means something to you, Stella."

"It means everything to me, Buck. Please don't make me wait any longer."

He reached behind him, tore open a packet, put the condom on, and rolled onto his back. "Come here," he said, holding out his hand. When I straddled him, he put his hands on my waist. "We'll take this nice and slow," he said, lifting me so the tip of his cock was at my entrance. He eased me down onto him while I guided his cock inside me.

"Slow," he murmured when I moved my hand so he could go deeper. "I don't want to hurt you." He kept his grasp on my waist firm when I rested my palms on his chest. I might be on top, but Buck was the one controlling how deep he went.

"I need to kiss you," he said before rolling me over and holding himself above me. I felt his hardness ease farther inside me at the same time he covered my mouth with his.

"God, Stella," he groaned. "You're so tight, so hot, so wet for me. I feel like part of me has died and gone to heaven."

I spread my legs wider when he started to move, wanting him to go deeper. I reached around and grabbed his ass.

Buck's eyes met mine. "Tell me what you want, darlin'."

"More. Harder."

When he tucked a pillow under my ass and pressed deeper, I thrust my hips forward.

"Wrap your legs around my waist and hold on tight, Stella. Ol' Buck is gonna take you for a ride."

"I thought you were young Buck."

He was so deep that groans came from both our chests as he filled me like I'd never been before. When he swiveled his hips, hitting my G spot, I felt my eyes roll back in my head. How was it possible for him to do that and angle his body in such a way that he rubbed my clit with every stroke?

He picked up his pace, and I met him, thrust for thrust, digging my nails into his flesh as I felt myself spiraling.

Both of us shouted out our release. As my breathing slowed, I felt Buck's lips on my neck, scattering cool kisses on my overheated skin.

"That was a little quicker than I would've preferred," he said between nips. "It's been a while."

That was quick? I ran my fingers through my hair that was damp with sweat. My God, what had I been missing all my life? "It was perfect, Buck."

"It isn't over, Stella." He rolled to his side, got off the bed, and went into the bathroom. When he came back, he had something in his hand. He eased my legs open and covered my pussy with the damp, warm cloth. "You're gonna be sore tomorrow."

"I'm okay."

He dropped the cloth at the end of the bed and used both hands to spread my legs wider. "Like I said, we aren't finished yet."

By the time the sun came up, I could barely move. Every inch of my body was sore, but in the best possible way. I'd never experienced sex on that level before. Maybe it was because, as Buck had said, it wasn't just sex; we were making love.

He was gentle and then demanding; he brought me to the edge of pain and then pulled me back into pleasure—over and over again. All the while, he'd tell me how beautiful I was, how good it felt to hold me against him, how hot and wet I was just for him. He lavished his attention on my breasts, my pussy, my ass, so much so that when I closed my eyes now, even without him touching me, I could feel his hands and his mouth on every part of my body. I moaned at the memory of how good it all felt.

"God, woman, you have to let me rest," he muttered, moving my hand that was on his cock, winking, and pulling me into his arms. I rested my head on his chest, above his heart, and fell back to sleep.

When I woke, the sun was high in the sky and the opposite side of the bed was cold. I saw Buck's t-shirt laid out at the end of the bed. I rolled out and threw it over my head, stuck my arms through the sleeves, and padded out to the main room, hoping that if Buck was still here, he was alone.

I found him in the kitchen, naked as he'd been when we fell asleep. "Good morning," I said, putting my arms around his waist and rubbing my boobs against his back.

"Mmm. I could get used to this."

He turned in my arms, pulled the t-shirt up, and covered both cheeks of my ass with his hands. When had I ever been so carefree with nudity? Granted, I was wearing Buck's shirt, but the idea that we could spend all day within the walls of this cabin not wearing a stitch of clothing, excited me far more than it made me nervous. That was all Buck's doing. In the course of only a few hours, he'd showed me I could be comfortable in my own skin. I didn't need to hide from him or cover up my fleshy parts. He liked me just the way I was. More, seeing me naked excited him.

I took a step back and pulled the shirt over my head. Buck slid his way down my body, kneeling in front of me. He shifted again so he was sitting on the floor and pulled me closer. "One leg here," he said, pointing to his shoulder.

"No, I can't," I said, laughing. "I'll fall."

Buck stood, grabbed me, and tossed me over his shoulder. "The bed's a better idea anyway for what I want to do to you."

"What do you want to do to me?" I wanted to ask what was left that we hadn't already done, but I was too afraid of what he might say.

"Everything I did to you last night, all over again."

We'd just turned the corner into the bedroom when we heard a knock at the front door.

"Nooo," Buck groaned, setting me on my feet. He put his arm around my waist and pulled me into him. I loved the feeling of his bare skin flush with mine and that the way he held me felt like possession. "When this is over, I'm taking you away. Somewhere we can spend days on end without interruption. You got it?"

I nodded, unable to stop myself from wondering if it would actually happen. I really wanted it to. Too much.

What if he was just talking? What if I counted on it? I looked into Buck's eyes; he was studying me.

"Do you know that when something is bothering you, the corners of your mouth turned downward and your brow furrows?"

"It does not," I said, trying to pull away from him.

"It does, or they do. I've seen it countless times. My question now, though, is what about my saying I want to take you somewhere we won't be interrupted is making you worry?"

"That isn't it." I tried to pull away again when there was another knock on the door.

"Keep your damn pants on. I'll be there in a minute," Buck shouted and then looked back at me. "Speaking of pants, I guess we should put some on."

"In order for me to do that, you'll have to let me go."

"Now, see, I knew you were going to say that. I also knew you were going to try to get out of answering my question."

"Buck, seriously—"

"No, Stella. I want an answer. Is it that you don't want to run off to the middle of nowhere with me?"

"That isn't it." God, how stupid was I? He'd just backed me into a corner.

"Then, tell me what it is."

"I don't like to plan too far in the future."

"Why not?"

I pushed against his chest with my hands; he didn't loosen his hold on me. "Buck, there is someone out there, waiting for us."

"Why not?" His tone was more demanding.

"Because I don't like looking forward to things."

"And then not having them happen?"

"That's right."

Buck rested his forehead against mine. "It's gonna happen, Stella. I guarantee it. Same way I guarantee that, as soon as I can, you're going to be on that bed, legs spread, with me so deep inside you, you won't know where I end and you begin."

I wanted that more than anything, and I didn't want to wait. And that was a problem. I'd told Buck that I couldn't afford distractions, and now the work I needed to do in order to find Barb's killer was becoming a lesser priority than having sex with him.

He brushed my lips with his, kissed my forehead, and let me go. I watched as he raced across the hallway to put on clothes I didn't want him to wear.

I stayed in the bedroom, eavesdropping when Buck stalked out to the main part of the cabin and unlocked the door.

"What can I do for you, Irish?" I heard him say.

"Decker is trying to get in touch with you. Stella too. He finally called and asked me to walk over and see if you were both okay."

"Hey, Stella," Buck hollered.

I peeked my head out of the bedroom door. "Yeah?"

"As you can see, she's okay and so am I. Anything else?"

"He wants you to call him." Irish spun around and stormed out of the cabin. Buck shut the door, locked it, and pulled out his phone.

"Hey, Deck." There were a few seconds of silence. "Yeah, Stella's here." More silence. "Sure, I'll go get her."

I stepped out of the bedroom and walked over to where he stood. I watched as he put the phone on mute.

"He wants me to put it on speaker."

"Go ahead."

"Okay, Deck, Stella and I are both here."

"'Bout damn time the two of you got up."

"Oh, yeah? Are we operating on someone else's clock that I wasn't aware of?"

Decker laughed. "Nah, just giving you some shit, young Buck."

"Why did you want me to call you?"

"Right. I have to go to Tennessee for a few days. Rip says they're about to wrap things up on the security system. Since I can't get there right now, you and Rock can handle the final testing."

"Roger that," said Buck. "If you don't mind my asking, what's in Tennessee?"

"You know Smoke Torcher, don't ya?"

"Of course I do."

"Putting in a system like yours at his place. And before you ask why I'm working on that one and not on the one at the Roaring Fork, I can tell you that his is going to be a hell of a lot more complex."

"Why's that?"

"He lives on top of a goddamn mountain, and it isn't the kind you hike on."

"Enough said. Anything else?"

I couldn't help but wonder why Decker had asked Buck to put the phone on speaker. So far, none of this had anything to do with me.

"Stella, you there?"

I chuckled. "Yes, Decker, I'm here."

"I wanted you both to know that I expect Cope and Ali will be showing up at the ranch sometime in the next two weeks."

"Okay," I murmured, my eyes meeting Buck's.

"Also, I've made arrangements for you both to have access to some of the Invincible's proprietary online resources. You'll be able to get into the facial recognition trackers along with a few other things you may find useful. Buck, you'll need to take care of getting Stella logged into the system."

"Roger that," he said like I'd heard earlier.

"Stella, it's somewhat complicated, but I'm confident young Buck can handle it."

"Gettin' tiresome, old Deck."

Buck and I laughed when he did.

"One other thing. Rip mentioned he and his team are going to start working on the other cabins."

"Decker, I—"

"He also told me you were worried about paying them. Since they're already on the Invincibles' dime, don't worry about it."

"I appreciate this, Deck, but—"

He sighed. "Stella, would you please set him straight?"

"I'll try," I answered, laughing.

"And if you're going to be out of contact, will you both please tell someone, so I don't send the cavalry out looking for you?"

"We're going to be out of contact," blurted Buck. I looked at him with wide eyes. "I'll check in periodically, but we're taking a couple of days."

"Copy that. Don't forget to check in."

Buck hit end on the call, dropped his phone on the table, and pulled me into his arms. "Before you freak out on me, hear me out."

"I'm listening."

"We can work all you want, but I want us to take breaks. That's what I meant by being out of contact. There are things we're waiting on, which means that there's no reason to keep spinning our wheels, trying to make something magically appear out of nowhere."

I got his point. In fact, I'd felt that way when I was re-reading Barb's emails. I'd "magically" wanted them to tell me something—anything—that they hadn't the first few times I'd read them. I knew there were clues buried in them, but I'd be damned if I could figure them out. "Okay."

Buck smiled. "Okay?"

"That's what I said."

"Then, the first place I want to take you to be out of contact is right in there." He pointed to the bedroom.

After spending the rest of the morning naked in Buck's arms, he suggested that it was time to venture farther off the Roaring Fork. While I got dressed after the bath we'd taken together, I overheard him talking on speaker to Rock.

"I'm going to need some backup today," he said. "I'm taking Stella out to run some errands and see the sights."

"Roger that. What's our departure ETA?"

"Thirty minutes."

Buck had given me the rundown of his plans for the afternoon, and I'd agreed to go along with them, even the stuff he was keeping a surprise.

At one on the dot, we were waiting on the porch when Rock pulled up in an SUV. There was a man I didn't recognize sitting in the front passenger seat.

"Who is that?" I asked, pointing as we walked toward the vehicle when the biggest man I'd ever seen in my life climbed out. I had no idea how he'd fit in the car in the first place.

"Hey, Ink. I'd like you to meet Stella."

The guy looked like one of those Transformers' characters after it turned from a car into a superhero. His arms were bigger around than my entire body, and his legs were twice as big as his arms. He was wearing athletic shorts and a ripped tank top, probably because no other clothes would fit him. His head was shaved except for a Mohawk that had been dyed platinum blonde.

"Stella, this is Breckin Ryan, also known as Ink. Ink, this is Stella Hunter."

When he took his time looking me up and down, I did the same thing right back to him. I had no reason to ask why he was called Ink. Most of his body was covered in it. He was trying to intimidate me, probably something he did with everyone he met to the point it had become a habit.

I had no doubt the man could snap me in two without raising his heart rate, but I also knew that if he tried, Buck would take him down.

I folded my arms and gave him another once over. "Nice to meet you, Breckin."

"Ink."

"Right."

"You did that to me the first time we met," Buck leaned in and said after Ink walked back over the vehicle and opened the back door for us.

"What's that?"

"You let me know in no uncertain terms that you wouldn't take any shit from me or anyone else."

"Isn't that what your friend just did to me?"

"He isn't my friend. Just someone I work with."

"Evidently, there's some history between you."

Buck put his arm around my waist and nuzzled my neck. "Don't go all reporter on me now, Stella. Most of the time, I think Ink and his attitude are bullshit. That's not history."

"Mm-hmm."

Buck leaned in and kissed the side of my neck. "Come on, darlin', a day of adventure awaits."

18

Buck

I wanted to end our day in downtown Crested Butte, so I told Rock to head toward Gunnison when we left the Roaring Fork.

I waited to see if Stella would ask where we were going, but as she'd said, she was willing to go along, even for the surprises.

While the drive into Crested Butte was one of my favorites, the reverse was pretty too. It followed along the Gunnison River until it reached the tiny community of Altamont, where it divided into two, the East River and the Taylor River.

Altamont was named for a famous racehorse, a favorite of the owner of Fisher Ranch, which eventually became the unincorporated community. There wasn't much there besides a couple of four-seasons resorts favored by hunters and fishermen, but it was a beautiful place. I knew Stella thought so too when she craned her neck to take it all in. Maybe on one of our adventures, I'd bring her back here to fish.

When we reached the historic downtown, I asked Rock to park.

"Looks right out of the movies," murmured Stella.

"As a matter of fact, Gunnison's Main Street has been in some. TV shows too." The two-block section of town was dotted with diners, shops, and bars that had been in business since before my great-grandparents were born.

I led Stella into a western wear shop and over to a rack of jeans.

"You've got to be kidding," she muttered.

I put my arm around her waist and pulled her close. "Try on one pair. For me." My smile broadened when she went into the dressing room with no fewer than six.

I stood right outside, hoping she'd model at least one pair for me. "Stella?" I said when I decided it had been long enough for her to take off the pants she was wearing and slip the jeans on. I held my breath when I saw the doorknob turn.

"Holy shit," I mumbled under my breath. She had her back to me, and damn, if the pair she wore didn't hug her ass in all the ways I imagined they would. I looked over my shoulder to make sure no one was close by and slipped into the room with her. I closed the door behind me and grabbed her ass with both hands.

Stella giggled. "What are you doing?"

"Making sure they fit." I squeezed both cheeks and then spun her around, admiring the way they looked from the front just as much. "Your body was made to wear jeans, Stella."

"There are a couple others I really like," she said, flipping through the hangers.

"Try them all on."

"Overkill much?"

"Overkill would be if I went back out there and grabbed all the pairs I wanted to see on you."

She put her hand on the waistband.

"Go ahead. Take them off."

"You need to step out."

I sat in the chair instead; I loved the way her cheeks flushed bright red. "Take them off, darlin'." I watched as she peeled them from her body, wishing I had offered to do it for her. "You are so fucking sexy," I murmured, pulling her over to me, so I could put my hands on her bare ass. I put my finger under the strap of her thong. "By the way, I love this." I leaned forward and nipped her pussy through the sheer lace before moving it out of my way and licking through her folds.

"Buck," she groaned, resting her hands on my shoulders.

"Shh. Don't make a sound, or I'll stop." I thrust one, then two fingers inside her, pressing my tongue against her clit. I wrapped my other arm around her to hold her still. When I did, I could see the outline of something unexpected under her arm. I ran my hand up and felt the shape of a gun. "Are you carrying, Stella?" I whispered.

Her fingers dug into my shoulders, and her body tried to writhe. "Are you fucking kidding me right now? God, Buck, I'm right on the edge."

I smiled and thrust harder, knowing the second she came.

"Good girl," I murmured, kissing her skin above her pussy and raising her shirt so I could check out her concealed carry compression tank. "By the way, this is hot as fuck."

"Um, Buck," she said, running her fingers through her hair. "If you want me to try on any other clothes, don't hesitate to let me know."

We left that store with all six pairs of jeans she took into the dressing room plus three more, two pairs of boots, and a few western-style shirts. My favorite thing, though, was the pair of Daisy Dukes she added to the pile when she didn't think I was looking. Man, I could hardly wait to peel those off of her.

"Hungry?" I asked.

"I am. Starving, actually."

I pointed to a place across the street. "They have the best sloppers I've ever had in my life."

"Sloppers?"

"It's an open-faced cheeseburger smothered in green chili."

Stella put her hand on her stomach. "That sounds so good."

"But?"

"You have to remember that I'm older than you and I have to think about things like indigestion."

I stopped dead where I was. "Why does this 'older than you' thing pop up all the time? You're six years older. Actually, I think it's closer to five. And what makes you assume I don't get indigestion?"

"You may get it once in a while, but I get it all the time," she mumbled, looking away from me.

"Have you ever considered there might be a cause of it other than age?"

"What do you mean?"

"When's the last time you saw a doctor, Stella?"

She shrugged and didn't respond.

"So anyway. How about a slopper? I hear that if you chase it with a beer and a shot of whiskey, no heartburn."

For someone who didn't eat much, Stella put that slopper away like she hadn't had any sustenance in days.

"What's next, or is it a surprise?" she asked, tossing her napkin on the table.

"We can walk the rest of the way down the block or head back to Crested Butte. Whichever you'd prefer. Oh, and by Crested Butte, I don't mean the ranch. I thought we'd take a stroll on Elk Avenue."

"What's that?"

"CB's version of Main Street. It's a lot like this one and totally different at the same time."

"I'm good with whatever."

I leaned forward and stared into her eyes. "I haven't known you that long, but long enough that I don't think I've ever heard you say anything like that."

"I've known me a lot longer than that, Buck, and I can tell you, in thirty-six years, I've never said anything remotely like that." She leaned over and kissed me. "Thank you."

We walked off part of our lunch in Gunnison before getting on the highway that would take us into Crested Butte. "I know we just ate, but I was thinking of seeing if Ben and Liv wanted to meet us for dinner tonight."

"I'd love that."

"I bet it never gets old," Stella mumbled shortly after we passed Altamont.

"What's that?"

"How breathtaking this place is. I'm with Rock. I don't know how you ever left it." She looked over at me and put her hand on top of mine. "Sorry. I know that's a sore subject."

"You know what? Being here with you makes me look at it differently. Maybe it's time some good memories replaced all those bad ones. What do you say we work on that?"

"I think we have been." She winked. "I know that there are things I'll *never* forget about being here."

I knew what she meant, and I liked her saying it. But there was a part of me that sure didn't like thinking about when we'd both have to leave.

If anyone had told me a month ago that getting out of Crested Butte would make me sad, I would've called them a damn liar on top of being crazy. But I loved being here with Stella. There were so many things I wanted to show her, share with her, experience through her eyes. I wasn't sure I'd ever run out of stuff for us to see and do together. Plus, every season brought more.

In autumn, we could drive over Kebler Pass to Aspen and see the most breathtaking fall foliage on the planet. In the early summer, CB turned into the wild-flower capital of the west. Thousands of people visited, and even with crowds like that, there were endless trails where we could hike and never see another soul.

The best season of all was winter, though. I'd never taken anyone to the cabin that sat near the top of Mt. Crested Butte, but when there was snow on the ground, we could take a sleigh up the mountain for dinner.

I'd nestle Stella under a pile of blankets, hold her close to me, and we'd look up at the stars as horses carried the sleigh up the ski slopes.

The cabin had once belonged to Uley Sheer, a miner, moonshiner, and mountain man who'd been born here and never left. Over the years, he'd added on to his original six-by-eight-foot cabin, and after he died, he left it to the town who'd turned it into a cozy restaurant.

"Buck?"

I rested my gaze on the woman who made me want to rediscover the place I grew up. "Yeah?"

"You're lost in thought."

I thought about telling Stella what I was thinking about, but I'd made her uncomfortable when I said I was going to take her to a remote cabin on the ranch. If I told her I was thinking about spending four seasons showing her around my hometown, she'd probably ask Rock to let her out at the next corner.

"I forget how much I love about this place."

"I hope you'll share those things with me."

I studied her. Was it fair of me to wonder if she really meant it?

"Ben's family owns this place," I said to Stella when we walked by the Goat, a bar on Elk Avenue. "He used to show up here and play sometimes. I don't know if he does that anymore."

"Buck?"

"Yeah?"

"Did you see this?" Stella pointed to a flyer hanging on the bulletin board by the entrance. "This is tonight."

I stepped closer, stunned to see my brother Holt was scheduled to play. "Wow," I mumbled.

"Can we come?"

"Sure," I blurted without thinking through the ramifications of my response. Could we? I mean, it wouldn't be difficult to set up security as long as I was able to do it in advance. It meant I might have to call in a favor from the Rice family, but considering it was my brother's show, I doubted they'd mind too much. I had suggested we have dinner with Ben and Liv if they were available. If we did, I could ask then.

When I heard the door opening, I pulled Stella to the side, out of the way. I was stunned when I saw it was the man I was just thinking about calling.

"Hey, Buck, how the hell are ya? Sorry we didn't get a chance to talk the other night."

"Hey, Ben, this is Stella," I said, putting my arm around her shoulders. "We were just discussing asking you and Liv if you were free for dinner."

"We are. In fact, we were planning on being here for Holt's show afterwards."

"Uh, do you have a minute?" I pointed behind him, toward the bar.

"Sure. Come on in. Ladies first."

"Hang on," said Ink, surprising all of us. "Excuse me, ma'am, but I'll go in before you."

"Holy shit," muttered Ben when Ink walked past him. "He's twice as big as anyone on my crew. Whose detail is he on?" Ben pointed first to me and then to Stella.

"Me," she said, half raising her hand. Ink motioned for her to come in a few seconds later.

"Have you figured out what I wanted to talk to you about?" I asked, laughing.

"My guess is we're gonna have a sellout crowd early tonight."

"Where can we set everyone up?" asked Rock, who had come in behind me.

Ben motioned toward the back of the space. "That's where I usually hang out." He then pointed to several other spots. "My guys will be there, there, and there. But seeing as you'll be here too, maybe I'll give a couple of them the night off." Ben motioned with his thumb at Ink. "He counts for at least three, doesn't he?"

"What are you doing here?" asked Holt, coming from the back, carrying his guitar.

"Figuring out logistics for your show."

Holt's eyes opened wide. "You're comin'? I figured with, you know, you wouldn't be able to."

Ben squeezed Holt's shoulder, threw his head back, and laughed. "Son, you think after all these years, I don't recognize a bodyguard when I see one?" He turned to me. "I'll give Livvie a call."

When he walked away, I looked at Holt. "I had no idea you were making such a name for yourself. Hell, I didn't even know you were touring with CB Rice. Why didn't I?"

"I kinda kept it on the down-low, given Pop's illness."

"His illness?"

Holt's cheeks flushed. "Okay, his opposition to my being in a band."

That didn't explain why he hadn't told me, but I'd already made my brother uncomfortable as it was. I'd bring it up another time.

"I'm excited to see you perform," said Stella.

Holt smiled. "I gotta admit, I'm happy you and Buck can be here." The look on his face changed.

"What?" I asked.

"Well, Flynn wanted to come too, bring that Irish guy, but I told her she couldn't."

"Livvie is all in," said Ben, walking back over to us.

"You think we can fit two more in tonight?" I asked.

"Hell, yeah. In fact, invite the whole damn crew from the Roaring Fork, and I'll do the same from the Flying R." Ben turned to Holt. "You got anybody else you want on the guest list tonight?"

"Is Sable working?"

Ben looked over his shoulder at the bartender.

"Nope, she requested the night off," the man said.

I saw my brother's face fall.

"Said she wanted to be in the audience, not serving them," the man added.

As hard as he tried, Holt couldn't contain his smile. "So, um, Sable."

"Yeah, I kinda got that," said Ben, nudging him.

"You sure you're up for this?" I asked Stella.

"You're kidding, right? I'm so excited!"

Holt, hearing her, beamed.

"The rest of your family will be here, then?"

"I guess so. I'll have to ask."

"Don't ask. Insist. They have to come and see Holt."

I laughed to myself at Stella's enthusiasm while, at the same time, I wanted to gather her in my arms and hug her tight for making my baby brother smile like I hadn't seen him do in years.

I thought about my old man and how he'd always made it impossible for any of his offspring to experience happiness. It was a damn shame. Rather than dwell on the negative, I watched Stella as she talked to Holt and Ben.

She caught me looking, and her cheeks turned pink. "What?"

I put my arm around her. "You make me happy, Stella."

She leaned in and kissed my cheek. "You make me happy too, Buck."

19

I knew damn well that Buck was trying not to react. Hell, I couldn't believe I'd said it either. But, what the fuck, right? I was happier today than I ever remembered being in my life.

Every time I started to think about Barb or the investigation we were in the midst of, or that Buck and the rest of the Invincibles team believed I was in enough danger that we had to plan out where I'd be sitting to watch a guy sing and play the guitar in a bar—I pushed it out of my head.

Here I was, Stella Hunter, hanging out with a hot guy who'd shown me over the last twenty-four hours that he truly was attracted to me. Over and over again, he'd told me how much he wanted me, including in the dressing room of a damn clothing store. Not to mention the mind-blowing orgasm he gave me while we were there.

It was more than that, though. I really liked Buck. Every other guy I'd ever dated either bored the shit or annoyed the hell out of me. Buck did neither. Sure, he made me mad, but that was different.

I slid my hand into his and leaned my body against his arm. "What time is dinner?" I whispered.

"I'll ask, why?"

I reached up so my mouth was near his ear. "I was hoping I could try on some more clothes for you."

Buck turned his head and kissed me. "Hey, Ben, what time are we meeting you and Liv?"

"How's seven-thirty sound?"

"What time is it now?" Buck whispered to me.

"Three. We have plenty of time," I whispered back.

"We're going to head back to the ranch," Buck told him.

"Instead of coming here while they're setting up, why don't we eat up on the mountain?"

"What's open?"

Ben smiled. "I'll get Hans to open up Uley's."

"How are we gonna get up there?" Buck asked.

"Two options. Horseback or ATVs."

I squeezed Buck's hand, not thrilled with either option. "I've never ridden a horse, and an ATV, well…" I whispered.

"Horseback," Buck said to Ben before turning to me. "You'll ride with me." He released my hand and put his arm around my waist.

"Ready?" asked Rock.

Buck nodded.

"I'll send Press and Jagger back, Ink," Rock said before escorting us out.

"Livvie and I will meet you at Base Camp at seven fifteen," Ben called out.

I thought dinner with Olivia and Ben was the most fun I'd had in my life, until we went back to the Goat to watch Holt perform.

As Ben had suggested, the place was packed with people I recognized from the Roaring Fork and others I remembered seeing at the Flying R's barn.

Given men once again outnumbered women five to one, I spent a lot of time on the dance floor. Every time someone else asked me to dance, Buck would cut in after a couple of minutes.

All night, I felt like one of those women I'd always envied—the ones with husbands or boyfriends who looked at them like the sun set and the moon rose with them. Buck was affectionate, but not so much that it made me uncomfortable, especially since Ben was that way with Olivia.

"I need a rest," Liv said, holding up her hand when a man I didn't know asked her to dance. "And so does Stella," she added, pointing in my direction.

"Thanks," I said, lifting my drink in a toast to her.

"I'm too old for this," she muttered, laughing. "I'm a grandmother, for God's sake."

"I don't believe that for a minute."

"It's true," said Ben. "We're grandparents."

The way he beamed made me smile. If I weren't with Buck tonight, I would've been eaten up with envy. Instead, I was happy for them.

Over dinner, Olivia talked a little bit about the accident that had almost paralyzed her, and about how she never dreamed that after she pushed him away, Ben would take her back. "The universe had other plans for us," she said, turning to cup her husband's cheek.

I thought about Ali and Cope, and how it seemed as though the universe had conspired to bring them together too. I'd watched it happen. At the time, I was heartbroken, but now, I was as happy for them as I was for Ben and Olivia.

Buck put his arm around my shoulders and pulled me close. He rested his cheek against my hair. "I can't stop thinking about your fashion show this afternoon."

I laughed. It hadn't been as much fashion show as striptease after I put on a pair of cut-off shorts that barely covered my ass. I'd wanted to surprise Buck with them, but when it was the first thing he wanted me to put on, I knew he'd caught me adding them to my pile of purchases.

The man made me feel more desirable than I'd dreamed possible. He was insatiable when it came to sex and never failed to make me feel like I was the only woman in the world he wanted to be with.

Fighting against doubt and insecurity was nearly impossible for me, but somehow, I managed to push it far enough back that I didn't allow it to ruin my time with him.

I felt someone watching me and glanced at the woman sitting on the far end of the table. She was the one who'd been watching Buck and I dance at the barn, although tonight she was here as Porter's date. It was obvious, to me at least, that she'd much rather be on Buck's arm.

When Holt announced he was about to play his last song, Buck pulled me to my feet. I didn't recognize the piece, but it was clear he did. "I met a girl who stole my heart," he spoke when Holt sang the same words. I looked into his eyes.

"I met a man who did the same thing."

"Am I that man, Stella?"

It struck me then that Buck wasn't teasing. It was unfathomable to me that a man as fucking hot as he was could be insecure.

"Answer me, Stella."

"Yes, Buck. You are that man."

He pulled me so close that our bodies were flush and I could feel his hardness pressing against me. We stayed on the dance floor until Holt's song ended and then clapped along with everyone else in the bar. I followed Buck's brother's line of sight and caught a look pass between him and the woman he hadn't been able to keep his eyes off all night.

"He looks smitten," I murmured.

"I don't know," said Buck.

I cocked my head and scrunched my eyes. He leaned forward and kissed my forehead. "Looks to me like he's in love. I don't think he's the only one who is, either."

I stiffened out of reflex, something Buck didn't fail to notice, although he didn't comment on it.

Love? Jesus. He couldn't be talking about him and me, could he? And if he was, how did that make me feel? Scared. No, wait. Terrified. At the same time, him loving me would be like a dream, wouldn't it?

Buck put his finger beneath my chin and lifted my head. "Stop worrying, Stella. We'll take every day as it comes, okay?"

He brushed my lips with his, and out of the corner of my eye, I caught Porter's date's scowl. There was trouble brewing there, and it left me feeling unsettled. More, I felt for Porter, who was clearly crazy about her.

Buck made the ten days between then and now, an adventure. He showed me around the ranch, on horseback no less, but always with me riding with him. He'd asked me a couple of times whether I wanted to try riding on my own, but each time, I told him I preferred being in his arms.

He took me back to Altamont and taught me how to fish from the bank of the river. At first I thought I'd hate it, but after an hour or so, I found it relaxing and was anxious to go again.

Today, he was taking me to see what he said were his two favorite buildings on the ranch—the farmhouse and adjacent barn. I'd seen both every time we drove in and out the main gate. To me, they looked like a house of cards waiting to fall, but I didn't say that when I saw the twinkle in his eyes when talking about them.

I was getting used to Ink and at least one other person going along wherever we went, so it was disconcerting when Buck and I climbed into his pickup to drive to the farmhouse without someone leading or following us.

When he parked by the barn, I could sense his excitement, and it made me smile. So many things he and I had done together had resulted in the same reaction.

"I can't wait to show you this," he said like he did every other time we visited a place I hadn't been before.

It was difficult to hide my trepidation, given the state of the two buildings, but I trusted Buck. He would keep me safe whether it was from spiders or someone trying to kill me. Both of which I feared equally.

"Let's check out the house first," he said, taking my hand. We walked up the steps of the front porch, and a warm feeling settled over me. I couldn't explain it nor had I ever felt it before.

"You okay?" Buck asked.

"Yeah. Fine."

Buck cocked his head.

"I'm not sure how to explain it, but I feel like I've been here before."

He smiled and opened the front door. What I saw in front of me was the last thing I expected. The interior looked as though it had been locked in a time capsule. As Buck walked through the house, opening draperies, I was shocked by how well preserved the place was. It was dusty, but otherwise pristine. "Who last lived here?" I asked.

"My great-grandparents. They were both long gone before I was born, obviously. I hardly remember my grandparents, but being here, always made me feel close to them."

I ran my hand over the staircase's dark wood banister. There were similar wood accents throughout the house; the door and window molding were made from the same type, but the floors were lighter.

"Want to see the kitchen?" Buck asked.

"Lead the way." When we walked through the archway that opened into it, the first thing I noticed were the spectacular views of Mt. Crested Butte that could be seen from all the windows.

"Wow," I said, running my hand over the edge of the farmhouse-style sink that had a hand pump. "Back before it was chic to have one of these." Buck smiled.

There was an old-fashioned-looking icebox, a wood stove, and a table that sat in an alcove that looked as though it had been carved by hand. "This place could be a museum," I murmured.

"That's what my mother said when my old man threatened to tear it down."

I gasped. "He wasn't serious, I hope."

"No, he was dead serious as soon as he heard me say I wanted to live in it one day. I think I was all of ten at the time."

"I'm sorry, Buck."

He nodded. "I'd say it's okay, but it really isn't. I spent most of my life hating the son-of-a-bitch. What he did with his will makes me hate him all the more."

I put my arms around his waist. "It's sometimes impossible to understand why people act the way they do. My father walked out on my mother and me when she became ill. If it weren't for Aunt Barb, I don't know how we would've managed."

"We should get back."

"Wait. What? Why?"

"You're such a reporter." He winked.

"I'm serious. Why do we have to get back?"

"I know we haven't been putting in the time you'd like on the investigation. That's on me."

"Whoa. Hang on a second. Everything we've done has been because I've wanted to. Not only that, I've enjoyed myself more than I have at any other time of my life, Buck."

"You told me you couldn't afford a distraction, and I've been nothing but."

"We took some time off because we kept hitting brick walls. What we have done this week, wasn't a waste. Sometimes investigations drag on longer than we'd like. You know that as well as I do. So, how about you show me the upstairs?"

"If you're sure."

"If you don't, I'll go up there alone."

Buck took my hand in his and led me back to the staircase.

"The wood carvings are spectacular," I commented.

"According to my mother, this is my great-grandfather's work."

What a tragedy it would've been if Buck's father had succeeded in tearing this place down.

There were four bedrooms on the second level and two bathrooms. Buck told me that was highly unusual when it was built, particularly given one was just off the master bedroom.

"Gramps was a man ahead of his time," he said as he led me down the hallway.

Each room was decorated with gorgeous wallpaper and accessorized to match it perfectly.

"What's in there?" I asked, pointing to a closed door and thinking it was probably a linen closet. Buck opened it and motioned me inside. "Oh my God," I gasped at the nursery that looked straight out of a decorator's magazine.

"Again, ahead of his time. No one had a whole room dedicated to a baby in those days."

"This is his work, isn't it?" I asked, running my hand over the crib's railing. A cradle in the room had similar carvings.

"I guess so. I mean, I don't know for sure."

"Do you want to get that?" I asked when I heard his cell ringing from somewhere downstairs."

"Won't get there in time anyway. They'll leave a message."

Seconds later, mine went off. "It's Cope," I said, looking at the screen.

20

Buck

Without looking at me, she answered. "He's right here," I heard her say. It must've been Cope calling me a few seconds ago.

"Sure, I can do that." Stella took the phone from her ear and hit the speaker button.

"Hey, Buck, you there?"

"Yeah, I'm here. What do you want?"

"Ali and I are about to pull up to the front gates of the Roaring Fork."

"We aren't far away. We'll swing over and meet you." Stella ended the call and put the phone in her pocket. I didn't like the look on her face. "What's up?" I asked.

She shrugged one shoulder. "Ali and Cope are here."

"And?"

"Nothing." She tried to turn away, but I put my hand on her arm.

"And?" I repeated.

"Things will be different."

I felt like she'd punched me in the gut. "Because your one true love, Sumner Copeland, has returned?"

Her eyes scrunched. "What did you say?"

"You heard me."

"That's rich, coming from you."

"Deny it."

"Deny that Cope is my one true love? You're joking." She moved away from me. "This is bullshit, Buck. Just because you have feelings for Ali, doesn't mean you can turn this around on me. I left Cope behind a long time ago. If you can't do the same with the woman who is now his wife, that's your problem."

She stalked out of the house. I followed and stopped her before she could step off the porch.

"I don't feel that way about Ali," I said, standing in front of her so I could block any of her attempts to get around me. "I don't love her. I never did."

"That isn't the way I remember it."

"What about you? You were just as in love with Cope."

"I know better now."

"How?"

Stella shook her head.

"Guess what? I know better now too."

"How?" she whispered.

"Because I know the difference. For the first time in my life, I know how it feels to really love someone."

"Do you?"

"I do and you do too. You just said you know better now. How, Stella? Because like me, your heart has finally found a home?"

"Buck…you told Cope you'd meet them at the gate."

"I don't give a fuck about meeting Cope at the gate. He and Ali can sit there until sundown, for all I care. I want you to answer me. Do you love me, Stella? Because I sure as hell love you." I heard the words come out of my mouth and hated that I sounded angry. I wrapped my arm around her waist. "I love you, Stella," I said in a voice that sounded like I actually felt. "I love you so much." I kissed her. Maybe because I didn't want to wait for her to say it back and be disappointed if she didn't, so I took away her ability to talk.

Our tongues twisted together, and I deepened the kiss, hating that she was right about Cope and Ali waiting for us. I'd just told Stella that I loved her. Now, more than anything, I wanted to show her with my body how much.

"Buck," she murmured, pulling back.

"I know. Cope and Ali."

Stella grabbed my wrist before I could walk away. "That isn't what I was going to say."

I held my breath, staring into her eyes.

"You were right when you said that I know the difference too. For the first time in my life, I know how it feels to really love someone. You aren't just my lover; you're my friend—my best friend if you want to know the truth. I trust you in a way I've never trusted anyone, and that's why I'm so certain."

I needed to hear the words. "Certain about what?"

"I love you, Buck."

I pulled her into my arms and kissed her harder, deeper than I had a few seconds ago. "I want to make love to you, Stella. I want to tell Ali and Cope to go away, take you back to the cabin, and spend the rest of the day and night, showing you exactly how much you mean to me."

"I want the same thing—"

"Don't say it. I know we can't. Can't fault a guy for wishing, though."

She smiled. "Maybe they'll be tired from traveling."

"Right."

"Can't fault a girl for wishing, though."

I hit the remote for the gate and motioned with my arm for Cope to follow me. I pulled up to the main house and cut the engine. Stella, sitting right beside me on the bench seat, looked up at me when I didn't get out. "I need another kiss to hold me over."

She turned and wrapped one arm around my neck before planting her lips on mine. She pushed her tongue into my mouth and pressed her lips hard against mine.

There might've been a time I would've wondered if Ali could see us. I didn't give a shit now. Did Stella care if Cope did?

I pulled back, cupped her cheek, and stared into her eyes. "You better be thinking about me, Stella."

"You know I am, Buck."

"Let's get this over with so we can be alone." I got out of the SUV, walked around the front of it, and opened her door. When she shimmied to the edge of the seat, I put both hands on her waist and lowered her to the ground. I wanted to kiss her again, but I stopped myself. She might think it was just for show, and the last thing I wanted was for her to doubt that I truly loved her.

"I'm so sorry about Barb," said Ali, running forward to embrace Stella. Cope was standing behind her, and when Ali stepped away, he hugged her too.

"I know how important Barb was to you, Stella. I promise to do everything I can to find her killer," I heard him say.

"I appreciate that," she murmured, taking a step back. I was right behind her and snaked my arm around her waist.

"Have you heard from Deck?" Cope asked, his eyes trailing from mine, down to where I had a firm grasp on the woman I loved.

"No, why?"

"He's supposed to meet us here."

"Let's go inside." I motioned for Cope and Ali to go ahead. "You okay?" I asked Stella.

"More than okay." She leaned into me and put her arm around my waist.

I silently cursed all the time I'd wasted by not admitting my real feelings sooner. We'd had two glorious weeks as alone as we could be, given every time we ventured outside the ranch gates, we had two or three bodyguards with us.

With Cope and Ali here and Decker on his way, God knew how many hours it might be before I could hold Stella's naked body in my arms again.

I was about to walk through the front door when Cope came back out, looking at his phone. "He says he's at the cabin. That make any sense to you?"

"It does. Follow me."

I drove up the dirt road and parked in front of the one I considered Stella's and mine.

"You're in that one down there," I said to Cope and Ali, pointing. "We'll let you get settled before we meet."

"We can do that later," said Cope. "We have a lot to talk about. Where's Irish?"

"He's in that one," I said, pointing at the same time my sister came out the front door.

"Who's that?" asked Ali.

"That's Buck's sister, Flynn," answered Stella. "Come on, let's go inside."

The front door opened before we got to it, and Decker stepped out. I opened my mouth to ask how he'd gotten in but thought better of it.

"Don't worry," he said, clapping my back. "I made sure you and Stella weren't here before I went in."

While we waited for Cope, Ali, and Irish to join us, I followed Stella into the bedroom.

"I'm just grabbing my laptop," she said when she saw me behind her.

Once we were over the threshold, I put my arm around her. "I'm just grabbing another kiss."

"You're insatiable."

"Does it bother you?" I asked when she kissed me just as hard as I had her.

"It's just one of the things I love about you."

"Oh! Excuse me," I heard a familiar voice say from the hallway. "I didn't mean to interrupt. I was just looking for the restroom."

"Other side of the hall," I said to Ali without releasing my grip on the woman in my arms.

"I'm adding incorrigible to the list too," said Stella, taking my hand and leading me out of the bedroom.

"Uh, did you forget something?"

She turned back, smiled, and reached up to kiss me.

"Thanks for the kiss," I said, pulling her laptop out from behind my back. "But I meant this."

Ali came out of the bathroom then and glared at me. Now wasn't the time, but soon, I needed to put that woman in her place. What was between Stella and me was none of her damn business.

"Shall we get started?" asked Cope, motioning for the rest of us to take a seat.

Decker caught my eye and winked. He stood and cleared his throat. "Before we do that, you should know that Stella is the lead on this mission. Anything related to the execution of it, has to be approved by her."

Cope's eyes opened wide. "Is Stella contracting for the Invincibles now?"

"That's right, and if this goes as well as I'm hoping and she's interested, we may offer her a permanent partnership. Her exceptional investigative skills are certainly worth adding to the team."

I didn't know if Deck was playing Cope, which was more than likely, but I had to contain my laughter at how effectively it was working.

"Take a seat, Copeland," I muttered before turning to Stella, who was looking between Deck and me with wide eyes. "Go ahead whenever you're ready."

"One place for us to begin is with the emails Barb sent to me over the course of several years. At first glance, they appear like nothing, but both Buck and I believe they hold carefully constructed and hard-to-decipher clues."

"Like the message I sent you about La Chapelle-Saint-Maurice," I said to Cope.

Irish's head snapped up. "You didn't mention that to me."

"I apologize. I wasn't sure it meant anything."

"Where's the email?"

"I'm forwarding it to you now, Irish," Stella said, leaning over her laptop. She bit her bottom lip and took a deep breath. "I apologize if any of this is redundant, but I think it's important we are all up to speed before moving forward. It might be best if we went back to the beginning."

Ali opened her laptop. "Review is good. Let's do it."

Stella's eyes met mine, and I knew she had this.

21

Stella

"The day after your wedding, I went to visit my aunt, Barb, like I do most Sundays. There came a point in one of our conversations when she brought up the book I've been writing about the mission that brought down Director Fisk. It wasn't the first time she asked me to walk away from it."

This wasn't news to Ali, and probably not to anyone else in the room. I'd told her before how much grief my aunt gave me about the book Ali and I first thought we'd write together. Before saying anything more, I waited until she finished typing and nodded.

"This time, though, she took it further. She told me that if I didn't let it go—and these were her words—the same thing that happened to her could happen to me."

I looked at Buck, who nodded for me to go on. "As all of you are aware, my aunt's career in journalism took a nosedive when she wrote an article accusing Nicholas Kerr, who at the time, was president of

Interpol, of accepting bribes in the cover-up of what she referred to as Operation Argead."

"So she was warning you the book might end your career?" asked Ali.

"That's right. At the time, I thought she was being melodramatic." I closed my eyes. When I opened them, I looked at Buck; he nodded like he had before. I took a deep breath and kept going. "She said that if I didn't drop the project, it might be over both our dead bodies."

Ali reached over and squeezed my hand.

"At that point, Barb showed me a key she had hidden in her piano. It was for a safe-deposit box. When I asked what was in it, she said, 'Evidence.'"

Ali's eyes opened wide. "Where is it?"

"The key, the box, or the evidence?"

"All three?"

"I have the key. I have no idea which bank the safe-deposit box is in and, therefore, no idea what evidence is in it."

Ali sat back in her chair and stretched her arms over her head. "If I remember correctly, she was accused of manufacturing evidence."

"That's right."

"Well, if she *had* it, why didn't she say so?"

"I can't answer that."

"I have a theory." Everyone seated at the table looked in Buck's direction. "Cope, why do you think Fisk won't make a deal?"

"Because he's more afraid of someone or something than he is of prison."

"You're suggesting my aunt was more afraid of what would happen if she came forward with the evidence than the demise of her career?"

"They threatened to kill her." Like we'd all turned to look at Buck, this time we looked at Irish.

Ali drummed her fingers on the table. "Why kill her now, then?"

"Exactly. Why now, instead of ten years ago?" I asked.

Irish looked over at Decker. "You said there weren't any bugs in Barb's apartment. Is that right?"

"Affirmative," Deck answered.

"What do we know about the other victim?" Ali asked.

"Nancy Jones worked for my aunt since shortly after the scandal broke. As I told Jinx at DC Metro, I don't know if she has any family."

"I'd say it's time to find out," said Ali. "Is there anything else you know about her that might be relevant?"

I told them Nancy was a quiet woman. She did Barb's shopping, prepared their meals, and kept the apartment clean. Outside of all that, which didn't seem relevant, I knew nothing about her.

"How did your aunt find her?"

"I can't remember the details, but I think it was through a temp agency."

Ali nodded. "I'll see what I can find on the housekeeper. What's next?"

"Irish, Buck, and I have been focused on making connections between the people we consider to be players. Let's start with Nicholas Kerr, he was Interpol's president when Barb's article came out, as well as director general at MI5."

"Got it," Ali murmured. "Wasn't there talk of an affair?"

"She never admitted it to me, and I have reason to believe those allegations were untrue. I'll circle back to that, though."

"You said that Barb accused Kerr of accepting bribes?"

"That's right."

"Just him?"

I shook my head. "All of the executive committee."

"Who else was part of it back then?"

This was one of the reasons I liked Ali as much as I did. Her mind worked in a similar way as mine. "As I said, Kerr was president. The VP was Antoine Moreau, the General Directorate for France's External Security. The secretary-general at the time was Stanley Donofrio, who was on leave from his assistant director job at the CIA. When his Interpol tenure ended, he was promoted to director within a year."

"Heavy hitters," Ali murmured.

"No kidding." I looked over at Irish, who was deep in thought, staring into space rather than at his computer. "What are you thinking?" I asked him directly.

"How many cold cases of murdered agents could be linked to these three men."

"And?"

Irish directed his gaze at me. "All of the older ones."

I shuddered.

"Let's delve deeper into Kerr's background, if that's okay with you," Ali suggested.

Before proceeding, I surveyed the room, mainly Cope, Decker, and Buck. All three looked as though they were waiting for me to continue. "Early in her career, my aunt and Kerr both worked at the Council on Foreign Relations. I'm making the supposition that's where they met."

"Logical, what else?"

"Ed Fisk also worked for CFR, but in the DC office. Barb and Kerr were in New York."

Ali looked up at Cope. Fisk had been his and Irish's main target in their investigation and the person responsible for both men coming close to dying.

"Go on," said Cope.

"An aside, but important to note. When Kerr left his position at Interpol, he also stepped down as DG at MI5. He served in more of an advisory or consultant role from then until his retirement. According to Z Alexander, that wasn't unusual. Anyway, that's connection number one."

I waited for Ali to finish typing. When she looked up and nodded, I continued.

"Kerr also has connections to Interpol's current executive committee. Daniel Byrne, the president, and Boris Antonov, the VP, both served as delegates under Kerr. We haven't been able to find a connection to the secretary-general, Kim Ha-joon, yet, but he is tight with Byrne and Antonov." I took a deep breath and let it out slowly.

"You okay?" asked Irish.

"Yes." I smiled at him, touched that he expressed concern, and then rolled my shoulders. "Another connection we were able to make was between my aunt, her editor at Associated Press, and Kerr."

Ali raised a brow.

"Within a year of Barb's fall from grace, Hennessey and Kerr got married," said Irish.

Ali gave a slight shake of her head. "Come again."

"Working theory is that Sally was the one having the affair with Kerr, and they took Barb down together to squelch her Operation Argead story. It was the first piece in years that the AP passed on. They probably acted on the assumption that no one else would pick it up," I added.

"Give me a minute to get caught up." Ali's fingers flew on the keyboard while she typed in her notes. "Have you surmised anything further?"

Irish cleared his throat.

"Go ahead," I said.

"Again, theorizing. Kerr knew Barb had enough evidence to bring him down, because Sally shared

Barb's story with him. Neither of them thought anyone would pick it up. After it ran, Hennessey wrote the follow up herself, and in it, accused Barb of manufacturing evidence."

"As well as accusing her of having an affair with Kerr that ended badly," I added.

Irish looked over to Buck.

"It makes sense that one or both of them threatened your aunt. Like Irish, I'm theorizing," he said. "Kerr, most likely, delivered the threat, demanding your aunt turn the evidence over to him or he'd kill her."

"And?" I asked, following where Buck was going with this but wanting him to continue.

"She refused, but he didn't kill her."

"Why not?"

"Mutually beneficial arrangement," said Decker, who had been mostly quiet to that point.

"Meaning?"

"She still had something on him. Probably whatever is in the safe-deposit box. And someone, like Barb's attorney for example, has instructions for what to do in the event of her untimely death."

"Wouldn't that come into play now?" asked Ali.

"Not if Kerr believed he could intercept it," Buck answered, stroking his beard.

"Because he finally knew where it was?" I asked.

"That's right, darlin'." Buck's gaze rested on me, and it felt like a warm blanket.

"Ahem."

Both he and I looked at Ali.

"Yes?"

"Back to what we were talking about, I have more questions."

I looked at Buck, who was smirking in the same way I was over Ali's tone.

"Go ahead."

"I still don't understand the timing."

"This was the first she told me of the key. There had to be eyes, ears, or both in that apartment, but Rock said Decker didn't find anything."

"Which means Kerr either had it all removed or—"

"Or the other eyes and ears weren't devices. They were on a person," I said, looking at Irish, who was typing something on his keyboard faster than Ali had been earlier.

"There's a connection, I'm sure of it," he mumbled.

"Between?"

"The housekeeper and either Kerr or Hennessey."

It seemed unlikely to me. I looked at Buck. "I need to find that damn safe-deposit box, and in order to do that, I need to go to New York and meet with Barb's lawyer."

"Have you spoken with him?" asked Deck.

"Not since the first time."

"I'll check with the medical examiner and see if the death certificate is available yet. If it is, then I agree. If not, I'd recommend waiting."

"Thanks, Decker," I said before he picked his phone up from the table and walked out to the porch.

"Stella, can I speak with you alone for a minute?" asked Buck.

"Of course." I stood and followed him into the bedroom.

"If we go to New York City, this is how it'll go down. We'll do everything we can to get there and back within my forty-eight-hour time frame."

"Okay."

"If necessary, I'll fly back to Colorado, set foot on the ranch, and turn around and come right back."

"I'm sure that I—"

"Don't say it."

"I just meant—"

"Stella." Buck stepped forward and wrapped one hand around my waist while he cupped my cheek with the opposite hand.

"Okay, I get it. I'm sorry."

"Call him."

22

Buck

"Hey, Buck?" Ali called from the other room.

"I'm okay," said Stella, waving me away.

"Be right back." Like Stella had waved me out of the bedroom, Ali waved me toward the front door. "What's up?"

Irish, Deck, and Cope were head to head over something on Warrick's laptop.

"You can head inside for a minute," I told Ink, who was pacing back and forth on the porch. Once the door closed behind him, I waited for Ali to say something.

She took a deep breath, let it out slowly, and then put her hand on the porch railing.

"Spit it out."

"Look, you know I love you like a brother and Stella like a sister—"

"Your attempt at making this inbreeding is your issue, Ali."

"Very funny." She swatted me. "It's just that I care so much about both of you."

"And?" I motioned with my hand for her to get on with it as much because this topic was irritating the crap out of me than because I was anxious to get back to Stella.

"You need to understand that Stella is—"

I held up my hand. "Stop right there. What makes you think—even for a moment—that you know her better than I do?"

"She's my friend, Buck—"

I cut her off again. "She's my friend too. Do you know that for the last few weeks, including before Barb's murder, Stella and I talked at least once a day? Sometimes more. Can you say the same thing?"

"That's different."

"How?"

"We're both women. The friendship is different."

"Are you better friends with Stella than you are with me?"

"No, I wouldn't say that. Again, it's different. Besides, you and I have spent more time together."

Ali's cheeks turned pink when she realized she'd just used my argument against herself.

I put my hand on the door handle. "I appreciate that you care about both of us, but, Ali, stay out of it. What is between Stella and me is none of your business."

"Don't hurt her, Buck."

I thought about that for a minute. "It's more likely that it'll go the other way." I opened the door and walked inside at the same time Stella came out of the bedroom. She was ghostly pale; I rushed toward her. "What happened?" I asked as I guided her back into the bedroom.

"He's dead."

"Barb's attorney?"

She nodded.

"Have a seat." When she did, I sat beside her on the bed. "Who told you that?"

"I called his office, identified myself, and asked for Mr. Owens. The woman who answered the phone told me she'd put me through to Mr. Clark and asked me to hold." She took a deep breath and blew it out. "When he answered, he told me he'd intended to get in touch with me."

"And?"

"He said that, last night, Mr. Owens had suffered a gunshot wound and, by the time paramedics arrived, he was pronounced dead."

"Where was he?"

"Leaving the building where their offices are located."

"Did he say anything else?"

"Only that he and the other senior partners had divided Mr. Owen's client list and were contacting them. Oh, and he asked if we had a meeting scheduled. I told him that's what I was calling to do."

"Anything else?"

"He said he'd get back in touch with me sometime next week."

"I'm sorry, Stella."

She looked down at her hands and then up at me. "I didn't know him, Buck." She stood, and so did I.

"You sure you're ready to go back out there?"

She nodded.

"I probably don't need to say this, but this will be information passed on as need-to-know only."

"I know, Buck."

"That includes Jinx."

She was on her way out of the room, but stopped. "I know that too."

"Just making sure."

It didn't matter if I'd pissed her off or not; it needed to be said.

"Anything else?" she asked.

"No, I—"

She was gone before I could say another word.

When I followed, Stella immediately approached Ali and started a conversation. I walked over to Decker.

"I'll check in with NYPD and see what I can find out." He'd obviously overheard Stella tell me about the attorney's murder. When he said he'd check in, I doubted it meant he actually would; more likely, he'd hack in.

"Is Irish still trying to find a connection between the housekeeper and either Kerr or Hennessey?"

"I believe so."

"Does IISG have any other resources I might be able to use to assist?"

"IISG?" Decker laughed. "That's gonna fry Rile's ass. I like it."

The other contractors employed by the Invincible Intelligence and Security Group and I had started referring to it by its acronym, given "the Invincibles" sounded ridiculous to us.

"To answer your question, we do. I'll send you access links to those like I did the others."

"Thanks, Decker. I appreciate this."

"Buck, there is no other mission I've worked in all the years I've been in intelligence as important as this one."

"Copy that. Irish said exactly the same thing."

"Oh, before you look for a connection between Jones and the other two, why don't you see if you can get into Barb's will."

"Will do. Thanks again, Deck."

"IISG." He shook his head and chuckled as I walked over to where I left my laptop.

"I'm still not following how this directly connects to Fisk," said Cope. "Or how you're linking Kerr to Barb's murder."

"I located travel records indicating Kerr flew from London to New York City two days before the murder," answered Irish.

"I've been watching facial recognition feeds," added Decker. "So far, I haven't gotten any hits, but Kerr would know how to avoid being picked up."

"Are you saying we don't presently know Kerr's whereabouts?" Cope asked.

"That's correct," answered Decker. "Although we have reason to believe he hasn't left the States."

Cope looked at me and then at Stella and finally at Decker. "Unless anyone here objects, I'm going to go to Money McTiernan with this." He turned to Irish. "That's to say, I will if you're able to establish enough of a connection to warrant it." Cope cleared his throat.

"Of course she did," answered Stella.

"Where is it?"

I almost laughed out loud at the look on Stella's face.

"Asshole," Irish muttered under his breath. I doubted anyone else at the table heard him. I had to admit that, at the moment, I agreed with his assessment.

"Well?" Cope asked again.

"Whoever killed her, took it," said Stella, who stood and walked over to the window.

Ali reached over and put her hand on her husband's arm.

During Cope's original investigation, it was Money who'd brought in Ali, a CIA internal affairs officer, to determine whether Cope was also a double agent working with Irish.

Once Money found out both men had created their own covert mission and suspected Fisk of leading a ring of double agents responsible for the deaths of some of the CIA's best operatives, he backed them with the full force of the agency, all under the auspice of internal affairs. Not to mention with support from the Senate Intelligence Committee, chaired by none other than Cope's father, Henry Clay Copeland, Senior Senator from the State of Louisiana.

If Cope planned to take this to Money, it also likely meant he hoped to secure funding to keep the mission going—something his Senator father would certainly approve.

Even if I'd asked Decker how all this was being funded, I doubted he'd tell me. I knew, though, that even if Decker had to pay for this out of his own pocket, he wouldn't walk away from this mission for anything outside of his wife and soon-to-be-born baby.

"No objections?" Cope asked again. When no one spoke up, he continued. "Deck, err…and Stella, do you have the next steps determined?"

Stella looked at Cope, but didn't respond. Instead, she focused on Irish.

"What?" he asked.

"What happened with China?"

"What about them?"

"You were on trial for spying for them. Was that part of the cover?"

Irish looked at Cope and then Deck. All three men were smiling. "They're pretty easy to make a scapegoat for just about anything," he said.

"To confirm, there was never an official connection to China?"

"Not anything we could confirm. That doesn't mean they weren't somehow involved."

"I've been looking into the current executive committee and Interpol. Antonov is rumored to be next in line to take over when the current head of United Russia 'retires,'" said Ali, looking up from her laptop. "According to the brief I received several months ago, he looks like a pretty bad dude."

"Several months ago?" Stella asked.

Ali set her phone on the table. "Sorry. Unrelated."

"What is it related to?" asked Irish.

"The poisoning of the Russian diplomat in London."

I saw it the minute Ali realized that it might, in fact, be related.

"We all received the brief," said Cope. "Including you, Decker?"

"Affirmative." Decker was studying something on his own computer. "You know what I want to know? How in the hell did Byrne get elected as Interpol president?" he muttered.

"The way it works is the delegates nominate and vote. There are only nine, eleven if you count the two nominated," said Irish.

"Twelve if you include the secretary-general," I added.

"Does he vote?" Ali asked.

"Affirmative," answered Irish.

"It wouldn't be hard to figure out who voted for him. Who are the current delegates?" I opened my laptop to look. "France, Scotland, UAE, Netherlands, Angola, Brazil, Jordan, Czech Republic, and…drumroll, please…China."

"While Byrne's election makes sense, how did Antonov get elected, given that lineup?" said Cope.

I had to agree, it was surprising.

"Maybe Byrne had a hand in it, or even Kerr. We need to research all the delegates too," said Stella.

"On it," said Irish.

"I can help," offered Ali.

23

Buck

The six of us—myself, Stella, Irish, Ali, Cope, and Decker—spent the next few hours silently staring at our laptops. We'd divided Barb's emails and were studying each, trying again to link them to Interpol, the CIA, other intelligence organizations, or Operation Argead. Periodically, someone would sigh or get up to stretch.

"I do think it's time to engage Money," said Cope.

"Agreed," answered Decker. "I'd like to get Casper in place at Interpol before their quarterly meetings. There's an open position as the secretary-general's administrative assistant. Once she's in place, we can determine what other support we'll need."

Cope laughed. "Just as long as we're going through K19 on this one."

"Fuck off," Decker said under his breath.

"What other kind of support do you need?"

"We'll leave that to Doc."

"What about Smoke?" I asked, remembering that Decker had recently installed a security system at his ranch.

"We'll see. There are some extenuating circumstances with his partner on his last op."

I figured if Decker wanted to tell us what that meant, he would have. "Have Casper search La Chapelle-Saint-Maurice," I suggested.

"I already did," said Irish. All eyes turned to him. "A murder took place there ten years ago. It involved the deaths of three members of a French family, one Brit, and one American citizen. There were two survivors."

I immediately knew where Irish was going with this and dreaded hearing it.

"The Brit was with Irish Military Intelligence. The American and one member of the French family, Pierre Martin, were CIA operatives."

I felt sick to my stomach but listened as Irish continued, his voice heavy with the pain of knowing the agents' deaths were most likely committed at the hand of their own employers.

"French police buried the case."

"And the CIA fucking let them," spat Cope.

"Martin's wife and son were also killed in the attack. His two daughters, then aged eight and six, survived with minor injuries."

"They'd be eighteen and sixteen now," said Stella.

Cope nodded in agreement with what she'd left unsaid. There was a chance one or both of them remembered something. Asking, though, would very likely put their lives in jeopardy.

When dinner time rolled around, Rock and Ink took mess duty and prepared a meal that would send a vegetarian running for the hills. We had an abundance of protein by way of steaks, chops, and chicken but not much else to go with it. Fortunately, my sister showed up with salad, bread, and potatoes before everything else was finished cooking on the grill.

When her eyes met Irish's and they both smiled, it told me exactly how Flynn had known what we needed and when.

Stella had mentioned Flynn and Irish's flirtation to me, but I'd brushed it off. Now it appeared they were communicating, probably by text since I didn't see him leave the room once.

I kept my eye on Stella throughout dinner. As usual, she didn't eat much. She seemed focused, like she always was whenever I'd seen her in work mode.

Ali would take more breaks, crack jokes every so often, before she re-addressed. Stella's concentration was razor-sharp.

"You getting anywhere?" I asked, nudging her with my shoulder.

"Not really. You?"

I shook my head. "I've got a call into Hammer with a couple of questions about what I'm looking for with the will, but he was in court all day. He said he'd get back with me tomorrow."

"What *are* you looking for?"

"The right document ID."

Stella set down her fork. "Seriously?" she whispered. "Oh my God. Then, I wouldn't have to go to New York at all. Unless that's where the safe-deposit box is located."

"That's the plan, darlin'." I leaned forward and nuzzled her ear. "You done?" I asked, looking at her still-half-full plate.

"I wasn't that hungry."

"How unlike you," I teased, going in for a kiss. I picked up her plate and mine and took them to the kitchen. "You cooked, I'll clean up," I told Ink.

"I got it. This is the most exciting thing I've done all day, boss. Watching cows stand in a meadow for ten hours isn't exactly taxing my brain."

"We'll try to switch things up tomorrow," I told him, patting him on the back as I walked away.

"If there's nothing else we need to cover tonight, I'll head out," said Decker.

"How'd you beat us here, anyway?" Cope asked.

"Same way I'm getting home."

Cope laughed. "You had to get your own plane, didn't you?"

Decker raised his middle finger.

"You do know the K19 fleet has grown to three or four aircraft, right?"

"Knock it off, or you can walk to DC to meet with Money."

Cope shook his head and laughed.

When Stella pushed her chair back and stood, I walked over and stood beside her then leaned in. "Let's get everyone out of here so we can be alone," I whispered.

"If there isn't anything else for us to discuss tonight, I say we let Decker be on his way," she said to the group.

"Whatever you say, boss." Cope looked from Stella to me as I draped my arm around her shoulders. I saw his jaw tense, but I didn't give a shit. My relationship with Ali had turned from one I wanted to be romantic, to me looking at her more like a little sister. Even though Stella was older than Cope and me, I was sure he thought she needed him to look out for her. Maybe with someone else, but not with me.

"I'll send the plane back in the morning," Deck said to Cope. "I'll let Stella determine who goes with you."

"I thought you and Cope were going to get into it there at the end," Stella said after everyone had left.

"He needs to understand you're my primary responsibility."

"Is that what I am? Your responsibility?"

I turned her in my arms. "I thought you might prefer me saying that over 'Cope needs to understand you're mine now.'"

I expected her to bristle, but she didn't. "And Ali also needs to understand you're mine. What was that earlier when you and she went out on the porch?"

"Her warning me not to hurt you."

"I'll give you the same warning." Stella leaned forward and kissed me.

"Wanna know what I told her?"

"Sure," she said, pulling her shirt off over her head and unfastening her bra. She put her hands on her hips, but I couldn't take my eyes off her tits. "Well?"

"Well, what?"

"What did you tell her?"

"Tell who?"

Stella unfastened her jeans.

"Let me do that." I sat on the bed and pulled her between my legs.

She put her hands on mine. "What did you tell Ali?"

"Oh. That."

"Yes, that." Stella took two steps back. "No touching me until you fess up."

"I said it was more likely it would be the other way around."

Stella sat down beside me. It wasn't where I wanted her, but at least she was close enough that I could put my hands on her.

"Why would you think that?"

I stroked my beard, wondering the same thing. "I guess it's because I'm tied to this ranch until this time next year."

"I see." Stella flopped back on the bed.

"What?" I asked, trying not to smile at her reaction. It was just so unlike her.

"What are we, Buck? Are we in junior high and if one of us changes schools, it means we can't still love each other?"

I laughed, but only because she was smiling.

"I told you I *love* you. Do you realize I've never done that before?"

"You haven't?" I asked.

"Have you?"

"I'm not gonna lie. I have."

"Oh."

"Tami Saunders. Second grade."

Stella slugged me.

"That's the same thing she did."

"Enough playing around, Buck."

"By playing around, do you mean I can't do this?" I stuck my hand down the front of her jeans, groaning when my fingers felt the lace of her thong.

"No. You can do that."

"What about this?" I leaned forward and swirled her nipple with my tongue.

"I'll allow it."

I rolled off the bed, stood between her legs, grasped the back of her jeans, and peeled them from her body. "I had a fantasy about doing that," I said, kneeling and pulling her toward me. "Put your legs on my shoulders, Stella."

"Take your hair out of the ponytail," she said, using the same demanding tone of voice I had. "Wait."

"What?"

She put her right leg on my shoulder and then her left. "Okay. Now."

After releasing my hair, I pleasured her with my mouth until I couldn't wait any longer to be inside her.

"Wait," she said again when I rolled the condom on and scooted her back on the bed.

"What?"

"I want you on your back."

I flopped down on the bed like she had. "My pleasure."

Stella straddled me, easing herself down on my cock. When I was as deep as I could get, I put my hands on her waist, stilling her. Stella rested her hands on mine and looked into my eyes. "I love you."

"I love you too, Buck."

"I wish you could stay here with me on the ranch, but I know that's too much to ask."

"Do you really want to have this conversation while we're having *sex*?"

"We aren't having sex, darlin'. We're making love. And I can't think of a better way for us to talk about our future than by me being balls-deep inside you. You wanna know why?"

"Why?" she asked. She started to move again, and I let her.

"Because there isn't a day that goes by that I don't want to spend at least part of it with my cock in your pussy."

I shuddered when I felt that pussy squeeze me. "Which part of what I said made you do that, Stella?"

"All of it," she groaned as she increased her rhythm.

I couldn't hold back; I needed to fuck her hard. I held her still and pistoned into her until she cried out her release. Only then did I let myself go too.

Stella rolled her body off of me and onto the bed. "Just so you know, I'm in favor of your cock in my pussy at least part of every day."

24

Stella

"Who's this Smoke guy you and Decker were talking about last night?"

Buck stroked his beard. "One of the baddest motherfuckers I've ever worked with. Makes Ink look like a little pussycat."

"He's bigger than Ink?" I asked with wide eyes.

"Nah, but he's a hell of a lot scarier."

"Also someone you worked with?"

"I have a few times, back when we were both with the agency."

"What about Casper?"

"I don't know her as well. She and I never ran an op together. She's got a vested interest in this mission, though."

"She does? How so?"

"Casper believes her husband was one of the agents killed by Fisk's crew."

"Oh my God. That's horrible."

"Decker and the rest of IISG do their best to keep her busy."

"Was she with the CIA?"

Buck nodded. "One day, she just got up and walked out."

"Why do they call her Casper? Is she friendly?"

He chuckled. "That's not a word I've ever heard associated with her. No, it's that she can ghost like Burns can burn."

"Wow. That's quite a statement."

"She's that good."

"I admire strong women," I murmured. "I wish I was friends with more of them."

Buck's phone vibrated, and he pulled it out of his pocket. "It's Hammer. I'll put it on speaker."

"I can wait out there," I offered.

"Or you can stay here."

"I don't want to intrude."

"Stella…"

I shrugged and sat on the bed.

"Hey, Buck, hope I'm not interrupting anything."

"You are." He laughed. "Stella's here. I'm going to put you on speaker."

"Copy that. Hey, Stella."

"Hey."

"I wanted to give you an update on your father's will."

I got up again to leave, but Buck pulled me back down on the bed, beside him.

"Go ahead, Ham."

"First of all, it's almost like he wanted you to fail. How in the hell could anyone who's been running a ranch in the red for even a couple of years expect someone else to make a profit in the next?"

"That's just the kinda guy he was."

I could tell Buck was trying to make light of something that was anything but.

"Even if you could get your hands on cash, an investment doesn't equal profit. To turn that in a year is damn near impossible."

"Decker said the money from the lease wouldn't be enough to make it happen. How bad is it, Hammer?"

"That's one small piece of good news. Not as bad as I thought, and I'm not sure why Deck said that. Depending on how long the lease goes on, it could be that it'll be enough."

"How many months of lease income would we need?"

"At least six, but I have another idea."

"What?" Buck asked.

"Have the Invincibles extend the lease for the full year. After the end of that year, once the cash is freed up, buy them out of the months they didn't use."

"But it'll be after the fact. We wouldn't be buying them out. We'd be kicking it back to them."

"Semantics, Buck."

"I can't do that."

I had a sick feeling in my chest. Buck's pride wouldn't allow him to do what Hammer was proposing, even if it meant saving the ranch.

"Then, you better pray they need the lease to continue for a minimum of six months. Preferably longer. It's your best chance of fulfilling the profitability stipulation."

"Anything else, Hammer?" Buck asked.

"There is. I'm still looking into it, but not with much luck."

"What's that?"

"When I received the lease agreement back, it wasn't signed by the attorney for the estate."

"So we have no agreement?"

"I didn't say that. It was signed, just not by him."

"By who, then?"

"That's just it. I can't read the signature, and in the typed version, it just says, 'On behalf of the Roaring Fork Trust.'"

"Then, how do you know it wasn't the attorney?" I had no business asking, but the reporter in me sensed there was more to this, and I couldn't stop myself from poking my nose in.

"Because I asked him."

"What was his response?" When Buck smiled at me, I mouthed, "Sorry." He shook his head and motioned for me to keep going.

"He confirmed he wasn't the trustee, and when I asked who was, he told me he wasn't permitted to divulge that information."

"Is that legal?" I asked.

"It isn't, but it'll take a court battle between Buck, his siblings, and the trust to demand the trustee's identity be revealed. That'll take time and, more importantly, money."

Buck was stroking his beard.

"Any ideas?" I asked.

He shook his head, but I could see something brewing in the back of his mind.

"Stella, as long as you're here, Decker asked me to look into the murder of Barb's attorney and where that leaves you with her estate."

"Oh," I said, not surprised that Deck had engaged Hammer on my behalf.

"I reached out to one of Owen's partners and asked that he forward a copy of the will to me."

"Did he?"

"Negative. In fact, he refused."

"Can he do that?" I asked. "Legally?"

"While lawyers do it all the time out of professional courtesy, he can and did refuse. Makes him an asshole, but that isn't illegal. Should be," he muttered at the end.

"What should I do?"

"He promised he'd be in touch with you by the end of next week. If you don't hear from him, I'll reengage. And Buck, I'll get back to you about the Invincibles' agreement."

"What about it, Ham?"

"Jesus Christ, Buck. You'd do it for them if you could. Let them help you."

"Before you hang up, what's the document number on Barb Hunter's will?"

Hammer muttered something. "I wish you and Decker wouldn't ask me this shit over the phone."

"As if the line isn't secure, Ham."

"Whatever. Check your email." Hammer ended the call.

I reached over and put my hand on Buck's. "He's right, you know."

"I'm not sure he is. It would be different if I were a partner, but I'm not. I'm not even on the regular roster of contractors."

"It isn't up to you to decide whether someone offers to help you. Once they have, that decision has been made."

"I don't know. It doesn't feel right."

"Does what your father's done feel right?"

"Not at all."

"Explain it to me, Buck. I've only caught bits and pieces."

He told me about how his father had threatened that once he left the ranch, he'd never own any of it. He also told me that when the attorney read the will, he learned he had to do two things. First, that he maintain full-time residency on the ranch for a period of one year, which was what the forty-eight-hour thing was all about. The second thing was that by the end of that year, the ranch had to be profitable.

"He knew that if it was just me, I'd walk away and never look back. He also knew I'd never do that to my brothers and sister."

"You're a good man, Buck."

"Am I?" he asked, shaking his head. "Wouldn't anyone in my position do the same thing?"

"Not everyone would be able to. What if you'd been in the middle of a mission when the call came in that he died? You might have had to choose between the lives of others and your siblings' inheritance."

"My father wasn't a good man, Stella. He wouldn't have cared. All that would've mattered was that he found a way to control me. I often wonder how long it took him to come up with this idea. The attorney said the will was drafted around the same time I left for college."

"He was hurt and lashed out."

Buck stood. "This isn't about being hurt. This is him being a controlling, manipulative bastard who found a way to hurt his son. He did it my whole life and not just to me."

"I'm sorry, Buck."

"Don't be. If we somehow manage to hang on to this place by turning a profit, then on day three hundred and sixty-six, I'll be signing my rights to this place over to my four siblings. I don't want a penny for it, I just want it out of my life."

I wanted to tell Buck not to be hasty in his decision, but it wasn't my place. He had shown me the utmost respect earlier when we were meeting with Ali, Cope, Decker, and Irish. I would do the same for him.

"I want you to know I'm here for you, Buck. The same way you're here for me."

"Because you love me?"

I smiled and put my arm around his shoulders like he so often did with me. "Because I love you."

25

Buck

I could feel the tension seep off of her the minute she came out of the bedroom and she found Cope was saying goodbye to Ali.

It didn't matter we'd spent last night and every night for ten days naked in each other's arms. I'd lay money down that Stella had convinced herself that the minute Cope walked out the front door, I'd only have eyes for Ali. It wasn't remotely true, but that I had to show her. Words wouldn't be enough.

In the world of journalism, she was a barracuda. When it came to a story, nothing would make her back down, not even her aunt's murder. Personally, particularly with relationships, Stella second-guessed her second guesses.

I'd never heard her mention friends other than last night when we were talking about Casper and she said she wished she were friends with more powerful women. I knew she and Ali were tight, because I'd witnessed it. I was her friend. Hell, she'd said I was her best friend, but that had only come after I put in the time and effort to get her to let me in.

Her insecurity was easy to understand. From the brief I'd read on her before I was assigned to Ali's detail, I learned that her mother had died from AIDS when Stella was nine. Her father had left her mother right after she was diagnosed, citing infidelity as his reason for filing for divorce.

From what I remembered from the brief, Stella had had no known contact with him since the day he walked out. I knew where he was, as did everyone else who'd been given the brief.

Her aunt had raised her without a replacement father figure. That explained her attraction to Jinx, a man far older. I even saw it in the way they interacted. Jinx took care of her without attempting to find out what she really needed.

My approach was the opposite. I saw what Stella needed; my relationship with her wasn't about something inside of me desiring to control or possess her. I loved her and wanted the best for her. Plain and simple.

"Cope, is there anything else you need to inform us of before you leave?" Stella asked.

I almost laughed out loud at the stunned reaction on his face. Obviously, he'd forgotten Decker's announcement that Stella was the lead on the mission. "I don't believe so," he responded. "Other than I reached out to Doc and he arranged for Smoke and I to meet after I've finished briefing Money."

"We'llexpectanupdateafteryourmeetingsconclude."

"Roger that," he muttered.

Unlike me, Ali couldn't contain her laughter. In fact, the drink of coffee she'd just taken, came out through her nose. "I'll walk you out," she said to him, covering her mouth.

I turned to the other men in the room. "Who's been assigned to Cope?"

"Me," said Jagger. He grabbed his bag and went outside.

"What about Irish?"

"That's me," answered Ink. I remembered he'd been on Irish's detail when he was in prison as part of the op we thought was over but now knew wasn't.

"Irish? You good with that?"

"Affirmative."

"Press and Rip, what're your orders from Deck?"

"Conclude the installation," answered Rip. "Then—"

"Press, you're on Ali's detail. Rip, you'll be with Stella and me."

"Roger that," they both responded.

"I need to find that fucking box," Stella muttered under her breath while we waited for Ali to come back inside.

"There's nothing stopping you from calling the other lawyer again. Tell him you can't wait until the end of next week."

"I guess I should. I'm assuming I'm her sole heir, but one never knew with Barb. She could've had a few surprises up her sleeve."

I saw the moment Stella realized the correlation between what she'd said and my father's will. Yep, that bastard had had few surprises up his sleeve too.

"Sorry," she mumbled.

I leaned closer because, really, any excuse I had to get closer to Stella, I would make use of. "No need, darlin'," I whispered.

Since she wasn't looking at me, I followed her line of sight. Stella was looking directly at Ali, who had just come inside. I slowly shook my head silently, reminding her to mind her business.

As if she'd heard me, Ali went back to whatever she was doing on her computer.

"I'll call the attorney now," said Stella, walking toward the bedroom. I wanted to follow, but since she hadn't asked, I stayed where I was. When the door closed, Ali looked up at me with raised eyebrows.

"I just told you not to go there," I said.

"You did?"

"Words weren't necessary, Ali."

"What do you see happening between the two of you?"

"Whatever that is, is up to us."

"You can't really see her staying here."

I felt Stella's anger before I saw or heard her.

"Why is that, Ali?" she asked, walking over to the table where we sat.

"I didn't mean anything derogatory."

"I didn't say you did. I asked why you don't see me staying here."

Ali shifted her chair so she was facing away from her computer and at Stella. "Was there ever a time in your life when you've lived outside a city?"

I could tell by the look on her face that Stella knew exactly where this conversation was headed and that she was in full command of it. Part of me thought I should offer to leave the room, but there was no way in hell I was going to miss this.

"Ali, do you know that the day before you and Cope arrived, Buck and I hiked to the top of Bachelor Mountain?"

"I didn't say I doubted you'd enjoy yourself while—"

"Do you know how *high* that mountain is? The elevation?"

Ali immediately showed signs of agitation. I knew exactly what they were. She'd drum her fingers or tap her foot. Sometimes both. I'd been on her detail, lived with her for several weeks. It had been my job to be aware of what was going on with her. Her foot was tapping a triple beat.

"What's your point, Stella?"

"I don't need to answer that."

"Me overcoming my fear of heights is a lot different than you living out in the middle of nowhere."

"Wait. You overcame your fear of heights?"

Ali turned and glared at me. "Yes, and that has nothing to do with this conversation. I'm not talking about Stella getting over her fear of wide-open spaces."

"Buck, can you give us a minute?"

Ali slammed her laptop shut. "I'll leave."

I looked at Stella, who motioned for me to follow Ali outside.

"Hold up."

"Leave me alone, Buck."

"Can't do that."

"It's none of my business. I won't stick my nose into it again."

I took a step forward and touched the tip of her nose with my finger. "Give us the space we need to work this out, Ali. I love Stella and she loves me."

"You can't be—"

"Ali," I warned. "Listen to my words. Stella and I are in love. We have been for a lot longer than either of us probably realized. And before you go spouting off about how long we've known each other, I'll remind you that you and Cope moved a lot faster than we have."

Her eyes filled with tears. "I'm sorry."

I put my arm around her shoulders and turned her to look out over the ranch. "I'll always be your friend, Al."

Her chin shot up. "I know that."

"Do you?"

"I just said I did. I need some time on my own, Buck."

"Actually, you need the opposite. Stella is in there trying to solve her aunt's murder, and she needs your help. Mine too. Quit being so selfish, get your ass back inside that cabin, and do the right thing." When I smiled, so did she. I breathed a sigh of relief when, instead of heading toward the cabin she and Cope shared, she went toward Stella's and mine.

"Thanks for calling me out on my shit, Buck," she said over her shoulder.

"Anytime, Ali."

Stella was seated at the table when we came back in, studying something on her laptop.

"Did you reach the attorney?" I asked.

"He's out of the office, but look at this."

"What did you find?"

"You read it," she said, turning the computer. "You too, Ali."

In the email Stella had on the screen, Barb had made reference to an international soccer organization whose board was fired and eventually charged with extortion, but within days, those charges were dropped.

Stella clicked on another window; a news article appeared on the screen.

The piece, written by a sports' watchdog organization, alluded to large sums of money that had flowed from the soccer organization into several international governments and one intelligence agency—Interpol.

"Look at this," said Stella, clicking on another window. This time, an obituary appeared on the screen. "The man who wrote the article you just read was found dead the day after the story was posted. It was ruled a suicide."

"How did you find this?" I asked.

"I didn't. Decker did. My guess is that, somehow, he found it on the deep web."

The story I continued to read unfolded into a series of allegations that had nothing to do with the soccer organization. Instead, it alleged that over the course of several years, Interpol had been the recipient of money not just from the international governments that had committed to fund the organization, but from private companies as well.

The amounts of what were called "voluntary funding contributions" were staggering, in the millions, year after year, significantly boosting Interpol's annual operating budgets.

Ali, who had been reading over my shoulder, sat down and opened her own laptop. "Interpol is required to list their donors annually," she said, turning her screen toward Stella and me. "Have you ever heard of these organizations? I haven't."

We broke the list into three groups and searched for the private companies listed on the site. As I expected and assumed Stella and Ali did too, all I was able to find were dummy corporations, proving that someone wanted to ensure whoever was really behind them was never discovered.

"Isn't Interpol also required to publicly post their annual report?" I asked.

Ali shook her head. "It's protected under classified information."

Stella sat back in her chair and looked over at me. "What the fuck did Barb get herself involved in?"

"The same thing Cope, Irish, and Decker did."

"Speaking of Irish, he needs to see this."

<h1 style="text-align:center">26</h1>

Stella

Only hours ago, I believed I was on the brink of finally finding the information Barb had so desperately wanted me to. Now, I felt defeated all over again. Not just me, I could tell Ali, Buck, and Irish—who Buck had asked to join us—were experiencing the same level of frustration and disappointment I was.

Through IISG, Buck had gained access to the deep web—which contained content encrypted in such a way that it cannot be indexed by conventional search engines. Deep and dark were often used interchangeably, but they weren't the same thing at all. In fact, the dark web made up less than one percent of the deep web.

Searching for anything, even with the use of Decker's apps, was nearly impossible. The four of us worked well past sundown, occasionally hitting on something we thought promising, only to be disappointed when it led nowhere.

"When is Cope coming back?" asked Irish.

"Tonight sometime," answered Ali. "In fact, he should land any minute."

"Pretty damn nice, having a private plane at our disposal," said Buck. "Although, like Cope said, K19 has three or four, whereas IISG only has one."

I smiled at Buck's attempt to lighten the mood in the room, but I was the only one who did.

"They have two now." Irish closed his laptop, pushed back from the table, and stood.

"What did you say?" Buck asked.

"According to Decker, they just bought another one." Irish walked out of the cabin without a word.

"Cope says he wasn't always like that," murmured Ali as the three of us watched the door close behind him. "He sees every death of every agent as his own personal failure."

There was no point in my commenting that he shouldn't feel that way. We all knew that. He probably did as well, but guilt was the kind of thing that crept in and took hold despite logic or reason.

Ali's phone vibrated, and she turned it over to look at the screen. "Oh, he's here already."

"Cope?" I asked.

"He just pulled through the gates."

A few minutes later, we saw headlights. Buck stood, walked over to the door, and opened it. "Long day?" he said when Cope walked in looking as haggard as I'd ever seen him.

"You should've spent the night," said Ali, standing to hug her husband.

"I don't like being away from you any more than I have to."

Buck's gaze met mine, and we both smiled. I wondered if he was thinking the same thing I was—that now I knew how Cope and Ali felt. I was so used to spending every minute of the day with Buck, just the idea of us being apart made my heart hurt.

"Is there anything we need to talk about tonight? Or should we regroup in the morning?" I asked.

"Just a couple of things," said Cope. "First, I met with Money and my father, who's approved emergency funding for this mission."

As the head of the Senate Intelligence Committee, Cope's father had that authority. I couldn't help but wonder what other kinds of missions had been funded through the years that maybe shouldn't have been. Perhaps even the mysterious Operation Argead.

"The only other thing is to tell you that Smoke Torcher is on his way to France, where Casper is already undercover at Interpol."

"What's her role?"

"Administrative assistant to all three members of the executive committee. Primarily to Kim Ha-joon, though."

Kim was the only member of the current executive committee we'd been unable to tie to Kerr.

"How's Irish?" Cope asked. His question caught me off guard even though Buck, Ali, and I had just been talking about the man.

"The same as he always is," answered Buck.

Further catching me off guard, Cope put his hand on the small of Ali's back and led her back to the table. I hadn't expected them to stick around, given it was almost ten.

"He wasn't always that way," said Cope, pulling out a chair for Ali before sitting beside her and reiterating what she'd said earlier. "His time in prison changed him."

"How could it not?"

"You're right, Stella. How could it not?"

Ali reached over and rubbed her husband's back. "You do the same thing he does. You both carry this mission like a gauntlet, which I completely understand."

Cope looked at her adoringly. "I am luckier than Irish is. I have you to take my mind off of it."

Ali had a soft shoulder for her husband to rest his head. She also had the maturity and life experience to know when Cope needed her.

I thought about the conversation Buck and I had had about his sister. She was twenty-one years old and, as far as I could tell, had never lived anywhere other than this ranch. I now understood why Buck had discounted what was happening between Flynn and Irish. At best, it was a romantic fling. At worst, she was in way over her head.

"Stella?" I heard Buck say.

I raised my head and looked at the three people seated at the table with me. "Yes?"

"If there's nothing else, Cope and Ali are going to head to their cabin for the night."

"Right. Of course. No. There's nothing else."

"You okay?" Buck asked after closing the door behind them, Jagger, and Press.

"I was thinking about Irish and your sister."

"I was too," he said, stroking his beard.

"You were right."

"About?"

"A relationship between them being inappropriate."

"Interesting," he murmured, putting his arms around my waist. "And here, I was thinking the opposite."

I looked into his eyes. "You were?"

"Flynn has the sweetest soul of anyone I've ever known."

"All the more reason for her to steer clear of Irish."

"I disagree. If anyone can make him see his way out of the darkness, it's her."

I wriggled out of Buck's arms, took him by the hand, and led him into the bedroom.

"You know, I can't think when you do that," he said as I unfastened the buttons on one of the flannel shirts I'd bought in Gunnison.

"I say we stop thinking for tonight."

"Oh, yeah. Now you're talking," he said when I added my bra to the shirt I'd already tossed on the floor.

It wasn't a secret to anyone that I wasn't a morning person, particularly to Buck, who opened his eyes right before I crept out of the bedroom.

"What are you doing?"

"I didn't want to wake you."

"Then, let's go back to sleep."

"You go back to sleep. There are some things I want to look into."

I wasn't much beyond the threshold when a naked Buck wrapped his arms around me, tossed me over his shoulder, and carried me back into the bedroom. "There is only one reason for either of us to be up this early, and that's if my cock is in your pussy."

"God, your voice…it's like it speaks directly to my clit."

He set me on the bed and pulled off the thong I'd just put on. "Arms up," he said, pulling his t-shirt over my head.

I scooted up on the bed and rested my head against the pillow.

"Like what you see?" Buck asked as my gaze traveled the length of him.

I shook my head.

"You don't?" he asked with wide eyes.

"Nope. I love it. I love you, Buck."

"If I could hear you tell me you love me every day for the rest of my life, I'd die a happy man."

I spread my legs, and he knelt between them. If I could feel Buck inside me every day for the rest of my life, I'd die the happiest woman who ever lived.

27

Buck

An hour later, I was on my way to the kitchen to make coffee when my phone vibrated with a call from Decker.

"I've got news," he said when I answered.

"What's that?"

"Stella is about to get a visitor, one I'm sure you'll want to meet too."

"What's going on, Decker?"

"I have it on good authority that Burns Butler will be arriving at the Roaring Fork Ranch in under an hour."

"Are you serious?" I felt like a kid on Christmas morning. Worse, I sounded like one.

Fortunately, Decker laughed. "Yeah, I'm serious. Rip is picking him up at the airfield. Give me a call when he arrives, and I'll patch in remotely."

"I'm surprised you're not on your way here too."

"Evidently, Burns didn't think my presence was necessary. I'll show him."

I couldn't help but laugh after Decker ended the call. He'd sounded as much like a kid over Burns' visit as I did.

"What's going on?" Stella asked, coming out of the bedroom freshly showered.

"We have a distinguished visitor arriving this morning."

Her eyes were wide. "Who?"

"Burns Butler."

"Get the fuck out," she gasped. "Is Decker coming with him?"

"Negative, but he did ask me to let him know when Burns arrived so he could video conference himself in."

I took Stella's hand away from her mouth and brought it to mine when I noticed her biting her nails. "There's nothing to be nervous about," I murmured, kissing each fingertip.

"Are you saying you aren't nervous?"

"He isn't coming here to see me."

"Who's he coming here to see?"

"You."

Forty-five minutes after Stella smacked me for teasing her, Rip called to say he was about to pull through the main gate.

"Why do you think he's here?" asked Stella, who had been antsy since I told her about Burns' visit.

"He must have found something on Operation Argead."

When I saw the SUV pull up, I opened the cabin door and went out to wait on the porch with Stella. I'd heard so many stories about the man getting out of the vehicle, I wasn't sure what to expect.

Burns raised his hand in greeting. "Ms. Hunter and Mr. Wheaton, I presume?"

"Please call me Stella, Mr. Burns…err…Butler," she stammered, shaking his outstretched hand.

Burns put his other hand on top of hers. "It's a pleasure to meet you, lass," he said before turning to me.

"I'm Buck," I said, shaking his hand like Stella had.

"I've heard promising things about you, young man." There was the slightest Scottish lilt to his voice.

"Thank you, sir."

"Shall we go inside?" said Stella, motioning toward the door before leading us up the porch steps. "May I bring you some tea?" she asked once we were in the living room.

"A glass of water if you wouldn't mind."

I motioned for Stella to sit on the sofa while I got both her and Burns a glass and poured water in a pitcher.

"Please join us," Burns said when I set the water in front of them before heading back to the kitchen.

I grabbed another glass and had just taken a seat when I heard my laptop ping with the sound of an incoming video chat. "That would be Decker."

I grabbed the computer and hit the connect button. "I was just about to call you."

"Sure, you were, young Buck. Hey, Burns," he said when I set the computer on the coffee table where all three of us could see him.

"Decker, what an unexpected pleasure." Burns raised his glass of water toward the screen and winked at Stella.

"What have you got for us?" Deck asked.

Burns set the glass down and leaned forward. "As Decker may have told you, I'd heard of Operation Argead several years ago but only in passing."

"I also told them you had an idea who burned the op."

Burns nodded slowly. "There are certain signatures, you see. They're hidden, of course. Meant to serve as a tip of the hat, if you will. In this case, I immediately recognized it to be the work of Ming Shen-Lin."

The name sounded familiar to me. "Is that the same Ming who disappeared a couple of years ago?"

When Burns turned to me, I saw a hint of a smile. "One and the same."

Ming was rumored to have been arrested by the Chinese, accused of being a double agent with ties to the Hong Kong triad.

"This, then, would be the Beijing connection," I heard Stella murmur.

"One of them," said Burns, pulling an envelope from the leather bag he'd had slung over his shoulder when he came in and that now sat near his feet on the floor. He handed it to Stella. While she opened and looked through its contents, I saw Burns motion with his finger at Decker, who smiled and looked away from the laptop's camera.

Stella raised her head, and her eyes met mine. "May I?" she asked Burns.

"By all means."

She handed the envelope to me.

"I'll be damned," Decker muttered at the same time I read the list of aliases for the current secretary-general of Interpol.

Kim Ha-joon was only one of a handful used by Chen Wang-Su, whose father had worked in Chinese intelligence for many years with Ming Shen-Lin.

"Not South Korean," I mumbled.

"That is correct," murmured Burns.

As one of the few countries in the world with a long-standing alliance with China as well as critical strategic ties to the United States, South Korea held a unique, albeit tenuous, position in global politics. That China had maneuvered one of their own spies into Interpol's executive committee didn't come as a surprise. The only thing that did was that Kim hadn't yet been discovered.

"They all know who he really is," I said under my breath, not intending to say it out loud.

"Burns, we need to read Irish and Cope in on this," said Decker.

"Agreed, but if I recall correctly, you are not the lead on this investigation." Burns turned to Stella.

"He wasn't serious. I mean, I'm not really the decision maker here." She looked from me to the screen.

"Yes, Stella, you are, but I'd suggest you consider not reading Ali in just yet," said Decker.

"Right. Buck, would you please ask Irish and Cope to join us?"

"Roger that." I stood and was about to walk toward the door when Burns held up his hand.

"Before you do so, there's one more thing I'd like to go over with Ms. Hunter."

I sat back down.

"Much in the same way Agent Copeland, Agent Warrick, and Mr. Ashford have stumbled into something much more far-reaching than they ever anticipated, so did your aunt. I caution you, as I have them, to be absolutely certain you are aware of what you're about to take on. It is my understanding that Barbara warned you that if you continued to pursue this story, the consequences may be dire."

"I'm not afraid," said Stella, raising her chin.

"You should be," warned Burns.

"I can't walk away. I could never walk away."

Burns nodded slowly like he had earlier. "In that case, I'll tell you what I know about Operation Argead, along with where their weaknesses lie: with the ringleader—Nicholas Kerr."

After filling Stella in on what he knew about Kerr then briefing Irish and Cope, Burns asked Rip to deliver him back to the airfield. When we came back inside after saying goodbye, Decker was still live on the computer screen.

"I've just received two pieces of information out of Lyon. First, Smoke and Casper met with the daughter of Pierre Martin, other than telling them she didn't believe the murders were random, there was little else she remembered."

"What's the second thing?" asked Irish.

"Casper's just informed me that Daniel Byrne assigned someone to track Siren Gallagher. She's the IMI agent who worked the Kensington Whitby op with Smoke."

"Has Siren been working this mission since then?"

"Negative," answered Decker. "We have no idea why Byrne has any interest in her other than he was the one who hired her to work for Irish Military Intelligence."

"Should we consider her a suspect?" I asked.

"Negative," he repeated. "I can't get into why not just yet, but I can confirm that she is not working for Byrne."

"Copy that."

"Buck, there's another matter I need to discuss with you."

I assumed it was about the ranch and offered to step outside.

"We'll take a walk instead," Stella offered.

"Don't go too far." I winked.

"How is she?" Deck asked when I walked back over to my computer after closing the door behind them.

"I'm sure she's as overwhelmed as I am."

"What about before Burns' visit?"

"Frustrated. She's been trying to reach the attorney that took over for Barb's. Evidently, he's been out of the office for several days."

"That reminds me of a couple of things. First, NYPD has ruled Owen's death a random act of violence. Wrong place, wrong time kind of thing."

"Do you think that's the case?"

"Not for a fucking minute. The other thing is, there's a holdup of some kind with the death certificate. I've asked my guy here in Hays County to reach out to the DC medical examiner to see if he can find out why."

"Barb has been dead close to a month. Even with a murder investigation, the death certificate is typically released without the official cause of death."

"Not in the District of Columbia. However, if this drags on another week, I'll engage Hammer."

"Copy that. Thanks, Deck."

I watched as Decker looked at something on his phone. "What's up?"

"I just got a text from Casper. Something's gone down." The screen went dark.

Within a few minutes, Deck called back. "I don't have all the details, but it's bad, Buck. I'm leaving for Ireland now. I'll be back in touch after I've assessed the situation."

"Do you need backup?"

"I'll engage Rile and see who we've got over there."

It had been two days, and there was no word coming out of Ireland or anywhere else.

While the information Burns had shared about Kerr and Argead provided background information, everyone believed that our only chance at tying Kerr to Barb's murder, and perhaps even proving what Stella's aunt set out to expose over a decade ago, was finding the evidence she'd told Stella was in the safe-deposit box.

Two things prevented us from doing so. First, the death certificate hadn't yet been released, and second, the lack of response from the lawyer now responsible for Barb's estate.

I'd hoped to get Stella off the ranch today, if for nothing else other than a change of scenery, but the weather didn't cooperate.

A storm hit the region the night before, bringing with it several inches of rain and causing flooding throughout the East River Valley. Fortunately, Rip and his crew had finished the roof work on the newly renovated cabins, so they, along with the rest of the structures on the Roaring Fork, hadn't sustained any damage. At least as of yet. The last weather report I pulled up on my phone said the front was slow-moving, so flood warnings would remain in effect throughout the day and maybe into the night.

"Hey, Flynn," I said when my sister answered my call.

"What can I do for you, Buck?"

I told her my plan to take Stella fishing in Altamont had been thwarted and that I wanted her help in coming up with something else to get our minds off this investigation for at least a little while.

"Why doesn't everyone come to the dining hall for dinner? I'll see if Holt will play a short set afterwards."

"That sounds really nice, Flynn. Tell me what I can do to help."

"As luck would have it, Cord put a half dozen briskets in the smoker yesterday, and I made a few quarts of ranch beans, potato salad, and coleslaw. I also have several berry pies that just need to be baked."

"Is there an army on its way here that I haven't heard about?"

"It's what we always do for the Fourth of July, Buck. You couldn't have possibly forgotten that?"

"Right. I just didn't know you and Cord kept the tradition going." The truth was, I hadn't even realized today was the holiday.

"Sounds like you're set with food. Anything else I can do?"

"Just make sure Irish comes along."

"Flynn, about Irish…"

"Whatever you're about to say, Buck, I don't want to hear."

"He's a lot older than you, sis, and—"

I heard the chimes indicating my baby sister had hung up on me. I was still staring at the phone, in shock, when Stella walked out of the bedroom.

"What's going on?"

I wondered if Stella had forgotten what day it was, like I had. "That was Flynn. She's making a big, ranch-style dinner for everyone tonight."

"I was going to ask you if there was anywhere we could watch fireworks, but with this storm, there probably won't be any."

"They usually set them off from the top of Mt. Crested Butte, but I don't know if they will tonight. I'll make a few calls and see if anyone knows."

"I'm sorry our fishing trip was canceled."

"Do you really like fishing, Stella, or you putting on a brave face just for me?"

She pulled me over to the sofa. "Would you mind lighting a fire?"

"Not at all. By the way, have you talked to Ali or Cope yet today?"

She shook her head. "I think they're getting as sick of us as we are of them."

I laughed. "I hope I haven't made it too obvious." The truth was, Cope was grating on my last fucking nerve. I finished with the fire and sat down beside Stella, who snuggled her body into mine.

"You asked me about fishing."

"That's right. If you don't like it, you can tell me." I stared into her eyes. "I love your smile, darlin'. Truth is, I love everything about you."

"Yeah? Well, let me tell you a little something about myself that you might not know."

"Go on."

"Turns out you were right about my inner mountain girl dying to get out and explore a place like Crested Butte."

"You aren't playin' me, are you, Stella?"

The teasing smile that had been there since she walked in, left her face. "I love it here, Buck, and I'm not just saying that." She rested her hand on my chest. "Barb's death is the worst thing that's ever happened to me besides losing my mother, and honestly, I was so young at the time I don't remember much." She took a deep breath and let it out slowly. "So it's going to sound psycho when I say this, but, Buck, I've never been happier. Don't get me wrong, I'm sad and angry and frustrated, but somehow, knowing that tonight when I crawl into bed, you'll be there—not just your voice, but your body—makes it possible for me to face tomorrow."

"Wow."

Her cheeks turned pink, but the smile was back. "I know, right? Who the fuck am I?"

I laughed. "You're still you, Stella. The woman I love."

"I love you, Buck."

"You wanna take a ride?" It occurred to me that it was unlikely anyone had checked on the old farmhouse or the barn.

"With you, cowboy? I'll go anywhere with you."

I pulled up as close as I could to the front porch since the rain was still coming down in sheets. I couldn't see clearly enough to tell whether the house had sustained any damage.

"Wait until I come around," I said before jumping out of the truck. I got to the right headlight and saw Stella was waiting for me on the porch.

"I didn't want you to get drenched," she said when I joined her.

Just as I put my hand on the doorknob, a bolt of lightning struck the rod in the center of the barn. The accompanying clap of thunder was instantaneous. I looked at Stella, whose eyes were wide and mouth hung open. "You okay, darlin'?"

She slowly turned to face me. "I've never seen any-thing like that, Buck. Not in person. It was like a stream of light flowed straight through the barn."

"Can't say that I have either. Not up close like that."

"It would've made for a better story if it had hap-pened the last time we were here."

I cocked my head.

"It's when we first said I love you. You know, struck by lightning and all that."

"You can write the story any way you want, Stella. I'll back you up with the fact-checkers." I opened the door and motioned for her to go ahead of me.

I'd left the window coverings open the last time we were here, but with the storm, it was still almost dark as night inside. "Let's see if we can find some candles."

Stella and I looked in all the kitchen drawers but didn't find any.

"I think I remember seeing candlesticks in the dining room," she said, pulling me with her. "Got a match?"

I laughed. "Sure don't."

"Check by the fireplace."

"Did they have matches back then?"

Stella rolled her eyes. "Matches have been around since the mid-eighteen-hundreds, Buck." She said it as though it were common knowledge, making me chuckle.

I found a box on the mantle and handed them to her. "I'd light a fire, but I have no idea what kind of shape the chimney is in."

"That's okay. Candlelight is nice. By the way, why are we here?"

I'd come to see if the house had sustained any damage, but now that we were here, I had an entirely different reason. "What would you think about living here someday?"

"Here, as in this house?"

I nodded.

"Um, wow."

"Never mind, forget I said anything." I was about to blow out the candles so we could leave when I saw a tear run down Stella's cheek. She wrapped one arm around my neck and put her opposite hand on my chest. "I'd move in tomorrow if we could."

I gazed into her eyes, looking for any sign that she was teasing me and saw none.

"When you first brought me here, we hadn't even walked in the front door and I felt a warmth descend on my whole body. I told you then I felt like I'd been here before."

"I remember."

"Maybe the house was welcoming me home."

"It'll take some work to make it move-in ready."

"Do you mean like putting in a sink with a faucet?"

"That would be a good start."

Before long, the sky lightened and the sun shone through the clouds. Stella and I spent the next couple of hours uncovering the treasures buried under sheets that had been used to protect things like sofas and beds.

"You sure wouldn't rather live in a newly renovated cabin?" I asked when all the dust sent her into a sneezing fit.

"I love this so much more," she beamed.

"Oh, shit," I gasped, looking at my phone. "I told Flynn we'd be at the dining hall fifteen minutes ago."

"Can we come back tomorrow?"

"To the farmhouse?"

Stella nodded.

"Of course we can. In fact, maybe I'll ask Rip to come along so we can see what it would take to modernize it."

Stella's head spun in my direction. "Modernize it?"

I couldn't help but laugh at the look on her face. "Just to make it livable."

"Livable is fine. Modernize, over my dead body." As soon as the words left her mouth, Stella covered her face with her hands.

"It's just an expression," I murmured, so glad I'd driven the old pickup, so I could stop and pull her into my arms.

"I said something so similar to my aunt."

"Stella, don't go there. Both are common expressions."

She wiped away a new set of tears. "Flynn is waiting for us."

"We can skip tonight, if you'd rather."

"No. I'm actually starving."

"Uh-oh. Look out. I hope there's enough for everyone else."

"Shut up," she said under her breath. All I cared about was that she was smiling.

28

Stella

"Stella!" shouted Flynn the minute I walked in the door of the dining hall. "I have something for you back at the house. It came yesterday, and I completely forgot to bring it to you."

"What is it?"

Flynn shrugged. "I have no idea."

"An envelope? A package?"

"A box."

My eyes met Buck's. "Would you mind?" I mouthed.

He shook his head. "We're gonna run over there now." He made a sweeping motion with his arm. "Looks like you've got plenty of help."

Cope, Ali, and Irish were all in the kitchen, as were Buck's brothers. Near Porter, stood the woman who'd given me the creeps every time I saw her. She raised her hand in a wave, but she wasn't looking at me. Her eyes were riveted to Buck.

"Ready?" he asked without even looking in her direction. Something that did not go unnoticed by her.

"What's Porter's girlfriend's name?" I asked as we walked back over to the truck.

"Beth."

"The two of you used to be together?"

"A very, very long time ago. As in high school long ago."

"Ah, childhood sweethearts."

"I wouldn't go that far." Buck opened the door of the truck, and I climbed in. "Look, I know I was an ass-hole about Jinx and even about Cope, but believe me when I tell you there is nothing between Beth and me."

"As I said before, she'd like there to be."

He walked around and got in the driver's side. "In the same way Jinx would like there to be something between you and him."

It took less than five minutes to get from the dining hall to the main house. If the weather had been better, we could've walked, but the rain had started up again as hard as it had earlier.

"Did Flynn say where it was?" Buck asked when we raced in the front door.

"No, but my guess is that's it." I pointed to a box sitting on the counter.

"Shit," said Buck, putting his arm around my waist and pulling me back toward the door.

"What are you doing?"

"Wait in the truck, Stella."

"But—"

"*Go! Get inside the truck, now!* Call Rip and tell him to get his ass over here."

I raced through the rain and did what Buck asked. "Rip, um, there was a box sent to me. It's in the main house. Um, I think Buck wants you—"

"On my way."

In what seemed like seconds, Rip pulled up in an SUV. Ink and Press were with him.

I watched as they climbed out and raced inside. Moments later, Buck came out and got in the truck.

"What was that all about?" I asked.

"Suspicious package, Stella."

"And?"

"The guys are taking a look at it now."

"What should we do?"

"You and I are going back to the dining hall, where we're going to have dinner."

"I've lost my appetite, Buck."

"Wait until you get a whiff of Cord's brisket. You won't be able to resist."

I could see right through Buck's attempt at quelling my anxiety. Until I knew what was in that box, I doubted I'd be able to eat a single bite of anything.

We'd been back at the dining hall for a few minutes and were about to sit down with Cope and Ali when Rip, Ink, and Press walked in.

"False alarm," said Ink when we excused ourselves and walked over to him. "Nothing but a bunch of mail. Most of it looks like the junk variety."

"Oh." I hadn't given a thought to my mail. Someone must've had it forwarded to me.

"Nothing suspicious in it, boss," I heard Rip say to Buck. "We sorted through all of it. Like Ink said, most of it was junk mail."

"There was a card, though. The way it was addressed seemed odd, so we opened it." Ink pulled something out of his pocket and handed it to me. "See?" he said. "It's your address, right?"

I ran my fingers over what was written on the envelope Ink had handed me, immediately recognizing it as belonging to my aunt.

"You know anybody named Tiffany Joy?" Ink asked.

I looked up at Buck, praying he wouldn't make light of what I held in my hands.

"Excuse us," I heard him murmur. He took my hand in his and led me back out the door. The rain, thankfully, had eased up.

When I climbed inside the truck, I saw the box of mail sitting on the seat. Buck moved it to the other side of me. "Scoot over close to me," he said.

"Buck, I—"

"Shh." He put his hand across my lap and moved me closer to him.

By the time we got to the cabin, I was crying too hard to even see to get out of the truck. Buck lifted me in his arms and carried me inside, over to the sofa, and covered me with a blanket. "I'll be right back."

I heard him go out the door and come in seconds later. He set the box on the table and sat beside me.

"Thank you," I said as he gathered me in his arms.

"Is that from Barb?"

"Yes."

"What's inside?"

I pulled out the folded piece of paper and handed it to him.

"Have you read it?"

"I can't."

Buck unfolded it, cleared his throat, and read the words my aunt wrote.

> *Tiffany Joy haunts the streets of New York.*
> *Diamonds light the way down Fifth Avenue.*
> *Her reflection—elegant as a nymph*
> *Smiles back.*
> *The stars are her jewels, the night, her veil.*
> *Too soon, the party's over.*
> *Precious gems return to the vault.*
> *Six notes.*
> *A singular tune wafts*
> *From her small voice.*
> *My sweet Tiffany Joy.*

Buck set the note on the table, near the box, and held me while I cried. Other than the day I sobbed more out of guilt than mourning, I hadn't let myself break down. Now, I couldn't contain the grief that squeezed my heart. It poured out of me as though my body overflowed with it. This wasn't guilt; this was missing the woman who had raised me. She'd been there for me even before my mother died.

Before the scandal, before my aunt let fear keep her hidden away from the world, she and I had had such fun. Our favorite thing to do at night and in the dead of winter, was catch a cab and have the driver take us by the monuments in Washington—all lit up and free of crowds. If the weather was nice enough, we'd ask the driver to wait while we got out and read the inscriptions at the Lincoln Memorial.

Barb took me to London, Paris, and Rome among countless other places where I learned the history of the world. My curiosity developed then.

She was a good woman, whose only mission in life, besides raising me, had been to educate people about both the good and the bad. She alone was credited with changing the public perception of AIDS.

My aunt had looked too deep into the wrong thing, and it had cost her life. Was I doing the same thing? Should I accept that some stories shouldn't be written?

When my tears subsided, Buck reached for the note. "Does anything written in this mean anything to you?"

I took it from his hand and read it silently. "Nothing. And before you ask, TJ stands for Tiffany Joy or Tiffany Jackson. For a while, I think my mom might've even called me TJJ. Equally as ridiculous as my given name."

"It's a beautiful name." I looked into Buck's smiling eyes. "That I promise never to divulge to another soul."

"Thank you. And thanks for not making fun of me for it."

"My full name is Roscoe Buchtold Wheaton Jr. I have no business making fun of anyone for their name."

Buck picked up the envelope. "This was sent the day you found your aunt. Did she send anything like this in the past?"

I shook my head. "Which means she either had a premonition, or someone mailed it for her, like Decker suggested might happen."

"Someone who knew she was dead."

"Her attorney knew. Inexplicably."

"My guess is, this contains a message beyond what's apparent, Stella."

"I agree. Like her emails, it's only a matter of deciphering it."

"Two things stood out to me," Buck began. "First, the mention of a vault. Second, 'Six notes. A singular tune wafts from her small voice.'"

"What do you think it means?"

"Maybe an address."

"I guess I should start looking for a bank whose address begins with sixty-one."

29

Buck

Stella and I sorted through the remaining mail that had been forwarded to her. I'd held out hope until we came to the bottom of the pile that there'd be something either from Barb, her attorney, or even a bank statement that would give us a clue of the location of the safe-deposit box. There was nothing besides the note.

We'd just finished when I heard someone banging on the cabin door. When I rushed over to open it, Cope, Ali, and Irish hurried in.

"We've heard from Decker," Irish began. "Something went down in Ireland. He asked if we were all together, and I told him I'd let him know when we were." Irish tapped his phone several times and opened his laptop. Seconds later, Decker appeared on the screen.

"First of all, Byrne, along with three of his henchmen, is dead," he began. "There was a hostage situation that culminated in us eventually finding a box that held the evidence he was after."

"Which was?" asked Cope.

"Nothing that referenced Operation Argead or to link him to anyone from Interpol, past or present."

Cope looked as though he was about to speak again, but shut his mouth when the rest of us in the room glared at him.

"What we did learn is somewhat shocking. Do you all remember the reporter Veronica Guerin?"

"She and my aunt were friends," said Stella.

"Turns out she wasn't investigating drug gangs as was reported at the time. She was part of a task force working on exposing corruption within Irish Military Intelligence. The rest of the members of the unit, save three, were killed within a week of her death."

"What happened to the other three?"

"Irish?" said Decker.

"Special Agents Pierre Martin, Leon Schmidt, and Alan Perry."

I wasn't the least bit surprised Irish recalled the names of the agents murdered in La Chapelle-Saint-Maurice.

"The father of the agent I mentioned the other day, Siren Gallagher, was one of the men from the task force who was murdered. Byrne kept track of her all these years, thinking she might have evidence related to the crimes. Turns out, her mother, who passed away a few years ago, had it in a box that was supposed to be given to Siren but wasn't located until after Byrne's death."

Decker continued. "Stella, my contact in the Hays County Coroner's Office said the DC medical examiner is getting ready to release the death certificate. As soon as that happens, I think you should press to get a meeting scheduled with the attorney."

"I'll do that."

"Deck, Stella received something in the mail that was forwarded to her. It was a note from her aunt, sent the day Stella found her."

"What's in it?"

"We haven't been able to decipher its meaning."

"Send it to me. It'll give me something to do on the flight back."

"Roger that."

"Anything else I need to know before I get in the air?" Deck asked.

When no one spoke up, he ended the call.

"Can I see the note?" asked Irish.

I picked it up from the table and handed it to him.

"What's at 610 Fifth Avenue?"

I pulled out my phone. "Tiffany's flagship store."

"Right," he mumbled, continuing to stare at the note. He set it down and took a photo of it with his phone. "I'll send it to Deck."

When Irish left, saying he'd come back later, Cope and Ali said goodnight and left too.

"I'm sorry about dinner."

"Don't be."

"Are you hungry?"

I smiled. "Are you?"

"Starving."

"You said that earlier, didn't you? Let me see what I can rustle up." I got up to go to the kitchen and heard another knock. When I opened the door, all four of my siblings stood on the porch. "What are you doing here?"

"We brought food," said Flynn, pushing past me.

"You might want to ask if this is a good time," said Porter, walking in behind her.

"Ironically, we were just discussing how hungry we were," said Stella, walking over to join me.

"Best brisket ever," said Cord, carrying in a large platter covered in foil. "If I do say so myself."

"I don't bring much to this party other than my guitar," said Holt, trailing behind Cord.

"This is very sweet," Stella said, walking over to help Flynn uncover some of the other dishes.

"I'm sorry I forgot about your mail," I overheard my sister say.

It was probably for the best since, no matter what, I would've wanted the package checked out before Stella opened it.

"We were so busy in the kitchen; we didn't get the chance to eat much," said Porter, picking up a piece of brisket with his fingers. "Mind if we hang out and eat with you?"

I looked back over to where Stella and Flynn stood talking. "We'd love it," Stella answered after saying something to my sister that I didn't hear.

I couldn't remember the last time I sat down to a meal with my siblings and heard so much laughter. I also couldn't help but think a lot of it had to do with Stella.

She had the ability to draw each of them out. I felt as though I learned more about my brothers and sister tonight than I ever would have on my own.

Porter, for example, had far more interest in the roughstock business than running the dude ranch. That was Cord's and Flynn's passion.

Holt, on the other hand, hemmed and hawed until Stella asked him outright if his dream was to pursue a career in music.

"That leaves the rest of the ranch," I said, trying to make it sound like a joke, but failing miserably.

"Well, I could help," Holt said, looking directly at me.

"So could I," said Cord.

"Or course we'll all help," said Porter.

I looked from face to face, not having any idea what to say. Did they really think I intended to run the ranch?

"Buck?" said Stella, resting her hand on mine. "Did you tell them our plans to live in the farmhouse?"

"Really?" gasped Flynn.

"We've been talking about it," I mumbled.

Flynn jumped up and threw her arms around my neck. "I'm so happy," she said, kissing my cheek before moving over to Stella. "And there will be another woman in the family. This is the best news! See?" She looked at each of my brothers. "I knew everything would work out."

"Is everything okay?" Stella asked after my family left.

"Everything's fine. By the way, what were you and Flynn talking about before we sat down to eat?"

"Nothing really. I asked where Porter's date was, and she said she'd left shortly after we did. What else is bothering you?"

"Nothing."

She wrapped her arms around my waist. "No lying. Are you angry I told them about living in the farmhouse?"

"Definitely not. I'm glad you're excited about it."

"What is it, then?"

"They all just assume I'll take over the ranch."

"Well, yes, that was obvious."

"That was never my plan."

Stella pulled her shirt over her head, unfastened her bra, and tossed both on the floor.

"You know I can't think when you do that."

"I do," she said as she unfastened her jeans and stood before me naked. "No more thinking tonight. Let's make love, Buck."

30

Stella

"It's Jinx," I said, holding up my phone.

"Do you want me to give you some privacy?"

"God, no!"

Buck smiled, walked over, and took the phone from my hand. "Hey, Jinx, what can we do for you?" He hit the button so the call was on speaker.

"Uh, is TJ there?"

"I'm right here, Jinx."

"I wanted to give you an update on the partial print."

"And?" snapped Buck.

"I can't say definitively, but I believe the print may belong to Nicholas Kerr. The computer made the match."

I felt the bottom go out of my stomach. "Thanks, Jinx," I muttered. "Was there anything else?"

"No. I'll try to give you a call later."

"Code for 'when I'm out of hearing range,'" Buck said after the call ended.

"Don't be like that."

"Nothing against you, darlin'."

"Good."

"Busy morning," he said when my phone chimed again, this time with a call from Decker.

"Hi, Deck," I answered. "Buck is here. Okay to put the call on speaker?" I moved the phone from my ear and hit the button.

"Hi, Stella. Hi, Buck. I'll make this quick. I got word that both Barb's and Nancy's death certificates have been issued."

"Do you know the cause of death?"

"As we anticipated, gunshot wound for both. I'm getting ready to have the plane leave for Gunnison. Stella, if you can't get the attorney to respond to you, let me know, and I'll have Hammer intervene."

"Do you think he'll have better luck than I do?"

"Why do you think we call him Hammer? Keep me posted."

It took twenty-four hours before I got a response from the attorney. In that time, the plane sat at the Gunnison airfield. The pilots on standby had come to stay at the Roaring Fork, where Cord put them up in two of the more recently renovated cabins.

When the call finally came through and I was able to set a meeting for the following morning, I was grateful to have a private plane at my disposal.

"We have forty-eight hours to get in and out," said Buck after I hung up. "However, if for any reason you need to stay longer, we'll figure it out."

Within minutes, Irish, Cope, Ali, and the team of bodyguards were gathered in our cabin.

"Ink and Rock, you'll travel with us. The rest of you stay put."

"Buck?" said Rip. "You sure you don't want me to go too?"

"You're needed here."

"Copy that."

"In order to make the most of our time, we'll leave at twenty-three hundred hours. That'll put us on the East Coast at zero six hundred. Stella's appointment is at eleven hundred hours."

"Has he said anything about the location of the safe-deposit box?" asked Ali.

"He has not. What he said was he had a great deal to discuss with me regarding Barb's will. I'm hoping that's part of it."

"What about the death certificate?" asked Irish.

"Stella made arrangements for it to be overnighted directly to the attorney."

"Are you sure you don't want me or some of the other guys to travel with you?" Cope asked Buck.

"I'm sure. We don't need more targets to cover, and you'd be one."

"Copy that."

"If there's nothing else, we'll move out at twenty-three hundred. Thanks, everyone."

"We'll sleep on the plane," Buck said after I spent much of the time between everyone leaving and when Ink and Rock showed up to take us to Gunnison either pacing or on my laptop. "There's a stateroom we can use."

I doubted I'd be able to, but I had to at least try. I needed to have my wits about me when I met with the attorney, and in order for that to happen, I had to rest.

31

Buck

As I'd anticipated, Stella didn't get any sleep on the plane ride, and while we were checking into a hotel shortly after we landed, I doubted very much she'd sleep before meeting with the attorney.

After driving from JFK to Manhattan and checking in, we still had four hours to wait. As long as we got in and out of the lawyer's office quickly, were able to find the location of the safe-deposit box, and the bank granted Stella access, given she'd have a copy of the death certificate and the will with her, we'd be back in Colorado with time to spare.

"I hope this isn't just another fucking wild goose chase," I heard her mutter from the hotel room's bathroom.

I finished brushing my teeth and came out to find her standing by the window, looking out at the city. I stood behind her and massaged her shoulders.

"Why didn't I just take the fucking key that day? She could've told me which bank the box was in, and maybe she wouldn't be dead."

I didn't think it would have made any difference and doubted Stella did either. It wasn't necessary for me to say it, though.

"Come lie with me."

"Buck, I can't."

"Just for a few minutes."

I kicked off my boots and stretched out on the mattress. When Stella did the same, I gathered her in my arms.

"I'm sorry I'm being such a bitch."

"You aren't, darlin'. You're stressed, and you have every right to be."

"I couldn't do this without you."

"Might make me an asshole to say this, but I'm glad. I like being needed."

"I have a bad feeling."

I kissed her forehead. "It's understandable that you would."

"Why did she make this so difficult? Is this how she lived her entire life? I mean, in fear?"

"She may have, Stella, and with good reason."

"Why didn't she just tell me?"

"My guess is she was trying to protect you."

Stella's breathing evened out, and within minutes, she began to snore. Even if she could only sleep for a couple of hours, it would do her good.

"Wake up, sleepyhead," I said four hours later.

Stella sat up with a start. "Oh my God. I can't believe I fell asleep. What time is it?"

"We have forty-five minutes before we need to leave."

"I'm here to see Mr. Clark." said Stella when we walked into the lawyer's office.

"Right this way, miss," said the woman before turning to Rock, Ink, and me. "I'm sorry, gentlemen, you'll need to wait here."

Stella stopped mid-doorway. "They go where I go."

"Excuse me." The woman left us standing in the lobby. Within a couple of minutes, she came back. "You can all follow me," she snapped.

We were ushered into a conference room where a man stood at the end of the long table, reading a document.

"Mr. Clark, Miss Hunter has arrived."

When he looked over the top of his glasses at her, I wanted to take him by the arm and tell him to show Ms. Hunter the proper respect, given she was a client. However, we had one goal, and that was to get what we needed and be on our way as fast as possible.

Two minutes into his small talk, I cleared my throat.

"Right," said Stella, interrupting him. "We need to move along."

"Very well. Shall we start with—"

"My aunt's will."

"Of course. Um, Miss Hunter—"

"Call me Stella."

"Stella, I'd like to suggest you consider we have this conversation privately."

"Not necessary."

When Mr. Clark leaned closer to Stella, so did Ink, Rock, and I. He leaned back. "The financial aspects of your aunt's estate are…considerable."

Stella picked up her phone that sat face down on the table, glanced at the screen, and put it back where it had been. "Please get on with it. You're not our only appointment while we're in New York."

"Very well," he repeated, pulling a document out of the folder in front of him and sliding it toward her.

"What is this?" she asked.

"That is the amount of assets in the trust Ms. Hunter established in your name."

"This can't be right."

"I assure you that it is."

"Where did she get this kind of money?"

"I'm assuming your question is rhetorical."

Stella turned to me, wide-eyed and speechless. She slid the piece of paper toward me. When I saw the amount listed, I too was wide-eyed.

"Gentlemen," I looked up at Ink and Rock, neither of whom were seated. "Step out and close the door behind you."

"I don't understand," said Stella, turning back to the attorney.

"From what I read in my colleague's files, your aunt inherited money from her mother, your grandmother." He rifled through the papers in the file. "Here it is. Ten million dollars, plus the ongoing income that came from your grandmother's films."

"But this says two-hundred million."

"It appears your aunt had an astute financial planner. She did live off of a portion of the income, but most, she reinvested."

"There's something I don't understand. You said my aunt inherited this money from her mother. What about my mother? Nothing was left to her?"

"I do remember seeing something about that in the notes. One moment." He flipped through several more papers. "Here it is. The trust allowed for your aunt to support your mother, and subsequently you, throughout her lifetime, but no money was left to her directly."

"Does it say why not?"

"Only that your mother forfeited her direct inheritance to her sister."

Stella rolled one shoulder and then the other. "I have reason to believe my aunt left certain things in a safe-deposit box. Do you have information about that specifically?"

"I don't recall anything about a safe-deposit box." He sifted through more of the document and shook his head. "This is where that information would be, and there is nothing listed."

"You're certain?"

"Quite." He handed Stella a thick envelope. "This is your copy. I encourage you to read it in its entirety. I'm not saying it doesn't contain the information you're looking for, only that it isn't where it should be."

"Death certificate?" I whispered in Stella's ear.

"Right," she said. "May I have the copy of my aunt's death certificate?"

The man cocked his head. "I don't have a copy."

"What do you mean? I requested it be delivered to you."

"Excuse me."

When he stood and left the conference room, Stella leaned forward and put her head in her hands.

"You okay?" I asked, rubbing her shoulder.

She turned her head toward me, and instead of crying, which I'd feared, she was laughing.

"Two hundred fucking million dollars?" she whispered before picking up her phone. "We need to get out of here. We've already been here an hour."

"We're okay." I counted down. With the time change, we still had thirty-eight hours before I had to be back at the ranch.

"I am not in receipt of the death certificate," the attorney said, coming back in and closing the door behind him. "Your best bet is to request that it be sent directly to you from the medical examiner in Washington, DC."

"Is there anything else you need to go over with Ms. Hunter at this time?"

"I don't believe so. Again, my apologies for the delays in scheduling the meeting. As you can imagine, everyone at the firm was shocked and devastated by our colleague's passing."

I stood and helped Stella with her chair. Not being able to get our hands on the death certificate presented a problem we'd need to figure out.

"What do we do now?" Stella asked when we left the same way we'd come in, through the shipping and receiving dock. Given Barb's attorney had been murdered right outside this building, I wasn't taking any chances.

"Maybe we should cut this trip short," she said when Rock pulled the SUV up near the exit and we climbed inside.

"We still have time. Let's figure this out."

"I contacted Deck," said Rock. "The plane is ready and waiting. My understanding is a flight plan has already been filed."

"How long is the flight?" I asked.

"A little over an hour."

"What kind of arrangements do we need to make with the medical examiner?"

"Decker is already taking care of it."

"We can do it," I told Stella. "There's time."

"But we don't even know which bank the box is at."

I patted the envelope. "Better start reading."

32

Stella

"We should just go back to Colorado now," I said a few minutes later.

"Nope. We're here; let's see it through."

"What's the point, Buck? I don't know where the fucking safe-deposit box is," I repeated.

"Rock, do you know if Barb's place has been cleared as a crime scene yet?" Buck asked.

"No, but I can find out."

"If it has, see who else Decker can pull in to help start a search."

"I'm no genius, but what about the bank where the trust is located?" said Ink from the front passenger seat.

"What did you say?" I asked.

"That's what the lawyer said before Buck asked us to step out, right? That your aunt left money for you in a trust?"

"What is wrong with me?" I mumbled, pulling the bound document out of the envelope. I put my hand on

Buck's arm. "Will you give me a job when I hand in my press credentials?"

"Why would you do that?"

"I'm not exactly what one would consider an investigative reporter anymore." I rested my head against the back of the seat. "I mean, Jesus. That's so obvious."

"Hold on a minute. This is Barb, who sends you cryptic emails and notes. I doubt very much that Ink is right. The last thing she'd do is something obvious."

I put my hand on my heart. "Thanks, Buck. You're right. I feel slightly better."

"Rock, my directive stands," said Buck. "See if Deck can get someone started on the search of Barb's apartment. We'll head over as soon as we've picked up the death certificate."

"Roger that."

Four and a half hours later, we were headed to Barb's apartment, death certificate in hand. So far, everything had taken twice as long to do as I'd anticipated it would.

When we walked through the door, there were two men I didn't recognize, sifting through my aunt's belongings.

"You okay?" Buck asked. "I can ask everyone to step out for a minute."

"I'd appreciate that. Thank you."

Buck walked everyone to the door. "Do you want me to wait with the guys?" he asked with his hand still on the doorknob.

"Just for a few minutes. You don't mind, do you?"

He shook his head and smiled. "I'd do anything for you, Stella. Don't you know that?"

"Thank you, Buck." I blew him a kiss.

"I'll be right on the other side of this door if you need me."

I turned back around and heard the door close. I had to hand it to Jinx. He and his crew did a good job of putting this place back together. The last time I saw it, it had been ransacked. Now, it looked much like it had the day I walked out on Barb never to see her alive again.

Now that I was in here alone, I wasn't sure I wanted to be. Too many memories flooded my brain. When my eyes filled with tears, I had to stop myself from running to the door and begging Buck to stay in here with me.

I walked over and opened the lid of the piano, running my fingers over the keys. This damn piano. Never once had I heard her play it. Nor did she ever suggest I take lessons. Why did she even have it? There were plenty of other places she could've hidden a key, a note, anything.

Where would she have? I turned in a circle, surveying the room I was in. The possibilities in here alone were endless. I walked back over to where I'd left the envelope containing her will. I thumbed through it, looking for the name of the bank that held the trust.

I almost laughed out loud when I found it. *Key Bank.* Barb was nothing if not ironic. I pulled out my phone and checked the time. It was a few minutes past five-thirty. Too late to call the local branch to see what they could tell me. It would be better to show up in person in the morning anyway.

I walked over and opened the door. Buck was leaning against the wall right outside of it.

"Changed my mind."

"Yeah?"

"Yeah. I have a different idea of what we should be looking for. Several other ideas, in fact."

The more I thought about Barb and what I knew about her, the more I knew we should be looking for the least obvious rather than the most. Like Buck said, she'd never settle for prosaic. Case in point—her note.

"Stella, this is Bronson Dunning. We call him Vex," said Buck.

"Nice to meet you."

"And this is Smith Lavery."

"The pilot?"

"Figured we should let him earn his keep rather than let him hang out in the stateroom, watching porn, and eating junk food."

"Fuck off," he muttered at Buck. "Nice to meet you again, Stella."

"Wait a minute. Everyone else has an aka. What's yours?"

"You don't want to know," said Vex, laughing.

"C'mon. Tell me."

Smith had long hair like Buck but didn't keep it tied back. When he looked over at me, it covered part of his eyes. "They call me Crash."

I laughed out loud. "You're joking."

"Afraid not."

"That's horrible."

"Tell me about it."

"Okay, where should we start?" asked Buck.

"Someone should start going through her books. Check for dog-eared pages, notes of any kind, either written in them or loose. After that, start with the least obvious place you think someone might leave a clue, and work your way to the most obvious."

I got sidetracked when I found Barb's photo albums. I couldn't remember how long it had been since I'd cracked one open. I ran my finger over the picture of my mom and me, taken not long after she was diagnosed. She still looked perfectly healthy. No one would've ever guessed the havoc the disease would wreak on her body in the years that followed.

"Is that your mom?" Buck asked, looking over my shoulder.

"It is."

"You look like her."

I'd never thought so before, but now I could see the resemblance.

"I'm sorry to interrupt, darlin', but Vex found something I think you should see."

"Okay." I closed the album, put it back in the bookcase, and followed Buck down the hallway to Nancy's bedroom.

"What in the world?" I stepped in and walked over to the bed. "What is all this?"

"Bank statements."

"Where were they? In the mattress?"

"Under it, yeah."

"What made you look there?"

"Usually the first place a novice hides something. That and under a dresser drawer."

I sat on the edge of the bed and looked at one Vex handed me. "These amounts are staggering. Barb couldn't have been paying her that much."

"I doubt she was. I also found this." Vex handed me a photo.

"Jesus fucking Christ." I was tempted to rip the thing into pieces.

"Who is that?" Buck asked.

"This is Nancy," I said, pointing at a younger version of my aunt's housekeeper then at the young woman standing next to her. "And that is Sally Hennessey."

"Now we're getting somewhere," said Buck, rubbing his hands together.

When we left Barb's apartment a few hours later, I didn't have much more than when we arrived, other than circumstantial evidence suggesting that Nancy was being paid to spy on my aunt for years.

"You wanna head back to your place? I think it would be safe to at this point since we know who we're looking for. Or, I could book a hotel room if you'd feel more comfortable."

"My place. Definitely. If you think it's okay."

Bucked nodded and broke out into a wide smile.

"What?"

He stepped closer and nuzzled against my ear. "You wanna know how many fantasies I've had about sleeping in your bed, Stella? Thousands. Literally."

"We've been here almost twenty-four hours, Buck," I said on the way from Barb's place to mine.

"We left the ranch at twenty-three hundred Colorado time, so we've actually only burned a little over twenty hours. As long as we're in the air by six tomorrow night, East Coast time, we'll be fine. It even gives us a buffer."

"What if something goes wrong?"

"We've got support here with us, Stella. If anything goes wrong, we'll fix it."

Despite all his unfulfilled fantasies about sharing my bed, the only thing Buck did was hold me until I fell asleep. Perhaps he somehow sensed that was what I needed more than anything else.

It was rare I woke before him, but since I had, I took the opportunity to study the features of his face. I'd never seen Buck without a beard but would bet he had the quintessential baby face.

Every moment I spent with him, I loved him more. I had no idea what our future held other than I wanted to spend as much of it with Buck as I could.

"You're awake," he said, propping himself up on his elbows. "Everything okay?"

"I was just thinking how much I love you."

Buck pulled me into him so my breasts pressed against his chest. "That's about the nicest thing that's ever been said to me right when I woke up."

"We have so much to do today."

Buck ran his finger over my furrowed brow. "We'll get as much as we can done."

"I just thought of something."

"What's that?"

"Did anyone search the piano last night?"

"I don't think so, but I'll ask."

"How could I have forgotten to look inside the piano?"

"Hang on," he said, typing something into his phone. A few seconds later, he received a reply. "Rock says he doesn't think anyone did, but he's sending Vex and Ink over there now."

Buck got out of bed and pulled me with him. "Which first? Coffee or a shower?"

"You *are* a heathen. Coffee before anything."

"Even making love?"

"You didn't put that on the table."

"What do you think I planned to do in the shower?"

"Sorry to be less than romantic, but I still have to go with coffee."

After coffee, sex, and a shower, I called the Key Bank location where the trust was held. As I could've predicted, they reported there were no safe-deposit boxes in either my aunt's name or in the name of the trust. I was getting ready to call other nearby branches when Buck walked in and handed me his phone.

"I knew it!" I said, zooming in on the business card that, according to Ink, had been taped under the tenth and eleventh keys from the left. "Oh, no."

"What?" Buck asked.

"This branch is in Manhattan."

"I'll call Crash…err…Smith and ask him to file a flight plan as soon as possible. In the meantime, is there anything from here you want to take back to the ranch with you?"

"Um…I guess I could pack a few more clothes."

"Not necessary on my account. I'd vote for no clothes as often as possible."

"I really have everything I need there."

"And if we need more, we can always arrange another shopping trip."

"Shopping trip or a fashion show?"

"The second is a given."

I put my arms around Buck's neck. "Thank you for keeping me distracted."

"Is that a good thing?"

"Definitely."

His cell buzzed, and I saw it was a call from Smith.

"The earliest I could get was ten," I heard him say. I checked the time on my own phone. We should still be fine since we finally knew where the safe-deposit box was. At least, I hoped that's what finding the card in the piano meant. I walked a few feet from where Buck was still talking to the pilot and called the number on the business card.

It took me a few minutes and several transfers to reach the right person. "Please send a copy of the will, the trust documents, and the death certificate to me. Once I've reviewed them and confirmed everything is in order, I can approve access to the vault."

"We're flying to New York from DC in about an hour. How long will it take you to verify what I send?"

"A week to ten days."

"I need this to happen much sooner. I'm here from Colorado and—"

"The best I can do is sometime tomorrow."

"What about with a warrant?" Buck asked from behind me. "How soon can you make it happen, then?"

I held the phone away from my ear so he could hear the gentleman's response. "Depending on when I receive it, I may be able to arrange access for this afternoon."

"We'll be there no later than one o'clock."

"Sir, I—"

Buck hit the button to end the call. "Contact Jinx. Tell him you need a warrant in the next hour."

"What if he can't get it?"

"He'll get it."

Jinx said he'd do his best and would meet us at the airfield.

"Can someone who isn't in law enforcement serve a warrant?"

When Buck grinned, I didn't ask any further.

It was ten minutes after ten, and I was just about to give up and tell Buck we needed to leave without it when a black SUV pulled onto the tarmac.

"Where the hell is he?" asked Buck, walking up and putting his arm around my shoulders.

I didn't bother responding. "When did the weather turn so nasty?" I asked, realizing the sky had darkened and it was starting to rain.

"Seems like in the last couple of minutes."

At the same time Jinx walked up the airstairs, Smith came out of the cockpit.

"Bad news," he said, looking from Jinx to us. "We're on a weather delay. Nasty storm has everything grounded. Here and in New York."

"For how long?"

"They aren't saying."

"Buck, let's just go back to Colorado instead of going to New York."

"Let's not make a decision just yet. We still have plenty of time to get to New York." He took a step forward and held out his hand to shake Jinx's. "Thanks for getting this to us so fast. You didn't have to deliver it yourself."

"I didn't want there to be any kind of holdup," Jinx said, looking from Buck to me.

Buck ducked down and looked out the window. "Looks like a holdup is exactly what we got."

33

Buck

I knew exactly why Jinx had hand delivered the goddamn warrant and made sure he knew what was what from the minute he arrived. I also knew from the smirk on Stella's face that she was aware of what I was doing.

From the minute he'd stepped into the cabin until he was halfway down the airstairs, I had my hands somewhere on Stella's body. If he so much as tried to shake her hand, I would've gotten between them and throat punched the *sonuvabitch*.

Well, maybe I would've stopped short of punching him just for shaking her hand, but if he tried to kiss her like he had the last time we were all together, I'd straight out kill him.

I wanted to ask Crash when the airport closed, but if it had during the time we were waiting for Jinx, that would only make Stella feel bad.

It was the same with me getting back to Colorado. I was worried about how much time we were burning, but I'd never let on to Stella how much.

We needed to get whatever was in the safe-deposit box, be on our way, and put this damn mission to bed once and for all. I intended to stay until the very last minute I could in order to get this part of the investigation over with.

"If this is anything like the storm we had in Crested Butte a few days ago, it might be hours before it lets up enough for us to take off," said Rock.

"It isn't like that storm," said Crash. "It *is* that storm."

"Does it look like it's picked up any speed?"

"Negative."

There wasn't a person on the plane not watching the minutes tick by while, at the same time, watching weather reports.

According to local news, the storm hadn't picked up speed as it traveled across the country but it had strengthened. Estimates were that fifty thousand homes were without power, and flood watches were in effect throughout the district.

On a national level, the path of the storm was predicted to hit hardest in New York City.

"We need to get back to Colorado," Stella said again. I'd lost track of how many times she had.

"We can't go anywhere at this point. When the weather lets up and we're cleared for take-off, we'll reevaluate."

At fourteen hundred hours, almost on the dot, Crash announced the airport was reopening and we were tenth in line for take-off. We could still do this. One hour in the air, thirty minutes max to the bank. Another thirty max to collect the contents of the safe-deposit box. Then, head back to the airport and fly to Gunnison and be back at the ranch with two hours to spare. Maybe even more than that.

Before Crash went back into the cockpit after making his announcement, Stella stood and put her hand on his arm. "I'm asking you not to fly to New York. I'm the lead on this investigation, and I'm ordering you to fly to Gunnison instead."

Smith looked from Stella to me and then back. "I'm sorry, ma'am, but I have to fly to the private airfield at JFK. That's the plan I filed. If I change it now, we might have to wait until tomorrow to get another take-off slot."

"What about when we land? How soon can we take off again?"

"I'll have Vex submit a flight plan now."

"Thank you." Stella sat down beside me. "Don't you dare say a word."

Once we were in the air, Vex came out of the cockpit. "The best we could get is an eighteen hundred departure."

Stella's eyes opened wide.

"That'll give us plenty of time to get to the bank and back to the plane."

"It's cutting it too close."

I motioned to Vex to walk away. When he did, I turned to Stella and cupped her cheek. "If we leave JFK at six, that's four in Colorado. We'll land at eight or eight-thirty mountain time and be back at the ranch an hour later."

"It's too close," she repeated.

"It's the best we can do regardless, Stella. You heard Vex."

"We never should've come."

"We're within hours of finding out what's in Barb's safe-deposit box. You aren't the only person waiting to discover its contents. Remember that. Every day we wait—hell, every hour—means there are more agents out there in danger of losing their lives. The worst part, Stella, is we don't know why. We have to see this through. If your aunt left behind any evidence regarding Operation Argead that could put an end to this bloodbath, we have an obligation to find it." I laid it on heavy, but Stella needed to hear what I had to say. Barb's death was only one of many that deserved justice and for those who killed them to pay for their crimes.

"I'm sorry," she whispered.

"Don't be sorry, darlin', see it through. Let's finish this."

"Buck?"

"Yeah?"

"You understand I was only trying to protect your family?"

"Of course I do, as long as you understand what I'm trying to protect goes way beyond a ranch."

She was quiet for the rest of the flight, and so was I. Driving home the point to Stella about what was on the line, struck me right in the heart too.

Shortly after we landed and were waiting for Vex to open the aircraft's door, Crash came out of the cockpit instead. "Have a seat."

"What's going on, Lavery?"

He ran his hand through his hair. "We have one hour, Buck."

"What do you mean?"

"I got word from air traffic. They're predicting the airport will close at six hundred hours at the latest. I called in a favor and got a slot in one hour."

"That isn't enough time to get to the bank and back, let alone the time we'd need there." I turned to Stella. "I'm sorry. We'll have to come back."

"No."

"What do you mean?" I repeated the same words I'd said to Crash.

"I have to do this, Buck. You said it yourself. It isn't just me who needs to know what evidence Barb had. Every day that goes by, is another day that someone could die. I can't live with that."

"We'll fly to Colorado, I'll set foot on the ranch, and we'll turn around and come right back."

"It won't be that simple, Buck," said Crash. "The airfield might not open right away, and when it does, it may take a day or two to get a flight plan approved."

"I'll go to the bank, empty the safe-deposit box, head back to the airport, and catch the next flight I can, even if it's to Denver."

"No."

Stella's eyes met mine. "With all due respect, Buck, this isn't your decision."

I looked up at Rock and Ink, who were listening to the conversation.

"We'll keep her safe, Buck," said Rock. "You trusted me before to watch over her."

"Give us a minute," Stella said to the guys gathered around our seats. When they walked away, she looked into my eyes. "I'm not asking your permission, Buck, but I would like your blessing."

"If anything happens to you—"

"Rock and Ink will make sure nothing does. You know that."

"My gut is telling me not to let you do this."

Stella shook her head. "My gut is telling me I have to."

"You're armed, correct?"

"I'm never not armed, Buck."

"Never?"

Her cheeks flushed pink, and I winked.

Five minutes and that many heart-wrenching, soul-crushing, I'll-love-you-forever, deep kisses later, I watched Rock and Ink escort Stella off the plane.

The hardest thing I'd ever done was ignore the war waging inside me that said to stop her from leaving. Stella said her gut was telling her she had to, and that, I had to respect.

34

Stella

I wasn't exactly honest with Buck. My gut was screaming at me, but not that I should do this without him. Instead, it was that I needed him beside me, now and every minute for the rest of my life.

I had to ignore it, though. I'd lived on my own a long damn time, fending for myself, doing what needed to be done to get the story. I'd put myself in danger more times than I could count. Taking a cab to a bank, walking into a vault, and peering into a safe-deposit box, no matter what it held, wasn't scary. Taking a cab back to the airport and catching a commercial flight to Colorado wasn't scary either.

I looked behind me. "Hey, Rock?"

"Yeah?"

"Are you and Ink still considered commissioned law enforcement officers?"

"Absolutely. Why?"

I patted the gun that was concealed under my arm. "I've gotten used to flying private."

Both men laughed.

"You got a locked case for that firearm, ma'am?" asked Rock.

"Um, not with me."

"Not a problem."

"Is being an LEO why you can serve the warrant too?"

"Yep."

"And here I thought you were going to pull some sneaky spy thing instead."

The cab ride from the airfield to the bank took twice as long as I expected it to with all of the rain.

Getting ready to take off? I texted Buck.

Negative. Delayed. Lightning within three miles. At the bank?

Just pulling up. I love you, Buck.

Update me when you're in the vault.

And?

I love you, Stella.

"The flight is delayed due to lightning," I said.

Rock looked over at me from the front seat. "If it continues, we may make it back to the airport in time to fly private."

I wouldn't say so now, but something told me that wouldn't be happening. That feeling only intensified when the man I was instructed to see kept me waiting for almost fifteen minutes.

Still waiting for the fucking bank guy, I texted Buck.

Have Ink go breathe down someone's neck, he replied.

Taking off soon?

No word. I love you, Stella.

I think the asshole is on his way now.

And?

I love you, Buck.

After the fuss the bank manager—I learned when he introduced himself—had made on the phone, getting me into the vault was nothing more than a formality involving him looking at my copy of the death certificate, the will, and the warrant. The latter of which appeared unnecessary once I showed him my identification and he reviewed the first two documents.

"Cutting it kind of close, aren't you?" I said, pointed at the time on my phone; it was almost five.

"This branch doesn't close until six."

I couldn't help but resent him for the time we'd wasted. Both Buck and I could be on our way back to Colorado by now if he hadn't pulled a fucking power trip.

"Gentlemen, you'll need to wait out here," he said when Rock and Ink tried to follow me into the vault.

"Is there another way in or out?" I asked.

"Of course there isn't," the asshole answered.

I turned to my two bodyguards. "I'll be fine."

"We'll be right here," said Ink, taking a step closer to the bank manager, who hurriedly opened the vault and escorted me inside.

"Here it is," he said, pointing to the number on the box that matched the key. "Would you like a privacy room?" He motioned to a door.

"That won't be necessary. I'll just take the contents and be on my way." I opened the lid of the box and pulled out an envelope that felt almost empty. My stomach sunk when I peeked inside and saw all it contained was a small, distinctly blue bag. "Fucking Barb," I mumbled under my breath.

"Everything okay?" he asked as I folded the envelope.

"I'll need that privacy room after all."

In the vault, and you are not going to believe this, I texted Buck once I was inside the room, pulled the blue bag out, and discovered all it contained was another key.

There was an immediate response that the message could not be delivered. That had to mean either I didn't have a signal where I was in the bank or Buck's plane had already taken off.

I tucked the Tiffany bag inside my tank, next to my gun, then folded the manila envelope it had been in, and put it in the pocket of my jeans. I signaled the manager that I was ready to leave and walked over to where Rock and Ink waited.

"Everything go okay?" Rock asked.

I shook my head, but only enough for him to notice. "Let's get out of here." We were about to exit through the revolving door when I pulled out my phone. My message had gone through to Buck, but he hadn't responded yet.

Just as I stepped out onto the sidewalk, my phone pinged. I pulled it out and was about to tap my passcode in when I felt something jab into my side. I raised my head and saw five men, all dressed in black tactical gear reading NYPD. I immediately heard two simultaneous shots fired and watched both Ink and Rock fall to the ground as two of the men led me away.

We rounded a corner, and a black bag went over my head. My phone fell out of my hand when one of the men tossed me over his shoulder.

A few seconds later, I was placed inside a vehicle that sped away as soon as I heard the door close.

35

Buck

I pulled my phone out when I heard an alert that I'd received a text. *In the vault, and you are not going to believe this,* it read. I tried to call Stella and then Ink, but when neither answered, I called Rock.

He answered right away, but all I could hear was rustling. "Rock, are you there?" I shouted.

"Officers down," he wheezed. *"They got Stella."*

"No!" The cry involuntarily escaped my lips; Crash and Vex raced out from the cockpit. *"Send a bus, two officers down!"* I shouted. "Help is on the way, Rock. Hold on."

I raced out the plane's door and down the airstairs. The other two men were right behind me.

"What's going on?" asked Vex at the same time I heard Crash calling for transport.

"Rock and Ink are both down. Someone has Stella."

My worst nightmare had come to life. Someone had Stella, and without her phone, I had no way to track her.

36

Stella

I recognized the man sitting in front of me the minute the bag was removed from my head. Nicholas Kerr had aged since the last photo I'd seen of him was taken.

"Leave us," he said to the two men on either side of me.

"You sure you don't want us to stay, boss?" asked the man to my left in an English accent similar to Kerr's.

"I said leave us," he bellowed.

As if I'd pressed play on a soundtrack, Burns' words began to repeat inside my head.

"If you find yourself in Kerr's presence, play to his arrogance above all else. He's a misogynistic narcissist who will not consider you the least bit of a threat."

I expected Kerr to get up, but he didn't. Instead, he motioned for me to sit in the chair opposite the desk he sat behind. I ignored him and folded my arms, incredulous that the assholes who had delivered me to him hadn't frisked me.

"Sit!" he shouted, standing and slamming his hands on the desk in front of him. He'd startled me and caught my reaction. He smiled, shook his head, and sat down. "Tiffany Joy, at last we meet."

I sneered but didn't respond.

"So much like your aunt. You're weak like she was. Your only power is in your pen. Otherwise, you are mute."

"You didn't know her very well, and you don't know me at all."

He smiled like he had when he startled me. "Ah, she does have a voice, but where is the reporter, eh? Are you too afraid I'll kill you to ask me any questions?"

"You're going to kill me whether I ask or not, just like you did Barb and Nancy."

He shrugged. "Yes, well, that is probably true."

"Does your wife know you killed her aunt like you did mine?"

He nodded slowly. "She knows I had no choice."

Burns' voice was back in my head. *"He'll want to brag, show you how powerful and almighty he is. He sees himself as a descendant of the Argead Dynasty—like Alexander the Great before him—he'll want you to know that no one has defeated him."*

"All those years, she bested you."

His eyes scrunched. "She did nothing of the kind."

"You had no idea where the evidence was, not until Nancy overheard Barb tell me about the safe-deposit box."

"You see patience as failure; that is your problem. You rush, so anxious to have the scoop that, in your haste, you miss the real story."

"Enlighten me, then. What *is* the real story?"

He sat back in his chair. "People like you believe you can expose the injustices of the world, sit on your high horse, and damn those who, for years, have fought for your freedom. You, Barb, the rest of the media, none of you understand how the real world works."

"I'm sure you're going to take the opportunity to tell me."

"I often wondered what Barb saw in you that she believed was worth saving. That's what it was all about, you know? It wasn't her own life she wanted to protect. It was yours."

"What do you mean?"

"The bargain she made with me. As long as you were left alone—left alive—she would not release the evidence she claimed she had on Operation Argead."

"Why did you kill her, then, and not me?"

"Once I knew it truly existed, it was only a matter of time until you led me to it. Unfortunately for Nancy, she couldn't produce the key. All she had for me when I arrived at the apartment was that you'd taken it with you. From that moment on, there was no need to keep either woman alive."

"You shot them."

He shrugged again as though the statement meant nothing to him. "As I said, it was only a matter of time before you led me to it. Once I left the apartment, I called your aunt's attorney to inform him of her death. I anticipated that within hours, I would have the evidence in hand that you now possess, and would be on my way back to England. But you made me wait, didn't you?"

"What was it you said about patience being a virtue?"

He smirked. "That isn't what I said at all. If you'd been listening, you would've heard me say it was people like you who see it as a failure."

"People like me." I smirked like he had. "If not a virtue, how do people like you see it?"

"Your aunt believed she could take on the world, that once she exposed the corruption she thought she'd found, that would be the end of it. What she—and you—and people like Veronica Guerin failed to recognize was that it is the very corruption they railed against that keeps the world spinning. Bribes, power plays, deals negotiated in back alleys, that is how it really works. You see world leaders on television, shaking hands as they sign agreements, flashbulbs going off around them—all of that is for show. The real deals were made months, even years, before the stage is set for the public to see. In that time, those who threaten to tear down the carefully mastered plans of men like me, are eliminated."

"Eliminated? As in agents around the world being assassinated?"

"You are so sure they were the good and I am evil. Your naivete is so common, so typical. Without men like me, you would be nothing."

"Because I'm a woman?"

"Because you're a stupid woman."

"You say that men like you are the real deal makers. Is that how you justify lining your pockets with millions of dollars? You say that all you do is for the greater good, but when your day of reckoning comes, you know as well as I do that you were nothing but a thief. A common criminal. A murderer who only ever knew how to steal, never how to earn your way in the world."

"So like her," he murmured, making me want to slap the smirk off his face. "What your aunt found was merely the tip of the iceberg, Tiffany Joy. As if anyone in the world truly cares what goes on at Interpol. It serves merely as a clearinghouse for those of us in the intelligence business to burn evidence before it lands in the hands of someone like Barb. Or you."

"Are you saying Operation Argead goes beyond Interpol?"

He laughed. "I'm saying that without the voluntary contributions that come through Interpol and countless other organizations like it, the intelligence community, even entire governments, would crumble with lack of funding. No, little girl, our reach is global. Even the most powerful countries—the United States, Russia, China—all rely on Argead. Without us, they would be nothing."

"Sounds like you've let a little power go to your head. You can't really believe that you and your little group of intelligence has-beens truly affect world governments."

He sighed. "As I anticipated, this is all too much for your small mind to comprehend. I've grown weary of your tedium. Hand over the evidence now so I don't have to dirty my hands with your blood in order to retrieve it."

Kerr reached for something I had no doubt was a gun, but was distracted by the sound of shots fired outside the room we were in.

"You know what? Fuck it," I said, reaching for my own gun.

37

Buck

I tracked Rock's location to right outside the Key Bank branch that held Barb's safe-deposit box. By the time we arrived, paramedics were already on the scene, and even from a distance, I could see both Ink and Rock were sitting up, talking to NYPD.

When Crash pulled up to the barricade, he, Vex, and I jumped out of the car.

Two police officers raced toward us to prevent us from entering. "They're with me. Let 'em through," I heard a familiar voice say. What the fuck was Jinx doing here?

"Here," he said, tossing me a phone. "Follow me."

"What the fuck? What is this?" I asked, looking down at the flashing red dot on what looked like a radar screen as I ran in the same direction he had.

"I knew you wouldn't be able to keep her safe."

"Like you did?"

"At least I know how to find her."

"The warrant," I mumbled, racing after him.

"In here," he shouted. I looked behind us and saw Crash and Vex right on our heels. Rock and Ink were a few feet back.

"What are the extent of their injuries?" I shouted at Crash. We sure as hell didn't need the two of them bleeding out while we went in search of Stella.

"Nothing life-threatening," Vex shouted back.

"Buck, you take the stairs with Crash," shouted Jinx, pointing at me. "Vex, you come with me." When he went in the direction of the elevator, I pushed him out of the way. The door closed before he could get to his feet and get inside.

"Fucking old man," muttered Crash as I watched the red dot on the screen increasing in size.

When the dot got significantly bigger, I hit the button for the seventh floor. I held Crash back before he raced out, easing myself far enough that I could see four men standing guard in the hallway. When I saw the stairwell door open behind them, I fired, hitting one before ducking back into the elevator.

"We're clear," I heard Vex shout after hearing three more shots fired. I was almost to the door where the four men lay when I heard a single shot go off from inside. I hurled my body against the door and raced inside.

"Hold your fire," I heard Stella's sweet voice say as I watched her blow away the smoke from the barrel of her Smith and Wesson Shield. "I always wanted to do that." She lowered her gun and set it down.

"Kerr?" I asked, pointing to the body slumped over the desk.

"None other."

I kicked Kerr's gun that lay on the floor farther away and checked for a pulse. "He's dead."

Stella smiled. "I could've told you that."

"But we aren't," said Ink, rushing in the room followed by Rock.

"Thank God," Stella said, rushing over to them at the same time two more men came through the door. "Jinx? What are you doing here?"

38

Stella

I expected the adrenaline crash, just not as hard or as fast as it happened. Fatigue set in so quickly, I felt like I might pass out. Along with it, came nausea.

"Let's get you out of here," said Buck, putting his arm behind my knees, lifting, and carrying me out of the room. There were police everywhere in what I now realized was the hallway of a hotel.

"In here," said Jinx, holding a door open for us. Buck carried me over to a sofa in the suite and sat down with me still in his arms.

"Give us a minute," he said to Jinx, who walked out, closing the door behind him.

"I have so many questions," I said.

"Me too," said Buck. "But first, I need to kiss you."

He brought his lips to mine, soft at first, but within moments, the kiss turned frenzied. "I was so fucking scared," he whispered, resting his forehead against mine.

"Buck! Oh my God. What are you doing here?"

"Do you really think I'd just fly back to Colorado when you were in danger? Or that Crash would?"

"But…the ranch!"

"I don't give a shit about the ranch, Stella."

"But…Flynn and your brothers!"

"I made one phone call on the way from the plane here. It was to Hammer. I told him you'd been kidnapped and that I wasn't leaving New York until you were safe and in my arms."

"Did he tell you you were crazy?"

Buck shook his head. "He told me he'd take care of it."

"What does that mean?"

"I don't know, and what's more, I don't care." He kissed me again. "I love you, Stella."

"I love you, Buck." Something occurred to me. "Hey, how much did Decker say the Roaring Fork would sell for?"

"I don't know. Fifty million maybe?"

"If I bought it, I'd still have a hundred and fifty mil left."

"Right." He laughed and leaned forward to kiss me again.

"I'm serious."

"First of all, you're delirious. Second, there's no way in hell I'd let you do that."

"Just like there was no way in hell you'd let me go to the bank on my own?"

"I don't think those were my exact words."

"Even if they weren't, it's what you meant."

"Speaking of the bank, I got your message. What did you mean when you said I wasn't going to believe it?"

I reached under my shirt, pulled the blue Tiffany bag out, and handed it to him. "Sorry, it's a little sweaty."

He laughed and opened it, looking up at the ceiling when he saw what was inside. "Another key? You've got to be kidding me."

"Can you imagine how pissed Kerr would've been if he'd killed me and then realized this was all he got for it?"

The look on Buck's face changed. "Don't make jokes about it, Stella."

I put my hands on either side of his face. "Okay, I won't." I kissed him and then pulled back. "But seriously, can you imagine?"

"What do you mean you know what the key is for?" Buck asked two hours later when we were in the air on our way to Gunnison, Colorado.

"This one was easy to figure out."

"I'm waiting."

"The key is to a storage locker."

"Where?"

"Tiffany's."

"They have storage lockers at Tiffany's?"

"They used to. I mean, they still do, but only for people who have had them for years. Families are grandfathered in, if you know what I mean. Anyway, I asked my mom once why she'd named me Tiffany Joy. She said that when she was a little girl, her mother, Stella, would take her and Barb to the store on Fifth Avenue. They'd go into the vault, and my grandmother would let them try on her jewels. She said that when I was born, she felt the same kind of joy she felt each time she visited the store with her mother."

"That's kind of sweet. Tiffany—"

"Stop right there. You start calling me Tiffany Joy and I swear, I won't love you anymore."

Buck nuzzled my neck. "Nothing will stop you from loving me."

"That might."

"Stop worrying," said Buck when he caught me looking at the time on my phone. "We're going to make it."

"It'll be close."

Buck shook his head. "By twenty-three hundred, I plan to be in bed in the cabin, both of us naked, and my cock buried deep inside you."

"It's a nice plan but—"

"But what?"

"We're scheduled to land at ten. It'll take an hour to drive from the airport to the ranch. You might make it in time if we land early."

"Something's wrong with your calculation."

"What?"

"You said it will take us an hour to get to the ranch. It'll only take us twenty minutes."

"How? Are we going to fly?"

Buck smiled.

"We are going to fly?"

"Holt made arrangements to have Ben's helicopter waiting for us."

"Better pray there's no storms in Colorado."

"We're gonna make it, Stella. Even if we didn't, Hammer said Porter, Cord, and Flynn had a plan."

"A plan for what?"

"What they'd do if anyone asked if I was on the ranch."

"What were they going to do?"

"Hammer didn't say."

"I suppose it's conceivable that they'd just lie. I mean, it is their inheritance at stake."

Buck's eyes hooded. "I wouldn't let them. I don't lie, Stella."

"I'm sorry—"

"There are other ways. They could challenge the will or get a judge to determine there were extenuating circumstances preventing me from being back within forty-eight hours. I would think that as long as the intent was to return, any judge would show some kind of leniency."

"I didn't mean to insult you, Buck."

"I know you didn't. I just don't want to cheat my way into ensuring my siblings get their inheritance.

My father spent most of my life trying to control it. I can guarantee this whole thing was him forcing me to make a choice between the life I want and the one he wanted me to have instead. I won't let him get away with it. I'll do what he asked, and I'll do it honestly. When I walk away, it will be with my honor and, more importantly, my soul intact."

"You're a good man, Buck."

"I don't know about that. All I know is that I won't allow my father to turn me into something I'd be ashamed of."

Buck's plan worked. At eleven o'clock, exactly forty-eight hours after we left the Roaring Fork Ranch, we were in bed, his cock buried deep inside me when we heard someone pounding on the door.

"Ignore it," said Buck as he thrust harder at the same time he pressed his finger on my clit. "Come on, Stella, give it to me."

I dug my fingers into the flesh of his back and came when I felt him pulse with his own release.

As he rolled off of me to dispose of the condom, I realized the pounding hadn't stopped.

"Buck, if you're in there, open up. If you don't at the count of three, I'll know you've violated the terms of your father's trust."

I jumped out of bed and peeked my head around the corner of the doorway in time to see Buck's naked ass as he stalked to the door and flung it open.

"What the fuck, Six-pack?" I heard him shout. I grabbed his shirt, threw it over my head, and rushed out to join him. I got there in time to see his ex, Beth, run her eyes down my man's naked body. Her cheeks were pink, and her opened mouth formed an "O."

"What the hell are you doin' here?" Buck asked her.

"Beth said she had evidence that you were off the ranch for more than forty-eight hours," Six-pack answered for her.

"Evidence? What kind of evidence?"

"Well…" stammered Six-pack. "That you weren't here."

"As you can see, I am very much here." Buck stretched his arms out on each side. "And as you can also see, you interrupted my time with my lady. If there's nothing else…"

He didn't wait for either of them to answer before slamming the door in their faces.

39

Buck

"We could've waited a day," I said when the plane that would take us from Gunnison back to New York City was about to take off.

"I want this over with, and so do you," said Stella. "If, and I'm saying if this time, everything goes as planned, we'll be back in Colorado before midnight."

Six hours later, we were back in the air, on our way to the place Stella and I had started calling home. Both of us were too stunned to speak as we lay on the bed in the stateroom and read through the hundreds of pages of notes Barb had handwritten.

"It looks like whoever took her computer, didn't get much," I muttered, turning another sheet over.

"It makes sense she wouldn't have kept anything on it. I mean, remember how cryptic her emails to me were? How would she have put all this into 'Barb code'?"

Most of what I read was circumstantial with a lot of conjecture thrown in on Barb's part. That didn't matter.

There was more than enough here for the CIA to pursue a deeper investigation into Operation Argead, most likely with the help of the Invincibles and maybe K19 too.

"Decker will be there when we get back, right?" asked Stella.

"He will be. I also have a hunch Burns might be too."

"Really?"

"We'll need him eventually just to help us figure out what some of this stuff means, even not written in Barb code."

"Most of this points a finger at Kerr, along with Donofrio from the CIA, and Moreau from French intelligence. There's nothing in it about Byrne, Antonov, Fisk, or even Kim, who is really Chen. Are Donofrio and Moreau even still alive?"

"I believe both are, and with Fisk in custody, I predict it won't be long before we can bring this whole operation down."

"Kerr made it sound like he ruled the fucking world," Stella spat as she flipped one piece of paper over. "He was exactly the way Burns said he'd be—arrogant, a misogynist, boastful—God, he was such an asshole."

"That reminds me, Decker asked me to tell you that he heard from Z. Sally Hennessey was found dead in the flat she shared with Kerr. An apparent suicide."

"I hope that's being investigated. I wouldn't be surprised if Kerr arranged for his own wife's death."

Stella stopped reading, flopped on her back, and closed her eyes. "Do you really think there's enough here to take them down?"

"I do, Stella. I also know that Decker, Cope, and Irish won't stop until they do."

"What about you?"

I knew that question was coming and had already given it a lot of thought. "We won't make any decisions until next year."

She opened her eyes and turned her head toward me. "We?"

"That's right. I'm not doing anything else to jeopardize my brothers and sister inheriting the Roaring Fork."

"Okay, but you said 'we.'"

"That's because by the time the year is over, I hope that the next day, you and I will be leaving on our honeymoon."

Stella sat up. "Are you asking me to marry you?"

"Yes, Miss Reporter. I am." I reached into my pocket and pulled out Stella's grandmother's diamond ring. "I hope you don't mind that I'm using this to propose with until I can get you a ring of your own, Stella." I slid off the bed and got down on one knee.

"Tiffany Joy, TJ, Stella Hunter, will you marry me?"

She put her arms around my neck. "Yes, I'll marry you, Roscoe Buchtold Wheaton."

"Junior."

"Huh?"

"I'm a junior."

"Right. Yes, Buck, Jr., I'll marry you."

40

Stella

On our way from Gunnison to Crested Butte, I told Buck that, if it was okay with him, I wanted to keep my grandmother's ring as my engagement ring. It was a perfect fit, and I loved it.

I also told him I wanted to start renovations on the farmhouse as soon as possible, along with investing the money we needed to in order to make sure the ranch was profitable when he fulfilled the other stipulation of the trust.

"Stella, I can't let you—"

"There you go again. If we're going to be married, you're going to have to accept the fact that you'll never be able to use those words again."

"But you shouldn't be using your aunt's money—"

"I rested two fingers on his lips. "Buck, I'm using my money, not my aunt's money, to build a life for my future husband and I. One in which we'll both be happy. I can't think of any better use for it."

As we drove up to the main ranch house, we saw five SUVs out front. "Looks like the meeting is here," Buck said to Rock.

"I told you that, Rock," Ink grumbled. "You didn't tell Buck?"

"It doesn't matter, Ink. We're here. Let's see who else is."

When we went inside, I saw Decker and Burns first. "Who's that?" I asked Buck.

"Let's see. That man talking to Irish is Rile DeLéon, who just for your information, is the one who named the Invincibles. My guess is the woman with him is Kensington Whitby, who may or may not already be his wife. The man talking to Burns and Decker is Doc Butler. He's Burns' son as well as the founding partner of K19 Security Solutions."

He led me through the testosterone-laden room and over to another group of men. "Razor Sharp and Gunner Godet, I'd like you to meet Stella Hunter. Razor and Gunner are Doc's partners in K19."

"Stella, it's a pleasure to meet you," said Razor, shaking my hand.

"An honor," said Gunner, doing the same.

"Look who's here," I heard Decker say from across the room. My eyes met Ali's, and both of us teared up.

"Excuse me," I said, rushing toward her.

"I can't believe you were here and gone before I even had the chance to talk to you." She hugged me hard. "I'm so glad you're safe, Stella. Cope told me…"

When her eyes filled with tears again, so did mine.

"It isn't over yet, Ali," I whispered.

"I know. Cope told me that too."

"Where is he?" I asked at the same time he walked in the front door with Money McTiernan.

"Stella," he bellowed, rushing over to me. Cope picked me up and hugged me harder than Ali had.

"Careful with my woman," I heard Buck say as Cope set me back on my feet.

"Stella means a lot to me too," said Cope. "I'm not going to apologize for that."

"No one ever needs to apologize for caring about someone." I put my arm around Buck's waist, reached up, and kissed his cheek. "I love you," I whispered.

"I love you too," he whispered back.

"If we could have everyone's attention please," I heard Decker say a few minutes later. "It might be easier if you all took a seat." I looked around the room and didn't see any of Buck's siblings. "Where are your brothers and sister?" I leaned over and asked Buck.

"My guess is Decker asked them to give the group privacy."

"What's going on?"

"I think we're about to find out."

Decker and Doc remained standing when everyone else found a seat. "In the absence of two, I'm going to speak on behalf of the four founding partners of the Invincible Intelligence and Security Group," said Decker, nodding at Rile.

"And in the absence of one, I'll speak on behalf of the four founding partners of K19 Security Solutions," said Doc, nodding at Razor and Gunner.

"What's with all the formality?" I heard Razor say to Gunner but loud enough for everyone else to hear. "We aren't getting married, are we?"

"We're already married," Gunner answered without cracking a smile.

"No," said Doc. "We aren't getting married. However, we are about to take on our first joint mission. IISG and K19 have been contracted by the CIA, backed by the full support of the Senate Intelligence

Committee, to proceed full-throttle in a mission designed to wipe every last person affiliated with Operation Argead from the face of the earth."

"I'm not sure that was the exact directive, Doc," said Money.

"You say tomato, I say annihilation," Doc responded. "Same difference."

"Irish Warrick will serve as lead," said Deck.

Every person in the room clapped when Irish stood and joined them.

"Well deserved," I heard a couple of people say. "Right decision," someone else said.

"Irish," said Decker, stepping to the side like Doc had.

"We'll begin at zero eight hundred tomorrow, if that's okay with Stella." He and everyone else in the room looked in my direction.

"Um. Sure." I shrugged. Irish motioned for me to join him.

"For the next three days, we'll review all the leads we have so far, most of which Stella brought back with her today." He leaned closer to me. "I've already briefed everyone in the room on the progress we made before you left."

"That's great," I said, a little confused as to why I was standing in front of this particular group of people.

"Stella, if she agrees, will serve as my second-in-command," Irish announced without looking at me. Once again, everyone in the room clapped.

He leaned closer. "Well? Will you?"

"Yes, Irish. I would be honored."

"Everyone heard that, right?"

I laughed when several people nodded. "Unless there are any questions, we'll convene back here at zero eight hundred tomorrow."

I saw a hand go up in the back of the room.

"Yes, Buck?" asked Irish. "You have questions?"

"Just one."

"Go ahead."

Buck stood. "I was just wondering who Stella works for. IISG or K19?"

"She works for us," both Decker and Doc answered.

Epilogue

Buck

One year after
Roscoe B. Wheaton Sr.'s death

A few more days, and the bullshit with the Roaring Fork Trust would come to an end. Thanks to my beautiful, amazing, generous wife and her investment in both the dude ranch and the roughstock business, the ranch had been operating in the black for six months.

As for not being able to be away from the place for more than forty-eight hours, Stella insisted she was happy to have a reason to stay home and continue fixing up the farmhouse, so it hadn't been an issue.

We ended up getting married over at the Flying R Ranch since they had a barn already set up with a stage, a dance floor, and tables. Holt and Ben Rice arranged for music while Flynn took care of having all the food catered and helped Stella order flowers.

Porter surprised us when he announced that he'd gotten his minister's license and could legally marry us, which meant best-man duties fell on Cord's shoulders.

He was disappointed when I refused to have a bachelor party, but perked up when I put him in charge of booze for the reception.

Stella asked Ali to be her matron of honor. When she said she didn't want any other bridesmaids, I was happy to keep it as simple as she wanted.

I think I was more disappointed than she was that we'd had to put our honeymoon on hold. But next week, after the meeting my siblings and I had scheduled with Six-pack, Stella and I would be flying to a private island in the Bahamas where, for one whole month, we'd be the only guests.

"How're you feelin', darlin'?" I asked when she came out of the recently renovated bathroom off the farmhouse's master bedroom.

"My back feels better after my bath." When she walked over to the end of the bed where I sat, I wrapped my arm around her waist and rested my cheek against her rapidly growing belly. She put both hands on the back of my head. "Careful, I think your son's got a couple of wild horses in there with him."

For the last week, the little buckaroo had been kicking up a storm, but at least Stella's morning sickness had subsided.

"Can we go into Gunnison today?" she asked.

I looked up at her and smiled. "We could always learn to make them here." Sloppers were about the only thing Stella craved—morning, noon, and night. That and banana bread, which Flynn kept well-supplied.

"They wouldn't taste the same."

"Are you insulting my cooking?"

She laughed. "Never, sweet husband. You just wouldn't use enough grease."

"Ouch!" I gasped when I felt a kick to my right cheek. "That little guy's rambunctious today."

"Just think how much worse it feels on the inside."

I put my hands on either side of Stella's belly, leaned forward, and kissed the place where the baby had kicked me. "I'm so in awe of you, darlin'."

My wife sat on the bed, beside me. "I wish we could get them delivered."

I laughed out loud. "Sloppers?"

"You're right. You should learn how to cook them."

I pulled Stella with me until we both lay flat on the bed. "Your wish is my command—" I repeated the few words that had made up most of the vows I spoke on our wedding day. "For the rest of our lives."

Keep reading for a sneak peek

at the next book

in the Invincibles series—

IRISHED!

1

Irish

Buck led me and the other people we were traveling with into the ranch's main house.

"Hello?" he called out.

"Hey, Buck," I heard a female's voice answer; she walked up and hugged him.

"Where is everybody?" he asked.

"Out surveying." The woman turned and looked directly at me. "Who are you?"

"Paxon Warrick," I said, stepping forward and extending my hand. When she took it, a feeling I couldn't explain, other than to say I never wanted to let go, washed over me.

"Flynn Wheaton," she said. Her cheeks flushed and I gripped her hand tighter.

"Great name," I said.

"Yours too."

When Buck tapped her on the shoulder, I dropped Flynn's hand and watched as she met and shook the hands of the other people in the room. More than once I saw her look over her shoulder at me.

I knew from the brief I'd received that Buck only had one sister, which meant Flynn was twenty-one years old. What I'd give to take ten years off my age and be five years older than her rather than fifteen.

When most everyone left other than me, Buck, and one person besides Flynn, she walked back over to me. When she looked into my eyes with her mesmerizing blue ones, all thoughts of age faded into irrelevance.

I longed to reach out and run my fingers through her long hair that was light brown with golden highlights. When she turned her head just slightly, I saw shades of red too.

Flynn took a deep breath when I stepped closer. I opened my mouth to speak, but words escaped me. If she and I were alone, I'd tell her how beautiful she was. But we weren't, as I was immediately reminded when her brother, who'd left momentarily, returned.

"Ready?" he asked.

"I should head out now too, but I'm sure I'll see you later," said Flynn, seemingly jarred out of the same trance I was in.

"I'd like that." I followed her to the front door and watched her walk away, wishing, maybe for the first time ever, that I could leave the wretched hell my life had become, and follow.

About the Author

USA Today and Amazon Top 15 Bestselling Author Heather Slade writes shamelessly sexy, edge-of-your seat romantic suspense.

She gave herself the gift of writing a book for her own birthday one year. Forty-plus books later (and counting), she's having the time of her life.

The women Slade writes are self-confident, strong, with wills of their own, and hearts as big as the Colorado sky. The men are sublimely sexy, seductive alphas who rise to the challenge of capturing the sweet soul of a woman whose heart they'll hold in the palm of their hand forever. Add in a couple of neck-snapping twists and turns, a page-turning mystery, and a swoon-worthy HEA, and you'll be holding one of her books in your hands.

She loves to hear from my readers. You can contact her at heather@heatherslade.com

To keep up with her latest news and releases, please visit her website at www.heatherslade.com to sign up for her newsletter.

MORE FROM AUTHOR HEATHER SLADE

BUTLER RANCH
Kade's Worth
Brodie's Promise
Maddox's Truce
Naughton's Secret
Mercer's Vow
Kade's Return
Butler Ranch Christmas

WICKED WINEMAKERS
FIRST LABEL
Brix's Bid
Ridge's Release
Press' Passion
Zin's Sins
Tryst's Temptation

WICKED WINEMAKERS
SECOND LABEL
Beau's Beloved
Coming Soon:
Cru's Crush
Bones' Bliss
Snapper's Seduction
Kick's Kiss

ROARING FORK RANCH
Coming Soon:
Roaring Fork Wrangler
Roaring Fork Roughstock
Roaring Fork Rockstar
Roaring Fork Rooker
Roaring Fork Bridger

THE ROYAL AGENTS
OF MI6
Make Me Shiver
Drive Me Wilder
Feel My Pinch
Chase My Shadow
Find My Angel

K19 SECURITY
SOLUTIONS TEAM ONE
Razor's Edge
Gunner's Redemption
Mistletoe's Magic
Mantis' Desire
Dutch's Salvation

K19 SECURITY
SOLUTIONS TEAM TWO
Striker's Choice
Monk's Fire
Halo's Oath
Tackle's Honor
Onyx's Awakening

K19 SHADOW OPERATIONS
TEAM ONE
Code Name: Ranger
Code Name: Diesel
Code Name: Wasp
Code Name: Cowboy
Code Name: Mayhem

K19 ALLIED INTELLIGENCE
TEAM ONE
Code Name: Ares
Code Name: Cayman
Code Name: Poseidon
Code Name: Zeppelin
Code Name: Magnet

K19 ALLIED INTELLIGENCE
TEAM TWO
Coming Soon:
Code Name: Puck
Code Name: Michelangelo
Code Name: Typhon
Code Name: Hornet
Code Name: Reaper

PROTECTORS
UNDERCOVER
Undercover Agent
Undercover Emissary
Coming Soon:
Undercover Savior
Undercover Infidel
Undercover Assassin

THE INVINCIBLES
TEAM ONE
Decked
Edged
Grinded
Riled
Smoked

THE INVINCIBLES
TEAM TWO
Bucked
Irished
Sainted
Hammered
Ripped

THE UNSTOPPABLES
TEAM ONE
Furied
Merried

COWBOYS OF
CRESTED BUTTE
A Cowboy Falls
A Cowboy's Dance
A Cowboy's Kiss
A Cowboy Stays
A Cowboy Wins